CRUNCH TIME

A DCI Henry Christie Mystery

Willing to do almost anything to escape his desk job, DCI Henry Christie leaps at the chance to go working undercover again. His task, to ingratiate himself with one Ryan Ingram, one of London's top criminals, who has relocated to the north of England. But the last thing Henry needs in this dangerous situation is the appearance of a man bearing a fatal grudge that will jeopardize not only himself, but also his family...

CRUNCH TIME

Nick Oldham

Severn House Large Print
London & New York

This first large print edition published 2011
in Great Britain and the USA by
SEVERN HOUSE PUBLISHERS LTD of
9-15 High Street, Sutton, Surrey, SM1 1DF.
First world regular print edition published 2008 by
Severn House Publishers Ltd., London and New York.

British Library Cataloguing in Publication Data

Oldham, Nick, 1956-
    Crunch time. -- (A DCI Henry Christie mystery)
    1. Christie, Henry (Fictitious character)--Fiction.
    2. Police--England--Blackpool--Fiction. 3. Detective and
    mystery stories. 4. Large type books.
    I. Title II. Series
    823.9'2-dc22

    ISBN-13: 978-0-7278-7952-3

Severn House Publishers support The Forest Stewardship Council
[FSC], the leading international forest certification organisation. All
our titles that are printed on Greenpeace-approved FSC-certified paper
carry the FSC logo.

Printed and bound in Great Britain by the
MPG Books Group, Bodmin, Cornwall.

One

The Jaguar XJS had seen much better days. Once called British Racing Green, this car's formerly proud colour had now faded to a patchy, lighter shade with numerous round, pitted craters where the paint had rotted from the acid in the bird shit from the branches under which the car had been parked and neglected for over five years. Rust blistered the bottom edges of both doors and all the wheel arches; the tyres, whilst not technically illegal, were treading a fine line, wearing very thin indeed. Add to that an engine which was temperamental at best from a lack of servicing and tuning – twelve cylinders, almost thirty years old, needed a lot of care and attention – and an exhaust blowing like a tractor, and the picture painted was one of dilapidation and decline, of having seen much better days.

This was a scenario compounded by the man behind the wheel.

He was just on the right side of fifty – not such a bad age – but he had the aura of a beaten, defeated man. His eyes were dark and sunken in their sockets, particularly his right, which squinted behind a cheekbone that had been broken months before and didn't seem to want to heal properly. Both eyes were bleary and blood-shot after four solid days on a bender of epic proportions.

The man's breath stank horribly of belched alcohol, a dirty, unpleasant odour to anyone not having lived alongside him for the length of his binge – and no one had. It had been a solitary road he'd travelled, bumping into fellow drunks for the occasional shared hour, but leaving even the best of them in his wake.

During those four days he had not found time to wash, shower, clean his teeth or change his clothing. In fact, he had been so utterly drunk at one point he had pissed his pants and not noticed. It was at that moment he'd been ejected from the pub and, down to his last tenner, stag-gered back to his car. Then, somehow, without mowing anyone down, he'd driven to his present location somewhere near his rented apartment on Salford Quays, Manchester, close to the Old Trafford football ground, the apartment he'd just received notice to quit having defaulted on the rent.

The man in the Jaguar had come to the end of the line.

He was broke. His latest business deal had turned to shit, leaving him owing serious money. His girlfriend had deserted him after christening him a loser and a drunkard. He was being thrown out of his property and his car was a heap of expensive-to-run shit. As he slumped with his head wedged against the steering wheel, having pulled into the side of the road and managed to manoeuvre three wheels on to the footpath, it seemed that, as he vomited copiously down his lap and shins and over his once beautiful brogues and into the turn-ups of his piss-stained pants, nothing else could go wrong for him.

But in such pitiful cases there is always something else that can – and will – go shit-shaped.

Although the man in the car wouldn't completely realize what the gravity of that 'something else' was until he was on the road to sobriety, that 'something else' was just about thirty seconds away. It took the form of two uniformed police constables who just happened to be in the neighbourhood when the call came through.

'Patrol to attend anonymous report of possible drunken man in a car on...' The comms operator gave the location and description of the car and the nearby double-crewed patrol responded immediately. They found the old XJS as described, looking as though it had screeched to a halt after having avoided a cat in the road.

The police car drew alongside and the female PC in the passenger seat opened her window and peered into the XJS.

'You or me?' she asked her partner.

'Be my guest.'

With a shrug of resignation the officer climbed out of the cop car, breath kit in hand, and slowly opened the driver's door. The man behind the wheel was now half-propped against the door and as the officer eased it open, he slithered slowly out and on to the roadside, lying half in, half out of the ancient sports car. The cop winced and stepped smartly back, crinkling her

7

nose at the terrible stench of vomit, urine, four-day-old body odour and alcohol, all combined into one awful package that cops were almost immune to, but not completely.

The officer bent slightly to look back into the police car and gave her partner one of those 'thanks a bunch, you bastard' expressions, but actually said, 'What a mess,' as she glanced down at the drunk driver.

On the ground, which he hadn't hit too hard, the driver groaned pathetically. Then his whole upper body heaved, giving the constable just enough forewarning to jump out of the way, as the heave turned to a retch and once more the man hurled. From his twisted position, the vomit shot out like a fountain, then splattered back down across his chest with a sound like hailstones hitting the ground.

'Call for the van, will you?' the officer said to her partner.

'Drunk in charge of a motor vehicle and failing to provide a specimen of breath ... oops!' The arresting officer had just presented the driver of the XJS to the custody officer at Salford nick in Greater Manchester. She'd propped the guy against the custody desk and then proceeded to outline the reason for the arrest and was just getting to the spiel when the driver lost his balance and staggered backwards on rubber legs. The officer caught him, prevented him from falling by getting a hand on his back, which seemed about the only part of him without a vomit-veneer covering. She manoeuvred him back up to the desk and held him there, the driver looking stupidly at the custody sergeant, unable to keep his head still on a neck that seemed to be without muscle.

The long-in-the-tooth custody sergeant, a gnarled, seen-it-all, don't-give-a-shit kind of guy, watched the episode with a contemptuous twist of his mouth. 'Circumstances?' he said wearily to the officer.

'Found him behind the wheel of a parked XJS, opened the door and he fell out. Keys in the ignition. Smelled strongly of intoxicants, he was sick all over everything, as you can see.' The officer indicated the prisoner's appearance with a wave of her hand. 'He sort of blew into the breathalyser, but couldn't provide enough for a sample. Too drunk, weren't you, mate?' she finished patronizingly, as though she were talking to a dumb child. She added, 'So I arrested him, but I'm pretty sure he's clueless about what's going on. Been on a real bender.'

'Right, mate.' The sergeant's eyes took in the swaying prisoner, who was having a bit of trouble focusing and preventing treble-vision. To him it looked as though he was being inspected by three sergeants all saying the same thing, just slightly out of sync with each other, like a digital TV gone wrong.

'Did you understand all that?' the sergeant asked him.

'Er – what?'

'Do you know why you've been arrested?'

'I've been arrested?' the prisoner blurted with surprise. 'I thought thish wush McDonald's.'

The sergeant scratched his ear with his ballpoint pen and declared, 'Too drunk to understand his rights.' He twisted to the keyboard in front of him and began to enter details of the arrest on to the computerized custody record whilst the prisoner continued to watch him with amazement, having to be held upright by the arresting officer.

'Name?' the sergeant asked.

'Oh, shit,' the prisoner replied. His watery but bloodshot eyes opened wide. A gush of sweat rolled down his forehead and temple and suddenly he became a pale grey colour – and heaved.

'Get him out of here!' the sergeant shouted at the PC. 'He's gonna chuck up. Get him to the toilets!'

The constable grabbed the prisoner's left arm and yanked him roughly away from the custody desk – it was very bad form to allow a detainee to spew his guts over the sergeant and his equipment – and steered him double-quick along the corridor to the toilets. They got there just in time so the prisoner could at least direct this bellyful into a toilet bowl. The prisoner sank to his knees, grabbed the porcelain – this was actually the staff toilet, not one for visitors – and retched and gulped and retched until there was nothing else to come out. This done, he hung his head in the bowl and groaned loudly, the perfect acoustics of the toilet ensuring that the sound travelled back to the custody office.

He turned his haggard face up to the constable, one eye slightly closed, a dribble of runny sick on his chin. 'That's better.'

'You look a real fucking mess,' the PC said. 'C'mon.' She hoisted him up by the elbow, flushed the toilet and steered him back to the patient custody sergeant, where she jammed him up against the desk.

'Right ... name?'

'What? My name?'

'Whose freakin' name do you think I want? Yes, you,' the sergeant said, with the irritability of someone who had dealt with a thousand inebriates and still had no time for them.

The prisoner's chin fell on to his chest and he looked up at the sergeant. 'Jagger's the name. Yep, Jagger.'

'Mick, I suppose? And I'm Keith Richards.'

'Duh-duh-do-dah-dah-duh-dah-dah...' the prisoner sang, attempting to replicate the riff of *Satisfaction*, the Rolling Stones' hit song.

The sergeant's face – his three faces – hardened. 'Do not fuck around.'

Something in the tone of his voice cut through the alcoholic haze and the triple image of the sergeant morphed into one slightly fuzzy one.

'No, itsh true, as God is my witness ... the name's Jagger.' The sergeant typed the surname into the computer. 'If you tell me your first name is Mick, you're straight into a cell, pal.'

'It's Frank ... Frank Jagger ... pisshead.'

'You got that right, pal. Time to blow.'

The legal drink-drive limit in Britain is 35 mg of alcohol per 100 millilitres of breath. Anything over that limit warrants prosecution, but most

11

police forces will warn a driver who blows between 35 and 40 mg, but anyone over 40 mg will end up in court. It takes a lot of alcohol to put an individual's reading to 70 mg – twice the legal limit – and those people who come into custody swearing on their mothers' lives that they only had a couple of pints or two small glasses of wine, yet blow over 70, are liars; they have been drinking heavily to get to that point and anyone blowing above that figure has been imbibing alcohol as though it's going out of fashion.

As was the case of Frank Jagger.

After allowing him to wash and freshen up, though this had little overall effect or benefit on him, Jagger was taken into the room in which the breath test machine, the intoximeter, was kept. Here he was seated next to the custody officer at the machine. Jagger watched through bleary eyes as the sergeant fired up the machine, tested it, then inserted the sterile mouthpiece into the extendable tube and gave Jagger the instructions: take a deep breath, put the mouthpiece between your lips and blow in one continuous breath until told to stop.

'You got that?' the sergeant asked.

'Sorta.'

'Here.' The sergeant pulled the tube. Jagger took it, put it in his mouth, started to blow.

'Keep going ... keep going,' the sergeant encouraged him. 'Bit more ... stop!'

Breathless, Jagger took the tube out of his mouth and slumped in the chair. 'Whassa reading?'

'You need to do it once more, then I'll tell you.' The sergeant waited for the machine to carry out the first reading, which he kept to himself, then to purge itself. He then asked Jagger to blow again, which he did, and, exhausted by the effort expended, he slithered down in the chair again, his head lolling uncontrollably.

The machine did its work. The sergeant snorted and said, 'Wow – you really have been drinking.'

'Yep.'

'One hundred and eight ... my highest score this year. Congratulations, three times the legal limit.'

'Do I get a prize?'

'Yeah, a night in the cells, a visit to Salford Magistrates Court in the morning, a three-year driving ban, probably and a helluva fine. How does that sound? First prize.'

'Sounds...' Jagger's head rolled in a wide arc as he tried to focus in on the sergeant, but in so doing he managed to overbalance and tip off the chair before the officer could catch him and before he could say 'good'. He hit the tiled floor hard and cracked the back of his head.

Two gaolers dragged him between them to a cell where they hefted him on to the bed, arranged his body in the recovery position – on his side, knees drawn up – just in case he was sick in his sleep so he wouldn't choke on his vomit and die. They threw a rough blanket across him and kept a fifteen-minute interval watch on him for the night. Too many drunks had died unnecessary deaths in police cells, but under the care of that particular custody sergeant, Frank Jagger – if that was truly his name – was not going to become another sad statistic. Jagger was asleep immediately.

It is police policy to rouse sleeping drunks every fifteen minutes – rouse them enough to get some sort of response – and this happened to Jagger for the remainder of that night, the cell door opening, the gaoler prodding him and making him talk, just enough for him to mutter, 'Fuck off and leave me alone.' So, although Jagger slept in fifteen-minute blocks, it was a disturbed slumber and not one designed to combat the excessive amount of alcohol he'd drunk.

When the cell door opened at 6.15 a.m. the following morning, he was still drunk and in desperate need of a serious spell of uninterrupted kip. He raised his head and peered groggily through one caked-up eye and said, 'Leave me alone, you fuckwits,' and yanked the blanket tightly over his head.

'You got company,' the gaoler announced, then Jagger heard him say, 'Sorry mate, you're in with a pisshead,' then the door slammed shut.

Underneath the blanket, Jagger's eyes flickered and he listened as hard as his drink-blunted senses would allow and at the same time started to try and get his brain working. It was a tough requirement. He felt worse than awful and a terrible clanging was going on in his head as if out-of-tune church bells were being rung by a vicious gang of demented campanologists.

It had been many years since he had felt so bad

from alcohol and it wasn't an experience he would be repeating any time soon. It was an age thing.

He had become totally aware, though, that someone else – another prisoner – had been put in the cell with him. He could hear that other person breathing, could hear them shuffling around.

Jagger peered over the edge of the blanket and peeked at his fellow prisoner. It was a man – obviously – about Jagger's age, looking lean and fit, dressed in tracksuit bottoms and a black tee-shirt. His head was bowed as he stood by the door and he looked deep in thought.

Jagger groaned. 'Wanna sit?' he asked, though his mouth felt as caked-up as his eyes. He was very dehydrated and needed about a gallon of cold, cold water, some food and a plateful of aspirin. He bent his knees to make room on the end of the bed.

'You must be joking,' his fellow detainee responded sourly. 'Stuck me in with a drunk, the shower of shit.' His lip curled and he shook his head. 'Bastards.'

'I'm a drunk-driver, not a drunk. There's a difference,' Jagger retorted. 'Suit yourself.' His legs extended again and he immediately fell asleep.

Two

It was 8 a.m. Jagger sat on the edge of the bed in his cell, hugging himself pitifully and rocking back and forth, eyes tightly closed, his head rotating. He hardly dared to breathe just in case he threw up again.

'I feel horrible,' he mumbled drily. 'My head's exploding.'

'Serves you right,' his unempathetic cellmate admonished. He was sitting on the floor in one corner of the cell, as far away from Jagger as possible.

Jagger didn't even bother to open his eyes. 'Prob'ly,' he gasped as his face screwed up with pain.

'Prick,' the other man said under his breath, pushed himself up and crossed to the cell door, jamming his finger on the emergency call button set in the wall and hammering with the side of his fist on the door. The door rattled and Jagger flinched at the metallic noise that penetrated his skull like shrapnel. The balls of his hands went to his temples and he braced his head.

Suddenly the inspection hatch clattered open.

'What?' the sullen voice of the morning gaoler demanded.

Jagger's cellmate placed his hands on the door

16

and he looked through the opening. 'I've been locked up here for two hours with a stinking pisshead of a drunk. I've had nothing to eat or drink,' he explained slowly with a seething undercurrent of anger. 'Nor have I had chance to speak to my brief – which I demand.'

'Breakfast is coming and I'll ask about your brief, OK?'

'OK,' he accepted stoically. 'And by the way, this fucker needs a shower, a change of clothes, Nurofen and water.' He thumbed a gesture at Jagger. The gaoler peered in, nodded, then slammed the hatch back into place with a crash that made Jagger jump.

'Thanks, mate.'

'One thing we ain't – it's mates.'

The thing about showers in police cell blocks is that they are always hot and powerful. There is no room for modesty, however, because for obvious security reasons there are no doors on the cubicles. But Frank Jagger couldn't have cared less that the gaoler was keeping one eye on him as he soaped himself down with a block of harsh white soap, shampooed himself with something rather like washing-up liquid, and rinsed off. He was beginning to feel human again as the aroma of vomit and urine was displaced by the cheap soap.

He shaved with a blunt disposable razor, using the soap as shaving foam, and though he nicked himself a couple of times, the process added to his slow re-emergence into the land of the living. He studied himself in the polished steel plate mirror screwed on to the wall – real glass mirrors were banned in the custody area – and thought he looked half-decent, even though the swelling under his right eye from the broken cheekbone of months before still distorted his face slightly, made his eye bloodshot and watery. Next he cleaned his teeth, using his first finger as a brush to apply toothpaste from an almost empty tube of Colgate.

'C'mon, gorgeous, here's your zoot suit,' the gaoler said, handing the naked Jagger a paper suit and slippers to replace his horribly stained and ultimately unsalvageable clothing. Jagger stepped into the generously proportioned suit and was herded back to his cell where breakfast and a huge mug of tea awaited.

The food was cooling on a plastic plate, but even so, the slightly congealed egg, lukewarm bacon and toast tasted like a feast. The tea was like gulping nectar and at the end of the repast Jagger was approaching some sort of normality, even though he knew he was still drunk ... well, perhaps not drunk as in the staggering, insensible sense, but still under the influence of booze.

He'd balanced his plate on his knees to eat and when he'd finished he placed it and the empty plastic mug on the cell floor and looked up at his cellmate. The man remained aloof, standing propped in one corner sipping his tea, not having touched his food which was on a plate at his feet.

Jagger exhaled. 'That's better ... you not eating?'

The prisoner toed his plate towards Jagger.

'Yours if you want it.'

'Nah, ta ... I'm OK now ... sort of ... smell better, anyway.'

'True enough, you were gross.'

Jagger shrugged. 'So what're you locked up for?'

'My business,' the man answered, giving Jagger a warning look.

Jagger held up his hands. 'Nuff said. Just instigating conversation.'

'Not interested.'

'OK, OK.' He breathed out again, then inhaled to get more oxygen into his lungs. 'What a fuckin' bender that was.'

The man chuckled, his guard dropping slightly. 'You're a fuckin' mess.'

Jagger nodded. 'Aye,' he said resignedly. 'Life has become a bitch.' He placed the tip of his right forefinger against his forehead and closed his eyes, still feeling bad. His broken, slowly repairing cheekbone had a throb all of its own. 'Not good,' he said, fighting a fresh wave of nausea which was interrupted by the cell door opening.

'Both of you,' the gaoler said, beckoning.

Jagger pushed himself up unsteadily and, despite the shower and food, he remained unstable. His cellmate supped the dregs of his tea, picked up his plate and handed the items to the gaoler.

'Not hungry?'

'Shit food.'

'Mind if I have it?' the gaoler asked.

'If you don't mind food that's been gozzed on,

be my guest.'

The gaoler glared at him, stood back and let both prisoners walk past him. They grinned at each other: any victory over the bastards was to be savoured.

The custody desk was a hive of activity. Detectives, uniformed cops, waiting prisoners, briefs, all milling about whilst a huge black guy with a tee-shirt emblazoned with the word 'Janitor' moved patiently around people with a mop and bucket. The desk was split into prisoner reception and those already in custody and now there were two custody officers on duty, one to deal with the new arrivals – of which there was already a queue – and one for those already banged up, of which Jagger and his cellmate were two.

Jagger looked despondently around and was pushed up to the desk alongside his new-found friend, who was then pulled slightly back by the gaoler when the custody sergeant pointed at Jagger and said, 'You first.'

The sergeant was a woman with harshly scraped back blonde hair and angular features, probably accentuated by her stressful role and tiredness.

Jagger gave her a winning smile, but that didn't stop her going through the process of ensuring that he actually understood why he'd been arrested and what had happened to him since, including his reasonably spectacular showing on the breath machine.

Jagger accepted it all with tired equanimity. He

declined the offer of a solicitor and also the opportunity to make a phone call. 'Thanks, but no thanks. I ain't got no one to call. Bitch dumped me, hasn't she? Just charge and bail me and I'll get going...' His voice trailed off as he saw the sergeant's head start to shake. 'No? What then?' he asked worriedly.

'You will be charged, yes, but you'll be going straight to court this afternoon. No bail ... standard procedure with drink-drivers. Get 'em banned as soon as possible.'

'You are fuckin' joking!' Jagger exploded. He banged the counter top hard with the flat of his hand, making everyone jump. 'I've things to do, you evil witch,' he snarled into the face of the custody officer. She did not flinch, but looked blandly at him, blinked, very unimpressed by the display. He jabbed a finger at her and shouted, 'You can't fuckin' well do this to me! I have things to do, people to see.'

'In this case, the magistrates.'

Jagger went rigid at her remark, then a seething, violent look came over his face. He raised his right fist, bunched it tight and held it for a moment, quivering with rage, before he drew it back.

'Hit me and it'll be the last thing you do,' she said coldly.

Jagger's cellmate, who had observed the interaction from a couple of feet behind, stepped forward and placed his fingers around Jagger's forearm. 'Don't be a fool,' he said into Jagger's ear. He looked harshly at the custody officer, then into Jagger's blazing eyes. He shook his head. 'The cunt isn't worth it.'

For a few seconds, his jaw rotating, Jagger seemed as though he would still drive his fist into the woman's face, but then the fight went out of him with a hiss and a flare of the nostrils. 'Twats,' he uttered.

The cellmate patted him on the back and moved away from the fray. Jagger was still shaking with anger, but he controlled himself by gripping the edge of the desk, knuckles white.

A man in an ASDA suit appeared behind the custody officer. He had a supercilious smirk on his face. He was late thirties, slightly over-weight, with a florid, drink-ravaged face. Jagger pinned him as a career detective. Cheap suit, with a know-it-all expression, tie an inch too short.

'And not only that' – the guy forced a victori-ous grin on to his face that lasted about a second, one of those 'gotcha' expressions – 'you would not have a car to go home in anyway. It's been impounded.'

'You what? What's—?' Jagger uttered, then his face drained as he realized something and tried to bluff it out, having shot a worried glance in his cellmate's direction which he then tried to cover up with a bit of bluster. 'There's nowt wrong with that car.'

The detective laughed mirthlessly. 'Other than the fact it's made up of two other XJSs, both of which were stolen fifteen years ago – so long ago they're not even on the computer anymore ... but as you know, that doesn't bother us half as much as the stuff in the boot, does it?' He winked at Jagger, whose shoulders sagged ever so slightly.

'There wasn't anything in the boot,' Jagger said, his voice a little hoarse.

The ASDA shopper sniggered, then held up a key which he waved in front of Jagger's nose. 'Well, we can talk about that later, can't we? First things first ... I've just got the inspector's authorization to spin your drum, search your hovel, and then I'm one hundred per cent sure we'll have a lot more things to chat about. Would you like me to bring you a change of clothes while I'm there? Or would you rather go to court in a paper suit – or really impress the bench with your sick-and piss-stained suit? Your choice, matey.'

The two cellmates did not see very much of each other over the next four hours, other than to pass shoulder-to-shoulder as they entered and exited interview rooms accompanied by detectives and solicitors. Eventually, just after one o'clock in the afternoon, they found themselves back in their original cell, sitting side by side on the bed with plastic plates on their knees, eating spam fritters and chips, each served with a huge plastic mug of sweet tea and a piece of Swiss roll.

Jagger ate as though he'd been on a starvation diet. The alcohol had more or less cleared from his system to be replaced by a constantly banging head and dry mouth. He was regaining his true self step by step and the food, crap though it was, tasted amazingly wonderful.

His cellmate, on the other hand, simply pushed his food around with his plastic fork.

They had eaten in silence until Jagger – to whom silence seemed intolerable – blurted, 'I never knew about that Jag ... fuck!'

His companion gave him a contemptuous, but amused look. 'Bollocks,' he said, 'and I've never exceeded the speed limit.'

'It's fuckin' true, I tell ya.'

'Pull the other one,' he said tiredly. 'Got my own worries.'

Jagger's attention returned to his thin, salty, lukewarm chips. He packed a couple into his mouth and ate with relish.

'Can have mine if you want.' His cellmate offered his plate.

Jagger stopped chomping. 'You haven't gozzed on 'em, have you?' he asked, bringing a laugh from the other man. A slight chink in the armour. Jagger took the plate and tipped the food on to his, then proffered his right hand. 'Frank Jagger ... and thanks for this morning, by the way.'

'Which bit?'

'Calmin' me down ... I was still feeling nasty from the drink, I reckon. I'd've been in real shit if I'd've smacked the bitch one, I suppose.'

'Deep, deep pooh.'

The man still hadn't shaken Jagger's hand, so Jagger waved it again, encouragingly, and reluctantly they shook. 'And your name is?'

'Ingram,' he admitted. 'Ryan Ingram.' The handshake continued, but Ingram seemed keen to detach himself from the grip. He looked sideways at Jagger. 'Do I know you? Your face looks a bit familiar.'

'Been about a bit, I suppose. Seen a bit, done a bit ... now it's all gone shit-shaped.'

'Hence the bender to end all benders?'

'Blew a hundred and eight, which is pretty good going, I'm told. Well worth a three-year ban and a grand's fine ... which I'll never be able to pay, which means I'll never get the cunts off my back.' He exhaled, a woozy sensation coming over him again. 'Still a bit pissed, I think. Four days does that to a bloke, especially one my age with no friggin' prospects and a real hard cunt breathin' down my neck.' He emitted an exaggerated whump of a sigh, wondering if he should go on to burden Ingram with further tales of woe. Or would it be too much? Would Ingram just close down? The building of a relationship, as Jagger knew, was a delicate thing. Too much, too soon could destroy something even before it began.

However, Ingram asked, 'What was in the "not-stolen" car that the detective was so interested in?'

Jagger froze. He tapped his nose, put his plate down on the bed, stood and crossed to the stainless steel toilet in the corner.

'Actually,' he said, pointing around the cell, then to his ears, to indicate the possibility of hidden listening devices, 'I've no idea. Whatever it is' – he placed his forefinger on the recessed toilet flush button in the wall – 'they must've planted it.' He pushed and the toilet flushed. He went back and sat next to Ingram and whispered three words into his ear, using his hands and the running water as a sound barrier.

Even when they were handcuffed and waiting in the holding cage in readiness for court, Ingram still did not divulge the reason for his own arrest to Jagger, remaining tight-lipped and mysterious. All Jagger had learned was that Ingram had been interviewed and charged with a minor offence and had bail refused by the custody officer for some spurious reason. Two other prisoners were also in the cage and Jagger did not get further opportunity to speak to Ingram as they were herded out into a van and conveyed to court. They were then placed in another holding cell to await their appearance, their handcuffs removed. This time Jagger managed to ease himself on to the bench seat next to Ingram, who looked disdainful at this invasion of his personal space and shuffled a couple of inches away from him.

'I reckon the cops'll give me bail after I've been dealt with for this drink-drive shit.'

'Did they find anything at your address?'

'Nope, just my clothes.' Jagger indicated his change of attire, out of the zoot suit and into a real one. He gave Ingram a sly look.

'But there is more stuff?' he guessed.

'Yeah, and that's one of my problems...' Jagger's trap shut tight as the cell door opened and a Group 4 security guard beckoned to him. 'Mega cash-flow problems, coupled with an angry man.' He shrugged and stood up. 'Maybe I could do with being sent down. At least I'd be out of circulation. See ya, mate – all the best, whatever you're in for.'

The court appearance was short, sharp and shocking, not assisted by the fact that, according to court records, this was Jagger's third drink-driving conviction in ten years.

He sat quietly in the dock and let it all happen, allowing the duty solicitor to argue his case – pretty weakly – for him. In the end the magistrates banned him from driving for five years, fined him £1,200 and ordered him to attend an alcohol rehabilitation programme, the details of which he would be informed of in due course. If he failed or refused to attend this, he was told sternly, he would be returned to court and a custodial sentence would be considered instead.

He meekly promised to attend.

Then, shell-shocked by the severity of the judgement, a muted Jagger was led back down to the holding area and pushed back into the cell with Ingram. He sat down heavily and put his head in his hands, emitting a loud groan. The other two prisoners were beckoned out, leaving Jagger alone with Ingram.

'Shit,' he breathed. 'Five years' ban and twelve hundred smackers. Utter, utter bastards.'

'Doesn't mean you really have to stop driving, does it?'

Jagger's eyes appeared from behind his hands and he grinned. 'Just don't get caught, eh? The fine's an issue, though ... as well as my other monetary problems and the associated, er, personal issues.' He was attempting to come up with some sort of nicety to call the people who were baying for his blood and money.

'Who are those issues?'

'Nah, rather not say. Sorry, mate.'

'OK.' Ingram shrugged. There was a pause, during which Jagger became aware that Ingram wanted to say something. Jagger didn't push it, simply allowed nature to take its course. 'I might be able to help you out,' Ingram said in a low voice. 'I'll need your mobile number, though.'

'How could you help me out?' Jagger responded glumly. 'Shit creek baaht paddle, me,' he said, playing the victim.

'Give me your number, OK?'

Jagger spread his hands. 'Pen? Paper? Business card? Don't see any of those things on me.'

Ingram leaned forwards and reached down to his feet, his fingers sliding down the inside of one of his socks, reappearing with a small ball-point pen of the type usually found in betting shops or Argos stores. Jagger smirked. 'Got anything stashed up your nose?'

'Kitchen sink ... what's your mobile?'

'Don't you want me to call you?'

'I do the calling.'

'Fair enough.' Jagger recited his number. Ingram jotted it down on the palm of his hand.

'I'll be in touch. Don't know where, don't know when.'

The cell door creaked open. The detective who had earlier spoken to Jagger in the custody area, the one possibly dressed in the fifteen-quid ASDA suit, stood in the frame. He beckoned Jagger with a stumpy finger and the expression a headmaster might have displayed before inflicting pain on a student. Jagger rose reluctantly, nodded at Ingram and followed the jack out.

The evening was cold. A bitter wind blew through the streets of Salford. Jagger stood outside the police station waiting for the taxi the custody officer had been cajoled into calling for him. He shivered, but grinned inwardly. It had been a good day, all told. Things could have gone wrong and he could so easily have ended up in detention, but it had worked out as planned – so far.

A black cab pulled up. 'Jagger?'

'That's me,' said the released prisoner, and climbed into the back of it.

'Any relation?' the cabby asked. He twisted around and looked at Jagger's face. 'No, guess not ... where to, pal?'

'Deansgate, please. Drop me off near Waterstone's.'

The pub was in a tight side street off Deansgate. It was a narrow building, bustling with a cross-section of clientele, and offered rooms by the hour. Jagger edged in and eased past the punters, emerging at the bar where, after an interminable wait, he ordered a large Coke and a bag of crisps. He was thirsty and famished, but he could not have faced another beer or wine. In fact his liver felt like a brick lodged just below his ribcage. It would probably need a few weeks of convalescence before it became pliable again.

As he paid for his goods, a woman sidled up beside him, blonde, about five-seven, trim, her nicely bobbed hair framing her face. She deliberately barged against him in a gentle way, almost causing him to spill his drink. He turned in a huff, ready to unleash a mouthful, but his annoyance morphed into pleasure on seeing who it was. They caught each other's eyes, but neither spoke. She did not apologize, but ordered herself a drink – white wine and soda – then turned to Jagger, who was placing a huge crinkle-cut crisp into his mouth, grilled steak flavour.

'I've got a room upstairs for an hour,' she said, leaning against the bar.

'Will that be long enough?' His tongue pushed out his cheek suggestively, causing her to laugh.

'How long do you need?'

'I can go on for ever once I get started,' he boasted.

'So I've heard. Room two, up the stairs, second right. I'm sure you'll like it. It's very tasteful given the nature of its general usage.' She pushed herself off the bar and disappeared through the crowd. Jagger popped another crisp into his mouth and washed it down with a gulp of Coke.

Room two was furnished nicely, for the price. It had a four-poster bed with a very flowery quilt and curtains; a table and two chairs; an en-suite bathroom for the necessary clean up, pre- or post whatever activity might be taking or have taken place. There was also a strong medicinal tang to the atmosphere.

The woman from the bar was sitting at the table set with two dinner places. She stood up as Jagger entered, extended her hand and they shook.

'Thought you might like a decent meal,' she said, indicating the place settings. 'The food is basic, but pretty good here.'

Jagger took a very deep breath, then exhaled. He was, and looked, exhausted. He plonked down at the table and regarded the blonde woman. She was in her late thirties, extremely good-looking now that her hair had been attended to. Last time he'd seen her was when it had been pinned sharply back off her face and she had been regarding him with harsh eyes across a custody desk whilst he had threatened to punch her lights out.

'I could do with a meal and a very long sleep, actually.'

'Actually, I've booked the room for the night. Thought you'd need a heads-down.'

'Thoughtful.' Jagger eyed the room, wondering how much action it had seen over the years. His mind boggled, then he looked back at the blonde, who was watching him with a half-smile, a million miles away from her earlier expression.

'I thought it might fit in with the Jagger profile.'

He acceded to the notion with a slight shrug and nod of the head. There was a knock on the door and a barmaid came in bearing a heavy tray with two plates on it, both stacked with wonderful smelling food. She placed it on the table and

31

Jagger almost swooned at the aroma from the grilled chicken and potatoes. The girl bobbed back out to the corridor and returned instantly with two bottles of red wine and two glasses. Then she left.

'The food I need; the wine might have to be avoided.'

'Understandable. I thought it might ease the meal down.'

'Whilst calcifying my liver, or whatever it does.'

'Up to you.' She smiled beguilingly and Jagger thought how completely different she looked out of uniform. Quite stunning, actually.

'So, Detective Chief Superintendent Makin of Scotland Yard,' Jagger said in a mock Queen's-English, upper-crust way, 'can we dispense with the formalities and can I tell Frank Jagger to go to hell for a while?'

'Well, Detective Chief Inspector Christie of the numbty constabulary, Hickshire, I think that might well be in order.'

And with that, Henry Christie, a DCI from Lancashire Constabulary, divested the mantle of Frank Jagger, his alter ego, his nom de plume, his legend, someone he had pretended to be for the last three weeks.

With a large sigh of relief he became himself again, at least for a short while, and said, 'In that case it'd be rude not to give the wine a try, wouldn't it?'

Three

Drinking the wine had been a mistake, even if it did ease the meal down. Problem was, one bottle became two and then, despite his best intentions, Henry drank too much and embarrassed himself, although on reflection he might have been more inclined to use the word 'humiliated' rather than embarrassed.

It was just fortunate that the debrief was done over the first bottle, before the alcohol had any chance to skew his recollections.

'So how d'you think it went?' Andrea Makin asked, eyeing Henry across the rim of her wine glass.

'You can only go so far with it,' he answered, 'otherwise suspicions get aroused.' He looked into her eyes, thinking – inappropriately, as usual – that suspicions might not be the only thing to get aroused tonight.

'Yeah, I know. It's a delicate path to tread.'

'Having said that, I think he pretty much took the bait ... we'll just have to wait and see, I guess.'

'You think he was interested, then?'

'He wanted my phone number ... let's just hope he doesn't want a date.' Henry forked a tender chunk of chicken into his mouth and chewed it pleasurably. 'He'll have a nibble,' he said, and immediately regretted the possible double entendre as Andrea's eyes glazed over, the corners of her mouth twisted upwards and then she turned her head away at a coy angle, blushing. And Detective Chief Inspector Henry Christie wondered how the hell he'd managed to get himself into such a predicament: somewhere between a deadly, high-class criminal and a sultry, sexy woman detective whose only goal in life seemed to be the capture of that criminal, and maybe Henry Christie on the side. A bit like a salad.

Four weeks earlier, Henry Christie had been sitting at his desk in his office set in one corner of the larger office housing the Headquarters Special Projects Team. He was shell-shocked and staring into space.

He was in that frozen state of mind in which he often found himself in the blurred but hurly-burly aftermath of the attempt to assassinate the American State Secretary on her official visit to Blackburn, Lancashire, some nine months previously. It had been an attempt that Henry had had a hand in thwarting – but at what cost? he often harangued himself. The answer he came to was the cost of the lives of two good people, lives that he, ridiculously, blamed himself for losing. However, in clinical retrospect, they would have died even if Condoleezza Rice had seen sense and cancelled her visit. Henry, un-knowingly, had set a violent express train going and lives would have been lost anyway.

He had almost been killed, too. A constant physical reminder of what had happened to him was his broken right cheekbone which even now remained tender to the touch and throbbed constantly as it steadfastly refused to heal properly.

And then, six months after that day of extreme violence, he had heard the news that his good friend, the American FBI agent Karl Donaldson, was fighting for his life in a Spanish hospital after having been found grievously wounded in mysterious circumstances in a square in Barcelona. It was an incident, Henry knew, that was connected to the hunt for the terrorist who had masterminded the assassination attempt on Rice.

Henry shook his head to try and rid his mind, at least for a while, of these horrendous musings.

He was not to blame for anything, he had been assured repeatedly by many different people, and he needed to put it behind him and move on.

Unfortunately, having a brittle character at the best of times, he had found himself clinging to the edge of nervous exhaustion, breakdown and depression. He had been there before and it was a place he did not wish to visit ever again because it was dark, bleak, featureless and very frightening.

He glanced at the stack of paperwork accumulated on his desk. His mouth twitched in distaste.

Things might not have been so bad if work had been more interesting and challenging. With the exception of a drugs-related death investigation he had been involved in, most of his time had been spent cooped up in the office, pushing unimportant pieces of paper and staring into space.

Through his office window he could see the Special Projects Team, the group of misfits who had been chucked together to do the projects no one else wanted to touch with a barge pole – and because no one else wanted those particular individuals in their departments.

However, Henry had tried very hard with his team and the work and been proud, in a perverted sort of way, that he'd managed to complete two very unsexy projects and launch three others which were going as well as could be expected, despite their unpopularity.

He rose from his chair, realizing he needed to move, get the blood circulating.

Passing through the Special Projects office he nodded amiably at his staff and emerged on to the narrow top-floor corridor of the headquarters building, making his way to the stairs.

It was his intention to have a mid-morning stroll and do some networking at the same time. He trotted down to the ground floor and snaked through along the ground floor to the Intelligence Unit where he had a chat with the DI in there; then he walked out of the HQ building itself and walked across the sports pitches to the Pavilion Building which housed the Serious and Organized Crime Unit, formerly the Major Crime Unit. He had a very pleasant conversation with the very nice female DCI, who was running a government-funded project on street crime. She declined his invitation to join him for a late breakfast, so he meandered back to the HQ dining room where he caught the tail end of the breakfast service. Then, armed with a bacon roll (which he promised himself he would run off at lunchtime) and a large coffee, he took up a position in one corner of the room.

He watched a few people come and go, his interest only perking up when a man he detested with a vengeance walked in, accompanied by a woman who Henry did not really take much notice of.

The man was Dave Anger, his former boss on the Force Major Incident Team, who had a massive downer on Henry because Henry had slept with his wife many years before, when she wasn't actually his wife, not even his girlfriend. It was something that gnawed relentlessly at Anger and he did not seem to be able to let it go, especially since his wife had left him and rubbed his nose in it. His vendetta against Henry was a growing legend throughout the force and had resulted in very bad blood between them.

Henry averted his eyes, looked through the window at the car park, sipped his coffee and ignored Anger's presence. He was soon lost in dark thoughts again, though, his mind's eye re-creating a scene of savage butchery. Two people lying dead, their throats cut so badly their heads were almost severed from their bodies...

'Henry?'

He twitched and looked up. Dave Anger was standing in front of him, a pretty unusual occurrence as both men steadfastly ensured their paths did not cross if at all possible.

'Dave,' Henry acknowledged the superior

officer dubiously, their eyes interlocking for one fleeting, flinty moment. He then glanced at the woman with Anger. She was standing slightly behind him, to one side, a grin on her face. Anger half-turned, 'Can I introduce you to...'

Her smile widened. She extended her hand. 'No need, Dave. We already know each other.'

Henry rose quickly, his chair scraping backwards, shaking hands with her, their eyes making an altogether different contact than his and Anger's had only seconds before.

'Andrea ... it's great to see you.'

Her name was Andrea Makin. When she and Henry had last met, some six years earlier, she had been a detective superintendent in the Metropolitan Police Special Branch. Henry guessed she would have probably moved up at least a rank by now. His eyes gave her the quick once-over – as hers did him – and he saw she had changed somewhat from the woman he remembered. She was still tall and rangy, but her facial features had tightened, her once wide nose now seemed pinched and her full lips were a little thinner. Her body, Henry guessed, from the appraisal, seemed pretty much as before. But she looked tired now. Stress or illness, Henry could not decide.

Still, he thought, I'll bet I don't look like the spring chicken she knew back then.

'Nice to see you, too,' she responded. 'You haven't changed a bit.'

'You mean I looked this bad six years ago?' he jested.

She smiled.

38

Anger's face had changed expression during this brief exchange – to annoyance that Henry seemed to have stolen some of his thunder. He coughed, bringing attention back to him.

'Seems a long time since the Nazis and Hellfire Dawn,' Andrea said, ignoring Anger.

'Yeah, yeah.'

'And how is Jane Roscoe?' she asked, like a minx.

'As far as I know, OK,' Henry answered, feeling himself redden up at the mention of a woman he was once illicitly involved with. He cleared his throat. 'So what brings you to this neck of the woods again? Still chasing Hitler lovers, or is it all Islam now?'

Anger, having been cut out, felt the need to interject. 'Neither of those things.'

'Ah, well, nice of you to say hello,' Henry said, lowering himself back down, thinking the encounter was over.

'It's actually you we came to see,' Anger said, causing Henry's eyebrows to ride up. There was a note of reluctance in his voice.

'Special Projects, me. Team misfit,' Henry said. 'What could you possibly want with someone like me?'

Andrea swooped past Anger into a chair opposite Henry, leaned on the table and said, 'Got a proposition for you – and your alter ego.' She smiled and Henry knew he was all hers from that moment on.

The trio retreated to Dave Anger's office in the FMIT block on the far side of the playing fields.

Once an accommodation block for students on residential courses at the force training centre, it had been commandeered several years earlier and refurbished to become a reasonably plush office suite to house the FMIT team and its administration. Henry had once had an office on the middle floor, on which Anger's office was situated, and it annoyed him to know that this now belonged to one of Anger's brown-nosed sycophants, a certain DI Carradine, the man who had replaced Henry on FMIT.

Being led by Anger across the playing fields, knowing he was being taken back to his old stomping ground, gave Henry palpitations and a shortness of breath. He tried to master his heartbeat and breathing, trying to slow everything down as discreetly as possible, so as not to draw attention to himself in the early stages of hyperventilation. He managed – just – and followed the two high-rankers into the FMIT block and up the stairs, feeling uneasy about what was going on.

What could Dave Anger want him for?

It had to be something unpleasant.

Seated in Anger's office – even more recently decorated than the block itself, Henry noticed, wondering how much the taxpayer had forked out for the wallpaper – Andrea Makin shot Henry a few worried glances, noticing the discomfort he was at pains to hide.

'You OK, Henry?' she enquired in a whisper.

'Yep, yep,' he clipped, obviously not.

They were sitting on the points of a triangle,

facing each other across a coffee table.

'Superintendent Makin,' Anger opened – so she hadn't gone up a rank, Henry noted – 'perhaps you'd like to begin?'

She gave him a thin smile and half-turned to Henry, her expression morphing into one of pleasure, something Anger clocked with a wry curl of his mouth. 'The thing is this, Henry,' she started, 'since we last met I've moved on to the Serious Crime Squad down in the Met and child pornography is in my portfolio.' Henry nodded. No wonder she looked drained. Dealing with that day-in, day-out can be an emotional killer. 'We're investigating the activities of a professional criminal by the name of Ryan Ingram.' She produced an A5-size photograph from her briefcase that she handed to Henry. It was a good quality surveillance photo of a middle-aged man with close-cropped hair, tough looking. 'He's a pretty big shot down in the Smoke, if you'll pardon my vernacular.'

'If I knew what one was, I'd be more than happy to pardon it,' Henry quipped. It brought a smile to Andrea's face, a scowl of disapproval to Anger's coupled with an under-the-breath 'tut'. He was clearly as uncomfortable with Henry, as Henry was with him.

'He's a drug importer at the top of a very long, complex chain, which we are constantly breaking the links of. Though,' she went on, 'it's the way of the world that those links get repaired very quickly. He's also into hardcore pornography, right across the board. He imports DVDs, finances filming in Holland and Belgium, and he's also hands on.' She paused, took a breath. 'He likes little girls in particular and we suspect him of abducting two children who've never been seen since. We think they may have ended up being murdered in snuff movies in Holland.'

Henry exhaled shortly, making a noise of disapproval. He peered closely at the photo of Ingram, then held it away, his brow furrowed.

'Henry?' Andrea enquired.

'Sorry ... he just looks vaguely familiar, that's all.' Henry was good-to-excellent with faces and names, and Ingram's image jarred something deep within the filing cabinet at the back of his brain. 'Having said that, I don't think I know him, if that's why you've asked me here.'

'No, that's not why ... just pin back your ears and listen, eh?' Anger said impatiently.

Henry shrugged and smirked, revelling in the knowledge that he obviously possessed something that Anger wanted and he, for a change, was in a position of power, a position he was eager to abuse, childish though this was. His eyes closed and opened and he looked disdainfully away from Anger, back to Andrea Makin, who seemed puzzled and unsettled by the vibes she was picking up.

'OK, go on,' he said to her.

'Ingram is a very violent man, suspected of disposing of business rivals and being behind some quite nasty crimes.' Henry nodded as he listened, now giving her his full attention, suddenly realizing that Ingram was just the sort of individual he should be investigating – not bloody well pushing reams of paper from desk to desk. 'Now, the thing is,' Andrea continued, 'we have been getting closer and closer to him and as we open doors, the heat starts to rise and he's become increasingly aware that his position is becoming ... vulnerable. Some of his lieutenants have been arrested, other people down the line, too. Don't get me wrong, he's well insulated and we have a lot more layers to peel away before we slot him, but he knows it's just a matter of time...'

'Sounds interesting.'

'But the problem is, because he's getting twitchy, he's decided on a move.'

Henry's eyes narrowed. 'Ooop north?' he guessed in broad Lancashire.

'Aye,' she responded likewise, 'ooop north. Living in a Travelodge at the moment with his mate, Mitch Percy. Separate rooms, that is.'

Henry pouted thoughtfully, a charge of excitement surging through him, which he tried to disguise. 'Which is where I come in ... somehow?' He tried to sound disinterested and hopeful at the same time.

'And which is why, if you agree to our proposition, I can't really be telling you much more about Ingram for your own safety.' She raised her finely plucked eyebrows.

And the penny dropped – with a thud.

Henry uttered a short laugh, whilst still experiencing the excitement.

Both senior officers gave him a quiet moment, sitting back, allowing him to cogitate. Anger eyed Makin. Both eyed Henry.

'Whereabouts up north has he come?' Henry

asked.

'Manchester,' Andrea told him. 'He's from the general area anyway.'

He nodded pensively. 'I take it that the proposition is not for me to move on to the National Crime Squad, say, and head a team dedicated to investigating Ingram?'

Both shook their heads. Anger chortled. As if.

'Thought not.'

'There's already a joint Met/GMP investigation under way,' Andrea said, 'but we're short of a particular angle on this guy.'

'And I think you know what's being suggested here, Henry,' Anger said, 'so stop horsing around.'

'First off, I need to point out that I haven't worked undercover for over six years,' Henry said warningly.

'We know that.'

'And I'd need a bit of time to get back into it – if I agreed to the proposition. Working under-cover isn't just something you pick up again, you know. I'll probably need a psychological evaluation.'

'Oh yes,' Andrea agreed. Anger tittered at the thought.

'And I think I'll need to run it past Kate. In fact I know I will.' Even though Henry said this as though it would be a joint decision, he'd already made up his mind.

A man called Frank Jagger was going to be resurrected and dusted off.

One thing did occur to Henry. 'Why me?'

The two looked at each other, then Andrea

said, 'Well, I could bullshit you, Henry, it's just that there was no one else available.'

'Gee, thanks.'

Four

'I need to be brutally honest with you, Henry,' the woman sitting opposite him in the pub said sadly. She was slightly older than him, but extremely well kept, with a lovely complexion, a neat bob of black hair, piercing bright blue eyes which were as hard as steel and seemed to rip away at every barrier he erected around his psyche, and a slim body clothed in a two-piece suit of auburn and gold. She looked spot-on and Henry had never seen her anything less than impeccably turned-out in all the years he'd known her.

Dr Carole Sanders was the force psychologist based in the Occupational Health Department. It was part of her job to psychologically profile and assess undercover officers for all the North-West police forces, ensuring they were mentally able to carry out such a stressful role where everyday undercover meant living on the edge where one slip could be fatal.

Henry looked down at his knees, preparing himself for the bad news. Before being allowed back on to the U/C rota, he had to be given a clean bill of mental health and he guessed that, following the previous day's appointment with Dr Sanders held in a room in a Travelodge near Preston, she was about to scotch his ambition. 'Go on, Carole, I can take it.'

She sipped her fizzy mineral water and regarded him warmly, like an old friend. She had crossed paths with him often over the last dozen years.

Henry braced himself, clasping his hands between his knees.

'You've been through a hell of a lot,' she said. 'I've spent a great deal of time going through your personal record and coupled with the discussion we had yesterday' – which had felt like wading through treacle, Henry thought on reflection – 'I have come to a decision.'

'Which is?' he blurted.

She held up a finger. 'Let me summarize first … in the very recent past you've had to deal with some major guilt issues regarding the deaths of your two colleagues; you've been in constant confrontation with your line management...' Henry's whole face twisted with loathing. 'You have dealt with the deaths of young girls—'

'That's just part of the job,' he interjected. 'Part of being an SIO.'

'I know, I know,' the doctor said gently. 'I'm just trying to pull together a picture of you personally and professionally, and it's the conclusions I come to from that that I base my recommendations on. I just want you to know my train of thought, OK?'

'Yeah, sorry for interrupting,' he said sullenly.

'You've told me a lot about your personal life,

including recent infidelities and your relationship with Kate and your American friend, Karl.'

'Yeah, Karl,' he sneered.

'A lot has been going on.'

'Admittedly.' Henry picked up his Coke and took a nervous sip, his eyes roving around the quiet pub in which they'd decided to meet for this follow-up 'chat' after yesterday's 'deep and meaningful', during which Henry had squirmed like a rabbit caught in a mantrap. He had not enjoyed it one little bit.

'And there are other considerations I need to take into account. Although not strictly in my field, your physical well-being has also to be considered.' Dr Sanders gazed sadly at him. 'You're only just on the right side of fifty, your retirement is looming should you choose to take it' – she held up a hand to cut off Henry's remonstrations – 'I know you can go on until you're sixty if you so wish ... but what I'm pointing out is that you're no longer in the first flush of youth. I know you run three miles a day, but your left knee keeps giving out on you, and you get up feeling like an old bloke sometimes.' She raised her eyebrows pointedly. 'Now I have no idea what's in store for you with this undercover operation, Henry, but I do know some things: it'll be tough, it'll be draining, it'll be dangerous and as well as your mind and body being spot on, you'll need the background support at home, too.'

She inhaled a deep breath, then regarded her patient with a shake of the head. 'What do you have to say?'

'Feels like the bloody X Factor,' he moaned. 'Feels like an audition.'

'Good analogy,' Dr Sanders nodded. 'Do you think you have what it takes?'

Henry steeled himself. 'Despite my ups and downs, trials and tribulations, guilt trips and infidelities, my answer's got to be yes.' He looked into her eyes and thought he saw a smidgen of relief there, respect even. 'I don't give up on things and, more often than not, I get results. They need the right profile of U/C officer for this job and my legend fits. I'm the right man for the job. I think it's going to be a fairly straightforward scam, maybe a month, two months tops to set it up. I've done it before and I can do it again ... and, yeah, I do have the support from home. Kate and I have discussed it at length and we're as solid as a rock.'

'Despite your infidelities?'

Henry blanched at that upper cut. 'I'm trying to curb that sort of behaviour. Like I told you, I even got one woman so drunk that she couldn't sleep with me. Pretty chivalrous and loyal, if you ask me.'

'But then you slept with the next one that came along.'

'Touché – but we are strong at home, honestly. Remarriage is on the cards – if I could just blurt out the proposal. Kinda sticks in my throat,' he admitted, and reached for his Coke, taking a long swig of it. He wiped his mouth with a pincer movement of thumb and forefinger. 'So come on, Doc, don't keep me in suspenders any longer. Am I fit, or am I fucked?'

'Do you definitely want to do this, Henry?'

'Yes.'

'Very well, I'll recommend you.'

He blinked with disbelief, which morphed into a huge Cheshire pussycat grin. 'Seriously?'

'Why – do you think I shouldn't?'

'No, no, no,' he babbled hurriedly. 'I just thought...'

'That you were an old, emotionally wrecked, physically burnt-out has-been?'

'Don't push it.'

'No ... you'll be OK and it'll probably do you a bit of good to get out of the environs of Lancashire Constabulary for a while, concentrating on something that'll take up all your energies and skills ... but the one thing I would warn is to keep an eye on the home front. It's the most important thing and it's the thing that trips up most U/C officers.'

'I will,' he promised sincerely.

In fact, Henry had played just a little fast and loose with the good psychologist in that he had lied about the reaction from Kate. The reason for that was because he hadn't had any sort of reaction at all as he hadn't quite got around to telling her about the possibility of working undercover again.

To Henry it had been a chicken and egg situation.

He figured that if he broached the subject with Kate and was then subsequently told he was not psychologically fit for undercover work, then the angst he would have gone through with Kate would have just been pain without gain. Instead he went though the process with Dr Sanders, telling a whopping white lie or two about his home life as he went along, so that when he went to Kate to tell her about the job, he would know he could do it. If the doctor turned him down, then he wouldn't even bother telling Kate about any of it.

When he revealed his intentions to Kate, her face said a thousand words, followed by her mouth, which said, 'You must be joking!' – at which a heavy sinking sensation dropped through his intestines. 'You're forty-nine years old, completely out of it in terms of working undercover and – big "and" here – it will not be good for us.' She made a circular, all-encompassing gesture with her hands.

Kate was only small framed. Not petite, but well proportioned, yet when her 'mad' was up she had the ferocity of a charging Pamplona bull at full tilt. Her eyes blazed and Henry almost expected her to paw the ground and blow steam through her nostrils. He would have liked to say how magnificent she was when roused, but in truth she scared the hell out of him.

He had raised the matter when he believed she was at her most approachable, just after a triple dose of soap operas and with a glass of Merlot in her hand, the second of the night.

'I can't even believe you're considering this. Do you think you're fit for it? Have you seen the shrink yet? Because you'll have to, y'know.'

He gulped, swallowing the contents of a very dry mouth. He was now caught in a quandary brought about by not being entirely truthful. If he told Kate he'd already been for a psychological evaluation, she would hit the Artexed ceiling because she would see it as him having gone behind her back, not telling her what was going on.

'I know I will,' he said, deciding to lie, wincing dreadfully inside. 'I just wanted us to talk about it first, then go and see the shrink once – if – you thought it was OK. There's every chance they'll think I'm pots for rags and tell me to get lost.'

'Mm.' Her pretty mouth screwed itself into the knot of disapproval he'd seen too many times for comfort. But then her lips unfastened and she turned to him, eyes a-glisten. She sighed and gave him a look of resignation. 'I know you'll do it anyway if you pass the scrutiny,' she said, 'so it's best if I just give you my blessing, isn't it?'

Henry's throat constricted as he looked at her and thought about the hell he'd put her through over the years, in spite of which, she was still here.

He exhaled. 'Tell you what – if I'm judged fit enough up here' – he tapped his skull – 'then I'll do the job for six weeks, tops. How about that?'

'Only if you promise to keep in touch ... I know it's impossible sometimes, but I also know you; you get so embroiled in it that you forget everything else. You must call every day and you must come home when you can ... that's all I ask. Keep me in the loop, OK?'

His head made exaggerated nods.

'Those are my conditions,' she finished sternly. She reached out and touched his face. 'You're still just a little boy, aren't you? Excited by dangerous things. Still playing cops and robbers.'

'You know me so well.'

'Which makes me so surprised that I'm still here.'

There is a fine balance with the amount of information and intelligence an undercover cop can be given prior to going into an operation, and Henry was adamant about how much he should be told on the subject of Ryan Ingram.

'I want to know as little as possible,' he said to Andrea Makin two days later as she briefed him. 'I don't want to know anything about any police operation, nor do I really want to know very much about Ingram himself, other than what he looks like.'

'Won't that be a disadvantage?' she asked. They had convened in a meeting room at Lancashire Police Headquarters to map out the way forward. She had set up a laptop computer and linked it to the ceiling-mounted data projector, ready and waiting for Henry's arrival. She also had a huge file with her which she had been leafing through.

On his arrival, Henry had purposely seated himself so he couldn't see any of the documents. He had been a trained undercover officer since the early Nineties, and was familiar with the lack of knowledge displayed by senior officers about the role and undercover policing in general, although to be fair to Andrea she did seem to have some idea, but not much.

'No,' he said in answer to her question.

'But surely knowledge is power?' she said naively.

'Only if you're supposed to have that knowledge in the first place. It can trip you up if you're not careful,' he explained. 'One innocent slip and suddenly the target is wary and suspicious. Next step means a gun in the face, maybe. What I need to know is my own story, not his, so that when I've made contact and when – if – he takes the bait, my background stands up to scrutiny. All I really need from you is his name, a look at his photo and some idea about how we're going to scam him, if that's what we intend to do.'

'So all this is a waste of time?' She flicked the pages of her fat file and tapped the laptop.

Henry nodded. 'It's the first contact that needs to be right – that's the important step. How do we meet? How does it come about? Do we get introduced? How does the ball get smashed into his court so he makes the moves, he's in the driving seat and I'm not suggesting anything that'll lead to screams of entrapment. That's the fun bit.'

Henry Christie's undercover legend – the person he became when working undercover – was Frank Jagger. He had chosen the name himself. Frank came from his dear departed father and Jagger from his favourite rock star.

Frank Jagger was a wheeler dealer, a bits 'n'

bats guy who operated on the fringes of criminality, dealing with the disposal of goods, usually stolen, from which he skimmed his profit.

Up until about six years before, Henry had known Jagger very well because throughout the Nineties he'd slid in and out of that persona for various operations, some of which had been very hairy indeed.

But his intimate knowledge of Jagger had lapsed, although the legend lived on, sustained by a small office situated within the monster that was now the National Criminal Intelligence Service, formerly the Regional Crime Squad, whose task it was to keep all legends alive and kicking even when they were dormant.

Henry and Andrea spent a while tossing around a few ideas about how to approach Ingram, and getting nowhere fast, when there was a knock on the door of the meeting room and a man, a detective known as 'the Keeper' came in, nodding at Henry and giving Andrea a muted, 'Afternoon, ma'am.'

Henry had met the Keeper many times over the years, never actually getting to know his name (nor wanting to), or where he operated from, because the Keeper, or 'Keeps', as he was referred to in conversation, was the man ultimately responsible for all the undercover legends in existence in the country, some sixty in total. He put together and maintained all the legends with the assistance of a very select group of people who, should they ever have been identified and targeted by crims, could divulge the identity and whereabouts of every undercover cop in England and Wales.

Keeps sat down and opened a folder. He looked at Andrea, who gave him the nod.

'Frank Jagger, fence, handler, petty thief,
fraudster, but mainly a handler,' he began. 'Last
used 2001 in the case of Jacky Lee.' He looked
pointedly at Henry, who recalled Lee very well,
and his sudden, violent demise at the hands of a
Russian hit man. 'Since then he's been lying
dormant, in as much as you haven't used him,
but I've been keeping his life going...'

Henry waited, breath baited, wondering just
what the hell he'd been up to in the intervening
years.

Henry was utterly astounded by the detailed
work the Keeper had been doing, giving a ghost
a life, especially when he was doing the same
thing for all the other U/C operatives. Many of
those legends would be up and running, not just
lying fallow.

The list was endless: passports, driving licen-
ces (with endorsements) bank accounts, tax
demands, supermarket bills, parking tickets,
library cards; letters from companies chasing
debts, mobile phone records and all sort of other
detritus people collect throughout their life-
times. The completely amazing thing was that
everything was authentic because it was all produced in collusion and cooperation with busi-
nesses and other organizations involved at the
very highest level.

'I'm impressed,' Henry said.

The Keeper gave a modest nod of acknowledgement and tried to mask his pleasure. 'I try.'

After further discussion, during which the Keeper gave Henry an overview of how he saw Frank Jagger's life having panned out over the last six years, he shook hands with Henry and Andrea, wished them luck, and left them to it. He'd given them the background, the life story, now it was down to them to take it from there.

Henry picked through the paperwork, wondering how Jagger would have continued his life after his involvement with Jacky Lee, the Manchester gangster, and the subsequent mess following his demise, which included a serious assault on Henry, one which he had buried deep in his mind and which still caused him to squirm when it surfaced.

'Thoughts?' Andrea Makin asked.

Henry's brow creased. 'Yeah,' he said at length. 'This guy would have laid very low ... he's no hard man and he would've seen it in his best interests to quit the scene, keep his head down...' he ruminated. 'He's not particularly good with money, as we can see from the debt chasers ... so he owes money to legitimate people and there would be every chance of him owing to loan sharks, drug dealers ... whoever.'

Andrea watched him, thinking.

Henry glanced across at her and his mind jumped back to the time when he had first met her. He could so easily have become involved – except that he'd been involved with someone else, an illicit relationship that had turned sour. Andrea caught his eye and he was certain she knew what he was thinking. He refocused his mind on the problem at hand.

'I think Frank Jagger could well be in hock to another crim ... I think he could've cadged a loan off someone with the intention of pulling off another deal, skimming his profit and repaying the loan with interest ... only, for some reason it's all gone tits up, he's left high and dry with a huge debt and a mountain of goods which he can't shift and which would be of interest to someone like Ryan Ingram.'

'Porn, in other words?' suggested Andrea.

'Of the worst kind – hardcore porn. Can you get hold of some if necessary?'

'Some? The Met has a shit load of the stuff piled up in warehouses all over London, mountains of it.'

'OK, then that's the premise ... now we need to start pulling the stories and characters together ... I have an idea on that score ... but I'm still not one hundred per cent sure how Jagger and Ingram get together.'

They looked at each other, their minds ticking over, then Andrea said, 'I have a plan.'

By the time they had finished – the scheming of mice and men – it was early evening. Henry was buzzing with delight and eagerness. They left the now almost deserted HQ building and strolled on to the car park.

'It's good to be working with you again, Henry,' Andrea said.

'And you, boss,' he conceded.

They walked across to her car, an S Type Jaguar, where they paused briefly. 'I'll start to fix up Ingram's arrest with GMP – somehow,' she said.

'Sounds good.'

He looked at her sleek car, then her sleek body.

'Are you sure you're up for this, Henry?' she asked with concern. 'I have to tell you that the report from the psychologist was quite detailed, no stone unturned. You've been through a lot recently ... I mean, it probably wouldn't be seemly for you to break down in tears in front of Ingram and blab it all to him.'

'I'm absolutely fine,' Henry assured her. 'And the bottom line is that I love it, absolutely love it ... which is why I'm keen to do this and why it hurt so much to be booted from being a detective.'

'OK, OK, I'm convinced.'

He stepped back a foot. 'I take it you've been assessing me as well?'

'Something like that ... y'see, I want Ryan Ingram and this may be one of the best opportunities we have to nail the perverted bastard and I don't want to blow it—'

'By having a weak link ... i.e., me?'

'Exactly,' she said stonily, 'so, as much as I like you, and it is good working with you, I do want to do a proper job.'

He watched her drive out of HQ. She was staying at a hotel somewhere near Bolton. He turned and ambled happily towards his car, his fairly recently acquired Rover 75, which in certain lights and wearing dark glasses, could have been mistaken for a Jaguar. Dream on, he thought.

Firing up the engine he felt light-headed and happy, though his thoughts clouded slightly when he wondered how he was going to deal with Kate again. He planned to tell her he'd seen the force shrink today and been given the mental all-clear, even though it was actually two days since he'd seen the doctor. He didn't want to reveal that the operation was already under way – that would have to wait for another day or two.

So whilst he wasn't actually telling Kate lies, he was rearranging the truth.

Maybe he could use this as a bit of practice ahead of going undercover, even though he knew that when he went under, his whole life would be a complete lie.

He drove through the HQ exit barriers, turned on to the A59, then headed in the direction of Preston, a journey he had taken many times, eventually cutting across on to the A583, which would take him to Blackpool. He could have done the journey on autopilot and in a way that's what he was doing that evening whilst listening to his thoughts and his CD player which had been mysteriously loaded with a disc by an artist called Mika who screamed tunefully at him. Kate would be the culprit. He would have to have strong words with her: don't mess with my Rolling Stones discs.

The evening was getting darker, rain had started to fall and he failed to notice the car that had been following him at a discreet distance since he'd left headquarters.

Once on the A583 he travelled along the dual carriageway up to the lights at Three Nooks, stopping as they were on red with just one vehicle behind him. He glanced in his rear-view mirror, but did not even register it, other than to note there was a car behind. Moving through the lights, the car stayed behind, matching his acceleration up to the 50 mph speed limit on that stretch of road.

The next set of lights was on green. He sailed through, considering pulling in at a petrol station before getting home and buying Kate some flowers and chocs as sweeteners for his news. The car was still behind him, but then it moved out into the right-hand lane and came alongside Henry's Rover. He didn't even glance at it. It was only when the car had remained parallel with him for a few hundred metres did he even acknowledge its presence, eye it once and think, Just get fucking past, will you?

He didn't look at the driver, but noted that the car was a Ford Mondeo, a similar colour to the one he'd previously owned and traded in for the Rover. He could not tell the exact colour in the fading light. He put his foot down slightly, aware that not far ahead was a dreaded speed camera on his side of the road. But he wanted to leave the Mondeo behind now because it was irritating him.

As he nosed forwards, so did the Mondeo, staying with him exactly.

Suddenly, it surged ahead.

A feeling of relief went through him, which evaporated instantly when the Mondeo slotted right in front of him and anchored on.

Henry had to slam the brakes on to avoid tail-ending it. He swerved towards the kerb. 'Shit!' he gasped, gripping the wheel.

Then the Mondeo accelerated away at high speed.

Henry cursed. What was the arsehole playing at? He caught his breath, considered a pursuit, then thought better of it. To get involved in a road rage incident was something he could do without. He decided it was just someone acting the toss-bag and let it go, reaching the next set of lights at Kirkham without incident or further sight of the Mondeo. A few moments later he was on the long straight stretch of dual carriageway which would take him up to Blackpool.

Fifty was the limit on this section of road, which had seen its fair share of fatalities.

A mirror check revealed a car approaching from behind, main beam on. With a pissed-off utterance, Henry flicked the lever on his interior mirror to cut out the glare. What was it with people tonight? he thought crossly.

The car sped right up his rear end, tailgating, only feet away from his chuff-box, the driver now flashing his lights angrily.

Henry knocked his mirror back into place and squinted at the reflection. He maintained his speed and position, refusing to be intimidated. Casually, he raised the middle finger of his left hand.

The car dropped back, lights lowered.

Henry recognized the outline of the car as a Mondeo. One person on board, probably a man. Same one as before, he guessed and thought, 'Whatever,' aloud, continuing to drive, coming on to another long straight stretch of dual carriageway. At this point the Mondeo swerved into the outside lane, moved forward and hung a few feet from the rear of Henry's offside wing.

Henry kept a cautious eye on the car through his wing mirror.

Then it came alongside, and they were like two racing cars on a Scalextric track, dead level, nose with nose, tail with tail, driver with driver.

Now seriously worried, Henry glanced sideways at the person who had become his tormentor – and what he saw sent a shock wave through him. The interior light was on in the car and he was able to see the driver clearly – as intended.

He was wearing a balaclava-type mask, with two eyeholes and a jagged mouth slit. The person was shouting something at Henry, who could see the mouth working obscenely behind the hole. Suddenly the person yanked his steering wheel down to the left, a jerk of a movement that Henry saw and reacted to instantly – but not quickly enough to avoid a collision.

He slammed the brakes on, but the two cars smashed into each other, edge to edge, with a horrendous scraping of metal and a sickening snap as Henry's wing mirror snapped off. Henry swerved into the roadside and the Mondeo tore away towards Blackpool. The driver threw a piece of paper out of his window as he disappeared down the road.

Henry sat behind his wheel, gasping. Someone had tried to ram him off the road. The same driver who had a few minutes earlier braked hard in front of him for no apparent reason.

Henry knew he hadn't done anything wrong in a motoring sense. He hadn't cut anyone up, or done anything stupid to make him a target for road rage. But the difference between road rage and this incident was that the former is usually a spur of the moment reaction to something, whilst what had happened to Henry was far more sinister ... and was proved by two things.

Firstly, by the car involved. A blue Ford Mondeo, exactly the same colour as the one he had previously owned. And Henry knew this for sure now, despite the darkness, because he had managed to see and note its registered number.

It was his old car.

Someone driving his old car had rammed him off the road.

Coincidence? Henry did not think so.

Henry got carefully out of his car. This was a fast stretch of road and though not busy at this time of night he still had to take care as he ran through the rain to retrieve the piece of paper thrown from the Mondeo. He managed to get it without being flattened, returned to his car and sat there with the hazards flashing whilst he carefully unfolded the paper.

It was A4 size, bearing a full-face photograph of himself.

And pasted over it was a gun sight consisting of concentric circles, the centre of the sight, the cross hairs, right above his forehead.

It was as though he was looking down the sights of a sniper rifle aimed at himself, ready to pull the trigger.

* * *

Henry's mind jarred back to the present.

It was part-way through the third bottle of wine that did it for Henry, as Andrea Makin poured out two large glasses from it with that pleasant glug-glugging noise as the wine cascaded out.

He had explained in detail, during the first bottle, the minutiae of how the first meeting had gone with Ryan Ingram; during the second, conversation had become more relaxed, gravitating from work to more personal matters. Andrea learned a lot about Henry and vice versa. The third bottle led to less conversation, with some quite lengthy gaps and meaningful eye contact, then to a meeting of bodies as the table was pushed away from between them, the tearing off of clothing and Henry pushing Andrea on to the bed and climbing hurriedly between her legs ... and then, unfortunately for both of them, erectile dysfunction and his subsequent humiliation.

Five

Henry awoke alone, feeling quite chilled in the room over the Manchester city centre pub. His head throbbed as a result of a combination of the wine intake, weeks of excess, tiredness and the stress he had been under thus far – but he knew he would in for much more pressure if Ingram took the bait.

He dozed awhile in the soft-mattressed, King-size bed whilst a series of emotions vied for attention inside him.

Part of him was glad he had not slept with Andrea Makin. It would have been another failure in his relationship with Kate, but the fact remained that he had *wanted* to have sex with her; another part of him was trying to deal with the fact that even though he had wanted sex, he hadn't been able to get a sustainable erection.

That had been so embarrassing.

As he'd clambered gamely over Andrea's more than willing flesh and her hands slid all over his body, ultimately finding their way to his penis only to discover not very much, their wild, breathless antics had ceased virtually immediately as she held him and looked into his eyes with disappointment.

He had looked down and said, 'Shit.'

Andrea's face hardened as he crabbed sideways off her and rolled on to his back, covering himself with the quilt. The back of his hand covered his eyes, an attempt to hide his utter shame.

'And I suppose that's never happened before?' she said stiltedly.

'I won't say never, but it's been a rare occurrence.'

'So it's me then?' Her voice was hurt.

'No, no, God, you're wonderful,' he babbled as she sat up on the edge of the bed, then stood up without shame, displaying her lovely peach-like rear to him, then bent over and collected her clothes, as Henry watched transfixed, gulping.

She hiked up her panties, picked up her bra and turned to face Henry whilst refitting it with jerky movements making her breasts bounce, and making Henry ache for the nipples he'd not even managed to get his lips around. Lifting the quilt and glancing down hopefully, he still had not reacted appropriately.

'It's just...' he began feebly.

'It's all right, Henry,' she said, hitching up her skirt. 'It was a foolish idea in the first place ... it would only have clouded our judgement. Y'know' – she tossed her hair back here – 'every debrief would've been just hot lust and dirty sex.' She shrugged. 'We wouldn't have wanted that, would we?'

'No.' It was a very squeaky, pathetic sound he made.

'Anyway, you're obviously drained and need a good night's sleep. We'd've only been fucking all night and that wouldn't have helped you, would it?'

She had completed her dressing and now looked down pityingly at Henry, her head tilted to one side as though she was inspecting a strange, horrible museum exhibit. Her mouth gave her face an expression of disgust, like she might have been looking at a medical display at Tussaud's waxworks.

'Let's pretend this never happened, eh?' She swung her bag over her shoulder and strutted to the door, stopping with her hand on the knob, turning back.

'I'm sorry, Andrea. It's not you, honestly.'

'Whatever ... let's meet at midday in the café in Waterstone's on Deansgate ... chat about the way forwards, eh?'

The words sounded pretty ominous to Henry, but he nodded assent.

'You have no idea,' she declared with a lioness-like swish of her head, 'what you've missed.'

'Oh, I think I do,' Henry mumbled to himself as, the morning after, he threw back the quilt and got out of bed following the mental rerun of his clash with Andrea. At least when she had gone, slamming the door dramatically behind her, he had simply fallen asleep for almost nine hours. He thought, hopefully, that maybe it was merely exhaustion that had affected his libido. However, as he glanced down at his presently acorn-sized member nestling in his greying pubic hair, there wasn't much sign of life.

Still, as a one-off, and as disappointing as it

67

had been, he decided not to worry about it. He shouldn't even have been butt naked with another woman, so perhaps it was simply a divine punishment for the sin.

He stood up with a groan. He had slept well and deeply, but the bed had been too soft for his liking and his lower back was killing him. Putting one foot ahead of the other and making his way to the en-suite shower, he felt about ninety and his liver like a chunk of Accrington brick.

The shower was hot, wonderful and reviving. He spent a long time underneath its powerful jets, shampooing and soaping off the last few weeks of grime and the remnants of his time in custody. Then he dressed and groomed himself, remembering that when he stepped back out on to the streets of Manchester he would again be Frank Jagger, ne'er-do-well and vagabond of this parish ... but before that he wanted to treat himself to an unhealthy breakfast, a couple of mugs of coffee and a chat on the phone with Kate.

'Hiya, babe.'

'Hello, darling,' Kate answered brightly, making Henry close his eyes in a pang of disgust at himself. 'How's it going?'

'OK, just getting to the interesting part, I guess.' He was on his personal mobile phone to her, sitting in a hot café in Manchester's Arndale Centre, staring down at a six-piece breakfast. Suddenly, on hearing her voice, his hunger deserted him as his guilt kicked in. 'How are you?'

'Oh, not bad, I guess.' She sounded slightly hesitant, something he detected straight away.

'What's up?'

'Er, well, neither of the girls were at home last night ... Jenny's away as you know and Leanne spent the night at Jason's.' Jason was *the* boyfriend. Henry's insides did a whoopsie at the thought of the long-haired, good-for-nothing, unemployed student layabout molesting his youngest daughter, now, god forbid, almost twenty years old.

'And?' Henry asked. It was still fairly rare for Kate to spend a night alone and she did tend to be a bit jumpy.

'I think we had a prowler ... in fact, I know we did.'

Henry went icy. His mind immediately panned back to the car which had tried to force him off the road, his old Mondeo. He had actually checked the car on the Police National Computer, but it had shown no current owner. He had not said anything to anyone about the incident, had lied to Kate about the damage to his car, and not had time to follow up anything because of the U/C job he was involved in. Also, he did not want to jeopardize the new job, either, by admitting that perhaps someone was after him. Once again he wondered if there was any connection between the incident and the job with Ingram, though he doubted it. The road rage had happened before he had even started working undercover.

Now he was wondering if a prowler at his house had any connection with the road rage incident. Connections, Henry thought. All connections.

'The security lights at the back of the house kept coming on,' Kate went on. 'I thought a dog or a fox might've got into the garden or something, so when they came on a third time. I went out to check, but the side gate was locked and there was nothing in the garden.'

The garden overlooked open fields and foxes had occasionally jumped the low fence, setting off the lights. Henry picked up on the wavering in Kate's voice. He frowned.

'Was it a fault?'

'I don't know. This was before I went to bed, by the way. So I locked up, then went to bed ... couldn't sleep without you next to me ... I had a mooch around to the girls' bedrooms and saw the light was on again.' The girls' rooms were at the back of the house, overlooking the rear garden. 'I peeked out and saw a man on the decking, staring up at the house. When he saw me, he legged it over the fence and disappeared down the field.'

'Did you call the cops?'

'No. I was too shaky.'

'Are you all right now?'

'So-so. I'll be OK.'

Henry knew there had been a few burglaries on the estate, but only in unoccupied houses. Maybe this incident was linked to those. Someone casing up a joint. He made a decision.

'Whatever happens, I'll be home tonight.'

At midday he wandered into Waterstone's on

Deansgate. He made his way up to the café, ordering a medium Americano for himself before joining Andrea Makin who was already there, drinking something very frothy, making her wipe her top lip after every sip.

She watched him coldly.

'I know I said we'd forget what happened,' she said immediately, forgoing any niceties, 'but no man who has ever been on top of me has been unable to get an erection. Do you know how that makes me feel?'

Henry blinked and made a sort of speechless, clicking sound with his tongue before he found some words to respond with. 'Not half as bad as I feel,' he said. 'I'm the one who couldn't do it and now I feel pathetic – OK? Let's just leave it, eh?'

Her face softened. 'I'm sorry, Henry. I guess I never saw that point of view. I just thought you didn't like what you saw.'

'Oh, I liked it,' he said, 'but' – he made a desperate squashing motion with his hands – 'can we just get on? I'm depressed enough.'

'OK.' She sipped her coffee and forgot to wipe the foam from her top lip, which cheered up Henry. 'So where are we up to?'

'Contact made – guess it's just a waiting game for now. That's assuming Ingram got released from custody.'

'He did. Take it he didn't tell you why he'd been arrested?'

'Nah – tight lipped.'

'And you don't actually want to know?'

Henry shook his head. 'Be better coming from

him.'

'Understood.' She paused. 'So we wait?'

'Correct.'

'And suppose nothing happens?'

'We'll have to think of a way of me bumping into him, naturally. But let's not hurry. He'll contact me.'

'How do you know?'

'Cos he's greedy – to see the product and make a profit. I could see it in his eyes when I whispered those words.'

'Which were?'

'Hardcore porn.'

She sighed, sipped some more coffee, wiped her lips this time.

'Re. Frank Jagger, we need to get him a banger to run around in ... in fact, maybe approach Ingram on that score,' Henry said, thinking out loud, his brain becoming de-fogged. 'Ingram knows Jagger has no wheels and that he's still got a load of gear to shift...' His words drifted off. 'But, whatever, I need to be seen to be in a panic because my debts are still unpaid and I've got that huge fine to pay off, too ... Jagger's pretty much in the shit, desperate, even...' Things were coming together slowly in Henry's mind, the next stage of the scam – but he suddenly pulled up short. 'I take it the wheels are in place to quash that conviction I just got?' He was referring to the fact that even though he had been convicted of the drink-drive offence under the name of Jagger, he would still be a disqualified driver in the eyes of the law. After all, he was the one who had committed the offence, whether he called himself Jagger or Christie.

'It's all being taken care of,' she assured him. Wheels within wheels, Henry thought, at the highest level of the criminal justice system in the country. However, any checks carried out by a third person would always reveal that Frank Jagger had been convicted and disqualified, which was part of the exercise.

'Good.'

A silence descended between them.

'What a waste,' she said at length.

'Meaning?' His brow creased.

'My hot arse,' she said delightfully.

'Don't,' he pleaded, mortified, 'don't.'

Henry shivered. The heating was off and it was very chilly inside the small industrial unit Jagger rented on the ground floor of a huge Victorian mill behind Great Ducie Street, not far from the Manchester Arena next to Victoria Railway Station.

The place was stacked to the rafters with cans of booze – the stock in trade of Frank Jagger, whose business consisted mainly of arranging the theft and then the selling of huge quantities of alcohol. Henry surveyed the cans and grinned because none of it was actually stolen, it was all provided by breweries and when this scam was finished it would all have to be returned.

He walked across the concrete floor and stood next to the fifty or so boxes containing several thousand DVDs, all of which were crammed full of hardcore pornography, including 500 with child porn. These had all come from the vaults of the Metropolitan Police, and once Ingram had been ensnared, they would all be returned for destruction.

As part of his preparation for getting back into the role of Jagger, Henry had sat through several disgusting hours of DVD viewing so that he could at least talk knowledgeably about the contents if necessary.

It had been harrowing to watch and as he recalled some of the scenes, he grimaced and wiped his face, then checked his watch: two in the afternoon. He started to wonder if Ingram would really contact him.

In the meantime, he locked the building and jumped into the beat-up Nissan Micra that had been found for him by Andrea. It had been decided to get him some wheels straightaway, otherwise it would have severely curtailed his ability to keep up with Ingram. The car was one from the GMP pound, had no current owner and would stand any scrutiny by Ingram.

It started first time, sweet as a nut in spite of its age and appearance, and he drove down to the A56, heading away from the city towards Bury. He pulled on to the forecourt of a motor dealership about two miles out of town, and stopped. The place specialized in the sale of Rover and MG cars and it was from here that he'd bought his Rover 75, part-exchanging it for the Mondeo.

Walking past a lovely display of MG TFs, the two-seater sports cars, he went into the salesroom and spotted the guy he'd done the deal with almost ten months earlier.

The salesman – Ken (how many car salesmen were called Ken? he wondered) – was chatting to a colleague by a coffee machine; as Henry closed in, Ken spotted him and cut away from the chit-chat, affixed his salesman smile and greeted Henry, who realized that he had not been recognized.

'Hello, sir, can I help you?' Ken eyed Henry's face and general appearance, then looked past his shoulder and clocked the Nissan on the forecourt.

'It's Ken, isn't it?'

A slight cloud of doubt scudded across Ken's honest visage as he speculated what he'd done – or not done, perhaps. 'I'm sorry, do I know you?'

'I part-exed a Mondeo for a Rover 75 about ten months ago?'

'Right.' Ken squinted, still not having put a face to the transaction.

'You did the deal.'

'Oh, I do hope there's no problem, sir.'

'No, not at all ... you don't recall me, do you?'

'I'm afraid...' Ken bit his bottom lip. 'We have so many customers.' He peered closely at Henry, then recognition dawned. 'You're the cop!' he said delightedly, jabbing a finger towards Henry's chest and coming a little too close. Henry caught a whiff of stale alcohol on Ken's breath. 'Now I remember.'

'Yeah, that's me.'

'So, is there a problem?'

'Not with the Rover, which I love and every-body else hates...'

'Such is the way of the world with that make and model, I fear. You either love 'em or hate 'em.'

'What happened to the Mondeo?'

'Why, do you want it back?'

Henry thought he saw something in Ken's eyes. Caution or worry, something like that. 'I'd just like to know what happened to it.'

'Err, not sure actually ... I'm presuming we sold it or it went to auction ... let me look up the records.' He indicated for Henry to follow him and then walked to a glass-fronted office where he plonked himself down behind the desk and told Henry to grab a seat. Ken then proceeded to flick through the lower drawers of a filing cabinet next to the desk. 'What was the name again?'

'Christie.'

'Here we go.' He extracted a slim file, tipping out the contents after clearing away a copy of the *Racing Post*. Henry recognized copies of some of the forms he had signed in triplicate. 'Part-ex,' he muttered. 'Mondeo for Rover ... um ... I recall you drove a hard bargain...' Ken raised his face from the documents. 'I know! It went to auction ... simple as that.' He gathered up the paperwork. 'Beyond that, I don't know.'

Henry looked at him, slightly puzzled – because he got the impression that Ken seemed to be hiding something, but couldn't say what. 'OK, did anyone show any interest in it before it went?'

'Not that I know.'

'Anyone come and test drive it, anything at all?'

Ken shrugged. 'Not through me.' He looked suspiciously at Henry. 'Why, has it been used in a job?'

'Sort of,' Henry said. 'Linked, shall we say?'

'How ironic.'

'Why?'

'Ex-cop's car being used in a blagging.'

'I didn't actually say that.'

'No ... literary licence ... but, back to your question, I don't know if anyone came to look at it. Another sales person might have dealt with them, if they did.'

Henry had noticed that CCTV cameras were dotted around the forecourt. He pointed at one. 'Do they work?'

'Sure do.'

'How long do you keep the recordings for?'

'Indefinitely – it's all digitally recorded. Very clever, state of the art, won't get wiped until the hard drive fills up.'

'So if someone came and enquired about the Mondeo, it could well be on camera.'

'Could well be.'

'Can you find out for me?'

Ken had obviously been expecting the request, but even so he could not keep his reluctance from showing behind the full-face smile. 'I'll do my best ... we have eight sales people here, two left since you bought your car.'

'I know it's a big ask,' Henry said in a vain attempt to keep the sarcasm out of his voice, 'but you'd be doing us, the police, a great favour. And also, which auction house did it go to?'

'That I don't know. Head office deals with that

side of things. Could be one anywhere in the country.'

Henry smiled encouragingly.

'I'll find out ... but can you give us a day or two?' He looked pained. 'Has your mobile number changed?'

'No.' Henry moved to stand up – but before he rose to his feet the mobile phone in his right-hand pocket rang. 'Speak of the devil,' he said, fishing it out.

It wasn't his personal phone, it was his business one.

Someone was calling Frank Jagger.

Ingram arrived in an old Peugeot 607, big enough for comfort, plain enough not to get noticed. It was driven by another man, a big, overweight slob with porcine eyes and a sneering disposition. Henry guessed he was Ingram's fists, even though the guy did not look capable of running more than twenty metres. Henry decided there and then that if it came to fisticuffs, he'd simply outrun the big guy, hopefully give him a heart attack.

They had arranged to meet somewhere neutral, a back street industrial estate behind a large biscuit factory in Bolton. Henry had been reluctant to go to Bolton as it meant creeping ever closer to Lancashire, thereby increasing the odds of being spotted and recognized. On the plus side, he'd never worked very much in Bolton, so not many crims in that neck of the woods would be able to point the finger at him. He decided to chance it.

Ingram climbed out and lounged against the side of the Peugeot.

His driver/sidekick rolled out and Henry walked towards them from his Nissan. He extended a hand, which Ingram shook with damp fingers, making Henry cringe inwardly. As he withdrew his hand, he knew he'd just shaken with someone suspected of abusing and killing little girls. Those fingers had probably encircled young necks and squeezed life out; they had certainly touched young girls. Henry looked into Ingram's eyes, which crinkled with superiority.

He hoped he didn't allow his distaste for the man to show, as this would show he knew too much, and it could be picked up by Ingram if Henry wasn't careful.

'You got out then,' Henry said.

'It was bollocks ... this is Mitch, by the way.' Ingram jabbed a thumb in the direction of the large guy. Ingram scratched his face, then nodded past Henry. 'Got a new car?'

'I had it anyway.'

'So what's your position, then?'

All three men turned as a huge HGV stopped a few metres down the street and began a slow reverse towards the biscuit factory gates, accompanied by the warning bleeper.

'In what way?' Henry turned back to Ingram. Mitch stood to one side of them, just out of earshot, his eyes taking in Henry, the Nissan and the environment. He was a lookout as well as a fist man, Henry noted.

'Financially,' Ingram said.

'Precarious ... if only I was in hock to a bank.

At least they don't have heavies.'

Ingram smiled knowingly. 'Don't you believe it.'

'OK, I won't. So what's this about?' Henry gestured with his hands to take in this meeting.

'I'll come to that when I'm good and ready, Frank.'

'Well, it better be sooner rather than later, because I got a lot of wheelin' and dealin' to do, as well as watching my arse for not-nice blokes who want to hassle me for loads of cash I don't have. I'm in a tight spot and unless you're here to stump up some dosh, then why are we talking?'

Ingram's eyes widened. 'Why the hell would I want to bail you out? Did I say this is what the meeting's about?' He sounded angry.

'No, no you didn't,' Henry conceded, 'but you did say you might be able to help me out, which is why I assumed...' He gave a helpless shrug.

Ingram looked critically at him. 'Let's go somewhere else.'

'Eh?' Henry said.

'After Mitch has given you the once over – and your car, too.'

'What the hell are you on about?'

'I'm very reluctant to get into bed with anyone who just happens to come into my life uninvited. I'm a careful person, Frank ... and if you really do want a favour, then you'll happily comply to my wishes. I'd hate to discover somewhere down the line that you were a cop all along, y'know.'

Henry stared open-mouthed at Ingram, shocked by the suggestion. However, this was one of those points in a budding relationship that needed cautious handling. A violent, OTT reaction, or a pathetically acquiescent one would definitely alert Ingram. It had to be just so...

'Everybody's afraid of undercover cops these days,' Henry said. 'Too much shit on the telly, that's what it is. For all I know, you could be one.' He smiled cynically. 'I don't know you from Adam ... you just got dumped in my cell ... I'm the one could be being set up here.' He raised his eyebrows.

'And why would the cops want to spend time setting up a lowlife like you?'

'Mmm, good point,' the man known as Frank Jagger conceded. 'Well anyway, I'm not a cop and you can do what you have to do. I don't like it, but I want you to say sorry when you don't find any hidden wires or micro-cameras.'

Ingram nodded to Mitch. 'Do him and the car.'

The big sidekick said, 'OK, boss,' in a high-pitched squeak of a voice which did not complement his appearance. A paddle-like instrument appeared in his right hand, having been secreted underneath his jacket. He took two steps towards Henry. 'Arms out, legs apart.'

Henry extended his arms, spread his legs slightly and allowed Mitch to run the detector across his body and under his armpits, down across his stomach to his groin and then up between his legs with a jerk which caught his balls. Henry scowled. Mitch smiled grimly, or it could also have been a scowl. Henry was not certain.

'Enjoy that?' Henry asked.

'Actually, yeah.' He jabbed the detector between Henry's legs again, then ran it down and around both legs, then back over the outside of Henry's jacket, causing it to beep.

Mitch eyed Ingram.

Henry extracted his mobile phone and showed it to Ingram, who took it from him.

'What're you doing?'

'I'll keep it for the time being.'

'I don't think so, it's my phone,' Henry bleated.

'I'd just like to have a look through it, see who you've been calling ... is that a problem? If it is, you can have it back and that's us done for good.'

Henry's jaw rotated. His eyes bore into Ingram's. 'OK,' he relented.

Mitch completed the last scan of Henry and said, 'Clean.'

'Good. Now the car.'

Mitch nodded and rolled to the Nissan, began to search it. Henry folded his arms and gave Ingram a slitty-eyed, pissed-off look.

'What's he looking for?'

'Anything that shouldn't be there.'

'What, like used condoms, that sort of thing?'

'Yeah, why not?'

'Clear, boss,' Mitch called from inside the Nissan. He seemed to be having trouble extracting himself, his wide backside trapped momentarily in the space between the front passenger seat, which had been tipped forwards, and the door post. He came out with a pop and a grunt.

Henry shook his head.

'OK, so far, so good ... now let's move on somewhere more comfortable.'

'Where to?'

'You drive this.' Ingram pointed to the 607. 'Mitch'll sit beside you and I'll follow in the wreck that you call a car.' He pointed disparagingly at the Nissan. Ingram gave Henry's mobile phone to Mitch and nodded at the big man.

The Peugeot was big and comfy, plenty of room for Mitch and his wide rear on the passenger seat.

'Head down the M61,' Mitch instructed him as he flicked the back off Henry's phone and peeled out the SIM card.

'What the fuck're you doing?'

Mitch opened the glove box and took out a small black box which Henry recognized immediately as a device for downloading data from SIM cards. Mitch thumbed a switch and a tiny green light came on. He slotted Henry's SIM into the device. 'Just drive,' Mitch ordered in his squeak of a voice.

Henry adjusted the driver's seat, fired up the big diesel engine and moved away. In his rearview mirror he saw Ingram set off behind, then as he turned his head and looked out of the windscreen, Henry saw the solitary figure ducking out of sight on the roof of the biscuit factory. He hoped to hell that Ingram had not seen the figure: the technical support officer who had, by means of a parabolic microphone, eavesdropped into their conversation, thereby having saved Henry the need to wear a hidden wire which Mitch would have found and probably enjoyed stuffing up Henry's backside.

Trouble was, Henry was now alone. He had insisted on having no other back-up than a listener on the factory roof, hoping that he would have got more out of the conversation with Ingram. But the man had proved much too wary and Henry now realized he would need to keep his wits about him more than ever.

Six

The man ran alone, fighting the pain that arced through his whole being like repetitious jabs of electricity.

So far he had run for four miles, the longest he'd managed since beginning his slow recuperation. It had gone well, but as he looked up the long, rising driveway leading to the huge house in the distance, he had to stop. It was no great incline and several months before he would have easily raced up the hill, taken it in his stride. That was before he had come face to face with one of the world's most wanted terrorists in a confrontation that could have gone either way. With a combination of luck, speed, skill and good health, it had gone his.

The terrorist, a man high on America's most wanted list, had been killed and the man out running had survived – but only just.

If the team supporting him in tracking down Mohammed Ibrahim Akbar had been only minutes later finding him in that deserted, hidden square in Barcelona, he would have bled to death. The quick thinking of his team and their first-aid skills had saved him, and for that, he was eternally grateful.

Akbar, on the other hand, had died, but no one mourned him.

The runner was bent double, the balls of his hands on his knees, his face looking up at the house, breathing heavily.

He gritted his teeth and grimaced as a shot of agony seared up the exact route the bullet had taken: in under the ribs, through his guts, nicking the bottom edge of a lung and then stopping as it thumped into the back section of his ribs by his spine – which, miraculously, it did not damage, just nestled against. Had it ploughed on a further three millimetres he would have been paralysed from there down. Knowing that, and if that had been the case, the man would rather have been dead.

He pushed himself up and stood tall, feeling the track of the bullet like it was a steel cable inserted through him. The sweat poured down him, even though the day was chilly and overcast. He braced himself to continue and, because every journey starts with one foot in front of the other, he placed his right foot ahead of his left and began to jog up the hill.

He was running in a wonderful setting, and that inspired him. The house he ran towards was called Bramshill and belonged to the national training body for the police in England and Wales. It was used as a base to tutor and train high-ranking officers and equivalent support staff.

The narrow road up to the house was bordered on either side by wide fields and trees. A herd of roe deer looked up in a fairly disinterested way at the runner before returning to their grazing.

The last 400 metres were pure torture, but the runner did not stop now. Though a snail's pace by his pre-injury standards, he made it in two minutes, coming to a halt near the front of the old house. He turned and looked back down the drive and across the amazing Hampshire countryside, thinking, I did good.

After spending a few necessary minutes warming down, he walked past the side of the house to the new gymnasium block where he had a long, hot-cold-warm shower and emerged with a towel wrapped around his waist into the men's changing rooms. There was one other man in the room, easing on his jacket after a session. They nodded at each other, then the other man's eyes caught sight of the runner's abdomen and the ugly, puckered bullet wound under the ribs. The man's face creased with empathetic pain. He turned away, slightly shocked, and hurried out as the runner allowed his towel to drop and display the remainder of his body.

'We need to talk.' Four words designed to strike terror into the heart of the listener. Despite his size and toughness, those words did just that to Karl Donaldson as he sat opposite his wife,

Karen, in the dining hall at Bramshill Police College. For a moment, Donaldson pretended not to hear them and carried on by saying, 'I did pretty well ... four miles. Agony, yeah, but I made it. I'm coming on all right.' Unconsciously he placed a hand on his shirt over where the bullet had entered his body.

Karen blinked. Her mouth twisted slightly and impatiently.

'Karl, you're not listening...'

His mouth clamped shut. He looked into her eyes and knew this was the horrible point his marriage had reached – the 'we need to talk' point.

He and Karen actually lived about four miles away from Bramshill in the small town of Hartley Wintney. From there Donaldson commuted to London daily, his job being at the American Embassy in Grosvenor Square where he was the FBI's legal attaché; Karen also commuted daily into the city where she had been a Metropolitan Police Superintendent for several years following a move from Lancashire in the mid-Nineties.

The couple had met years before when Donaldson, then an FBI field agent, had been investigating serious American mob activity in the north of England at that time. He had also met and become friends with Henry Christie.

At that time Karen had been a police officer in Lancashire and when she and Donaldson had fallen in love, he had secured a move for himself from America to the London Embassy and she had transferred to the Met so they could be together and get married. Which they did.

She was currently attending the Police College on a course for high-ranking officers.

'I'm not certain I want to listen,' Donaldson whispered hoarsely across the bowl of clear, tasteless soup in front of him.

'You've got to,' she said firmly.

A group of rowdy police officers on an adjoining table burst out in raucous laughter. Donaldson scowled at them. One caught his eye and sneered. The American felt a surge of rage pound through him, completely unnecessary.

'We can't talk here,' Karen said. 'Let's have a stroll.'

Donaldson stacked his unfinished meal on a tray and stood up stiffly, the run having taken more of a toll than he had bargained for.

Karen followed him out of the dining room and they headed towards the lake in the grounds, walking side by side, but two feet apart.

'You shouldn't have come,' she said.

'Darling, you're on a four-week course, less than four miles from home, and you're not coming home each night...'

'I told you,' she snapped, 'I needed time to think.'

'And what exactly is there to think about?'

'Us,' she said softly, and walked on ahead of him whilst he stopped in his tracks, dumbfounded.

He caught up with her, remembering in a flash the first time he had ever walked behind her over ten years before and, like a rude schoolboy, had made a remark to Henry Christie, who he had been with at the time, about how much he would have liked to make love to her. The words he'd used at the time had been less than romantic, though. To him, she was the most beautiful woman in the world and marrying her had been the happiest day of his life.

'C'mon, babe,' he said reasonably, 'what's going on?'

This time she stopped, causing him to bundle into her. Her eyes were moist and she was close to tears. Her chin wobbled unsteadily and an overwhelming feeling of love enveloped Donaldson. He opened his arms, wanting to embrace her, hold her tight – but her right hand shot out, palm up.

'No,' she said.

The whole of his body language grasped to understand fully what was happening here. His hands shook, his head wobbled on his neck.

'You almost died,' she said accusingly.

'But I didn't, darlin',' he defended himself.

She held up a finger, jerking it at him. 'You put yourself in danger, unnecessarily so. You did not have to go hunting down one of the world's most dangerous terrorists...'

'He—' Donaldson stuttered.

Karen gave him no chance to cut in. 'I know what he did and I know why you went for him, but knowing a reason does not mean I agree with it. Without even asking me, you volunteered to join the team hunting him down, without even thinking of the effect on your family – me and the children.'

Donaldson bridled. 'I thought about you all the time.'

She gave him a withering look and shook her head. 'You forgot us,' she challenged him. 'You went on a crusade and you hunted him down – and he nearly killed you!' she shrieked the last five words. 'What about us in your thoughts then, eh? If you had died, I would've had no husband and two children would have been without a father ... did you ever think to consider that in your eagerness to go gung-ho?'

'Someone had to do it,' he said pathetically.

'Yeah, but not you, Karl.' She exhaled and looked at the picturesque lake. Her jaw jutted out as she turned back to him. 'You're a changed man, Karl. Not the person I met. You've become more and more distant ... I feel that danger surrounds you all the time, somehow, and hunting down Akbar was just the icing on the cake...' Her voice trailed off sadly.

There was a pause.

'I love you, but I can't live with it and I don't think the kids should either.'

'I...'

She shook her head.

'Shit,' he said.

'I've stood by you, I've nursed you back to health ... you've run four miles today, you're OK now...'

'And now you're doing a runner, as they say?'

'I want to think about things.'

'I love you,' he said simply, hardly able to breathe as he watched her stony face.

'I know.'

'So what happens now?'

'I would like to go home every night, actually,

and sort out the kids...'

'But you don't want me there?'

Karen stayed silent.

Donaldson nodded. 'I understand. I'll get one of the embassy bolt-holes in London. Won't be until tomorrow, though.'

'I'll stay here tonight.'

'And I'll sort out the kids.'

She nodded, her face ashen, brittle. She gathered herself together, turned away and continued to walk around the lake. By herself.

Donaldson watched her for a few moments, then span in the opposite direction, amazed at how such a small woman could tear up the heart of such a big man.

Following Mitch's directions, Henry drove on to the westbound side of Bolton West motorway services on the M61 and parked up. Ingram drew the Nissan alongside, jumped out of it and got into the back of the Peugeot behind Henry.

'We leave that here,' Ingram said, referring to the Nissan.

'Are you fuckin' jokin'?' Henry snarled, twisting around to glare at Ingram.

'You can still take it or leave it.'

'I want dropping off back here,' Henry demanded.

'I'm already getting pissed off with you, Frank,' Ingram growled.

'OK, OK,' Henry gave in, raising his hands off the wheel in defeat. 'Whatever.'

'Ungrateful git,' squeaked Mitch.

Henry gave him a sidelong glance that Mitch

locked into with his piggy eyes then blew him a kiss. Henry had a premonition there and then that the two of them would come head-to-head in a very unpleasant way in the near future.

'Where are we going?' Henry asked.

'You two need to swap seats now. I don't want a dizzy driver driving me around just yet,' Ingram said.

When this was done, now with Mitch squashed in behind the wheel, the car set off west again, Henry increasingly uncomfortable that they were very nearly back on his home turf of Lancashire, dramatically increasing his chances of an encounter with someone who might blow him out, intentionally or otherwise.

They journeyed in silence as Henry watched the familiar countryside flash by, dropping down from the M61 on to the northbound M6.

'Just going somewhere for a chit-chat,' Ingram said eventually as they shot over the River Ribble, motoring in the fast lane at about 85 mph. It might not have been the best looking of cars, but the Peugeot was fast and comfortable.

'Where might that be?' Henry enquired.

'A room with a view.'

Which turned out to be another service station, this time the Lancaster South one at Forton on the M6, the one with the huge water tower-like structure opened in the 1960s shortly after the M6, Britain's first stretch of motorway. The structure, reached by a lift, housed a restaurant and Mitch led Ingram and Henry up to it, then queued up at the serving hatch and helped himself to an all-day breakfast. Ingram and Henry made do with a coffee, seating themselves by a window overlooking six lanes of motorway.

Henry felt reasonably relaxed now. He was unlikely to be recognized here. Even so, he kept his face low but watched all the comings and goings keenly.

He waited for Ingram to begin as Mitch inserted himself on to the seat of a table behind them and began to devour his feast noisily.

'OK, Frank, spill the beans.'

'Er, don't really know where to begin.' He rubbed his eyes and they squelched. 'I'm usually a middleman, mostly fags, booze, that sort of stuff. It comes my way, I dispose of it, take a cut. Still do, but I saw a window for some diversification, but it went kind of awry, y'know?'

'Awry? Nice word.'

'Yeah, y'know, down the shitter,' Henry said hurriedly, realizing that Jagger would be unlikely to use a word such as awry. His vocabulary would be far baser, at ground level. Point noted, he thought: take care. Ingram is watching, ready to pounce on anything that doesn't hold up. 'Anyway, I saw this opportunity but I needed some upfront cash because of cash-flow problems, if you know what I mean?'

'What was it for?'

'DVDs.' He closed his eyes appreciatively. 'Do you know how big the porno market is in this country? Worth fucking millions. Well, I'd come across this guy on my travels, a Paki or an Indian or summat ... got chatting, hit it off and he said he could supply if I could find the dosh and that was that.'

'What was what?'

'It was an opportunity I couldn't, didn't want to miss ... I'd seen the samples...' He shook his head in awe. 'Awesome, real hard stuff, and kids too.' As he said that, he tried to gauge Ingram's reaction to the last revelation and thought he saw some spark of interest in the eyes. 'But,' Henry added, drawing himself back slightly, 'obviously not to everyone's taste, I admit.' He peered quizzically at Ingram. 'It might be something you're not interested in, I dunno.'

'From a business point of view, I might be,' he suggested. His eyelids hooded over.

Henry sipped his coffee, which tasted rather good, and sniffed. His cheekbone was starting to throb, affecting his nasal passages, causing his nose to run.

'What went wrong?'

'The guy I'd set up to take the stuff got nicked and banged up,' Henry said with melancholy. 'The guy I bought them from wouldn't take 'em back sale or return. Guy who stumped up the cash for me wants repaying ... and I don't know what to do with the fucking things.'

'Good market research, then?' Ingram smirked.

Behind them, Mitch belched, drawing looks of disgust from other customers nearby.

Then Henry's pulse began to pound when he looked across the café and saw two motorway cops enter and tag on to the queue at the self-service area. He knew both of them. They had not spotted him. He squirmed in his chair, turning edge-away from them.

94

'What's wrong?' Ingram glanced over his shoulder and saw the officers. He turned back slowly. 'They spook you?'

'So-so,' he said blandly, swallowing something the size of a brick. 'Anyway,' he ploughed on, as though nothing was amiss, 'the bottom line is the guy who bankrolled me wants his cash for something else and now he's snapping at my heels, know what I mean?' Henry pulled a pained face. 'So I'm up bollock street. No liquid assets.'

'Why don't you go to Ocean Finance?' Mitch guffawed over the remnants of his hash browns, making it clear to Henry that whilst he was not at the table, he had picked up every word.

Henry grimaced at Ingram, part of his gaze clocking the two cops moving along the self-service bar with their trays. They were in deep conversation, probably discussing their latest multi-fatal pile-up.

'I might be able to help out,' Ingram declared.

Henry Christie experienced a wave of guilt and shame as he picked up the phone. He was back in his flat on Salford Quays, overlooking the Imperial War Museum. He was about to call home and give Kate the bad news: he would not be coming home tonight.

He felt so tight, especially after his earlier promise, but he knew it had to be done. The opportunity to get close in on Ingram was unfolding and if he didn't take it, the whole operation could fail.

He swore, braced himself, then tabbed in his

home number.

There was a ring at the front doorbell.

Keeping the cordless phone cupped to his ear, he crossed to the door and peered through the security spyhole.

'Shit,' he breathed: Andrea Makin.

'What?' Kate said as she answered and heard Henry's expletive.

'Sorry, nothing, love.' He opened the door and, placing a finger to his lips, stood aside to allow Andrea to enter, which she did with a very serious expression on her face.

'I thought you were coming home tonight,' Kate said. 'It's gone eight thirty.' Her voice was full of resignation.

'I know, love...' He followed Andrea into the apartment. She went to the wall-sized plate glass window looking down on to the basin of the Manchester Ship Canal and the museum beyond. 'Look, something came up. I need to deal with it. You know how it is.'

A very annoyed silence greeted his words.

'I'm sorry, love ... I will be back, but it'll be later ... early hours?' he added hopefully.

The line went dead when Kate cut him off.

Andrea Makin turned to him. 'Something came up? In your dreams, Henry.'

'What are you doing here?'

'I was worried about you.'

'Well, you've got to go because I'm off to see Ingram again.'

'Shouldn't you have reported in? I am your controller, you know.'

'Andrea, let me do my job.'

'Can you actually do it when you're being harassed by a needy ex-wife?'

'None of your business.'

'Yes it is. I can't have officers operating under cover who are having pain on the home front ... it tends to skew the perspective, makes them vulnerable.'

'Everything's fine.'

She breathed down her nose, flared her nostrils. 'OK,' she relented, 'but I want a quick update.'

'OK. He is very careful, as you'll have picked up from this afternoon's meeting. He even downloaded the info from my SIM card. It's a damned good job I went in there sparse. If I'd been wired, he would've found it. If the car had been kitted out, he would have sussed that too. And I think he would've sussed a tail. So, he's very wary, but interested. I could see it in his eyes and I think I can build a rapport, but I don't need hassle.'

'Just basic health and safety.'

'Fair enough ... did you manage to get anything from the roof of the biscuit factory?'

'Yeah, but nothing of value.'

'For the time being I won't be going in wired or anything, but I will try to keep in touch, promise. Now I need to shoot, got some DVDs I need to watch with my new pal. It's a man thing. He's having a look at the merchandise.'

'A pervert thing, you mean.'

'And don't come here again. He knows this address now and I wouldn't be surprised if he gets someone to keep an eye on it occasionally – at least until I get thrown out of here.'

The children had gone to bed and settled quickly as always. Good kids, polite, brainy and good-looking like their mother, occasionally showing the reckless streak of their father.

Donaldson pulled a suitcase down from the loft and carried it quietly into the bedroom. He began filling it with his clothes, then took it downstairs and placed it in the hallway by the front door.

Next he went to the kitchen where he grabbed a bottle of Jack Daniel's, threw some ice cubes into a glass and slumped back into an armchair in the lounge before almost filling the glass with the bourbon.

He gazed around the room, feeling empty yet full of pain, constantly replaying Karen's words over and over in his brain.

She had been right, of course. No one had forced him to go head-to-head with a terrorist. It had been his choice, his desire, obsession – call it what you will – and he had nearly died because of it and nearly left his family fatherless.

'Reckless, idiotic fool,' he said, and took a big mouthful of the whisky. And now Karen could not take any more. She had been by his side throughout the dark, touch-and-go days, stayed with him throughout his recovery, done her duty and now he was fit enough, she was splitting them up.

The problem was, he thoroughly deserved it.

He drank another mouthful.

* * *

Henry relaxed. He was sure he had not been followed, had made certain by careful driving, looping back on himself, stopping without warning, constantly checking on traffic and people – not that there was too much of either on the roads after midnight. He worked his way out of Manchester and by the time he hit the motorway in the Nissan, he knew he was alone and his whole metabolism shifted down a gear. He settled back and put his foot down just to see how much he could get from the lively little engine.

Thirty minutes after leaving the city, via a short detour up the M65, he pulled up to the gates of an industrial unit on the eastern side of Blackburn, near to the Blackburn Rovers' football ground at Ewood Park. He let himself through the gate using the keypad and into the unit itself using a combined keypad and fingerprint recognition system. The shutter door clattered open, revealing the interior of the unit. There was an array of motor vehicles inside, including the XJS he had been arrested in, and his own car, the Rover 75.

The unit had been inherited by the Serious and Organized Crime Agency from the NCIS, who had in turn inherited it from the Regional Crime Squad. It was one of the bases of operations for undercover officers in the North-West region, its location known only to a few people.

He dumped the Nissan, dropped the keys in the office, collected his own car keys and reversed the Rover out of the unit. He ensured everything was locked up and then drove back on to the M65 to resume his journey home.

He would be there within the hour.

Seven

The house was lit up, a police patrol car parked outside.

A nauseous feeling of dread coursed through Henry as he pulled on to the driveway and jumped out of the car, entering the house to face two uniformed constables in the hallway, Kate behind them, looking very small indeed. Her dressing gown was pulled tightly around her middle.

On seeing Henry, relief flooded her pale face.

'What's going on?' he demanded of the officers, neither one of whom he recognized.

'Hello, sir, are you Mr Christie?' one asked.

'I am.' Henry's eyes rolled between the three characters in front of him like balls in a bagatelle. 'What's happening?' he asked nervously.

'You've had a prowler,' the officer said. 'We have searched the area and he or she is now gone.'

'Are you all right?' he asked Kate, standing between them.

She nodded, looked scared and shaken. 'Yeah.' Her eyes were dark, tired.

Henry's attention turned to the officers. 'What

happened?'

'Someone in the back garden playing silly buggers, banging on the kitchen window ... did a runner when the house lights came on,' one said. The other continued: 'We were here within five minutes, searched the garden ... no trace.' He turned to Kate. 'You sure you're OK now, Ma'am?'

'Yes, I am now. Thanks for your quick response.' Some colour flowed back to her face. 'I'll be fine now my husband is back,' she added, Henry noticing the verbal slip.

'We'll be off, then.'

Together they watched them leave, closing the door to the world as the police car drove away. Kate immediately fell into Henry's arms, clutching him tight and burying her forehead into his chest. She was shaking. He held her tightly, his nose in her ear.

'It's all right, love.'

She raised her tear-stained face. 'I was so scared.'

'You would be.' Henry did not like prowlers. The word itself always sounded scary to him. It was so descriptive, had an ugly, nasty feel to it. He felt Kate relax, so he steered her gently into the living room, sitting her down on the settee. 'I'll get you a drink.'

She nodded. 'Firewater would be nice – on ice. The good stuff, not the cheap.'

'Sounds good. I'll join you.'

He went into the kitchen, but instead of getting the drinks, he opened the back door and looked down across the garden to the big open field at the rear, which was just blackness, the only light on it filtering from a lane a few hundred metres to the left. He walked across the lawn to the wire fence and peered towards where he knew there was a large pond on the opposite side of the field. It was a magnet for bird life and he could hear some muted night-time clucking, but saw nothing.

Back inside he fixed two Glenfiddichs with lots of ice and was about to return with them when Kate came into the kitchen. He handed her a drink, which she sipped with a shiver.

'What happened?'

'I went to bed early. The kids are both out for the night again, so I had a long soak first, then a long read, but I just felt a bit thirsty, so I came down for a glass of orange from the fridge. As I was at the sink, I heard a tapping noise at the window. I don't know, I thought it was a bird or something, so without thinking I just pulled up the blind and a masked man had his face squashed to the glass. It was horrible.'

'What sort of mask?'

'Like a balaclava with holes for the eyes and mouth.' Henry nodded. Kate continued: 'I screamed, but he just stayed there banging the glass, terrifying me.' She took a long drink of the whisky.

'What then?'

'I was petrified. I ran into the hall, grabbed the phone and dialled nine-nine-nine. Even when I was doing it, I could still hear him banging at the window.'

Henry was feeling cold, impotent and furious.

Another example of why he should be around more.

'Kate,' he said softly, 'I'm sorry I wasn't at home.'

'Not your fault, love.'

He raised his eyebrows in a way that indicated otherwise. 'Was he wearing gloves?'

'I don't know.'

'Let's have a peek.' He put his drink down on a work surface and went into the back garden again. For the first time he noticed the security light was not working. He squinted at it, high on the wall just below one of the girls' bedrooms, and saw it had been smashed. 'Looks as though a brick's been lobbed at it,' he said. Using the light cast from the open door and the kitchen window he poked around the patio and found two fist-sized stones near the back wall that he picked up. He knew they were not from the garden. 'Culprits, I'd guess,' he said, bobbing one of them up and down in his hand. 'Must've made a noise when they broke the light. Surprised you didn't hear a smash.'

'I might've done, actually,' Kate said, thinking back. 'I did hear a crack, or something, a few minutes before I came down. Didn't think anything of it. Just a bang.'

Henry shrugged and dropped the stones. 'No worries.'

He inspected the kitchen window for smudges or prints but in the available light he could not see that the prowler had left anything.

Kate stood on the threshold of the door. 'How long are you going to be away for, Henry? Is this thing going to take any longer than you promised?'

'I hope not ... undercover ops are always suck 'n' see things ... I mean, if I get through to this guy sooner rather than later, I could have enough to quit within days.' Kate stepped back as Henry came back into the kitchen. 'Who knows?' he said, closing and locking the door behind him, picking up his drink.

Kate sidled up to him. 'I'm glad you came home.'

'Me, too.' He stooped slightly, glass still in hand, and kissed her on the lips. As ever, her mouth tasted wonderful, her breath smelled great too, a combination of toothpaste and whisky, a great mix. She was holding her drink and slid one arm around his neck, pulling him tight to her lips. A tiny groan escaped from her throat. He bit her bottom lip, then drew slightly away.

'You called me your husband to them cops.'

'You are, aren't you?'

'Not officially.'

'Maybe that's something we need to—' Kate was going to say 'change', but the word never came out. Instead a rock the size of a brick smashed against the kitchen window with a huge crack, not breaking the double glazing, but making Henry and Kate jerk apart and spill their drinks.

'Jesus!' Henry uttered. He put down his glass and wrenched open the kitchen door to witness the black-clothed figure of a man vault the low fence into the field. 'Call the cops!' he yelled over his shoulder and immediately sprinted after the figure, bawling, 'C'mere, you bastard!'

'Henry, be careful!' Kate screamed after him.

He raced across the garden and flung himself over the fence in pursuit of the prowler, who was already thirty metres ahead, running swiftly through the shin-high grass. Henry stumbled, feeling his left knee give way momentarily, then come back, and powered after him, arms pumping, sheer rage driving him. Who was this bastard invading his privacy, terrifying his family? He had no right to violate his home.

The figure ran fast and Henry knew he was getting away. He then leapt into another garden and disappeared from view. Henry vaulted across the same fence, but by the time he landed the prowler had run off down the side of the house. Henry ran on, bouncing off the wall, and reappearing at the front of a house about a hundred metres from his own.

No sign of the man.

Gasping, Henry scoured the dark places with his keen eyes, but saw no one lurking or moving. 'Shit,' he said, shaking his head as he stood in the middle of the road.

An engine started behind him.

He spun and jogged towards the noise.

Was this just a coincidence at this time of night?

No way.

Henry headed up the avenue, through a tight ginnel and appeared in the next one as a car lurched out from the side of the road and accelerated at him. The main beam was on and for a

ent he was blinded, shading his eyes with a
arm.

he car was coming right at him.

e sidestepped in front of another parked car
he watched his old Ford Mondeo scream past
m in first. Henry aimed a useless kick at it.

So he hadn't dreamed it. Someone driving his
ld car was stalking him and his family.

He sniffed, got his breath and, very troubled,
nade his way home.

For the second time in a matter of days, and to
his utter shame and embarrassment, he could not
get an erection when he cuddled into Kate. His
saving grace was that she was exhausted, didn't
want sex, just the cuddle and reassurance. For
once he was happy to oblige and when he heard
her breathing become deep and regular, almost a
minor snore, he extracted his arm and lay awake
with his hands clasped behind his head, thinking
about the day.

The cops had rushed back, searched the area,
found no one, nor a car, then left Henry and Kate
alone.

Henry thought about the car and the previous
attempt to run him off the road.

Someone was definitely gunning for him. It
couldn't be Ingram because the road rage incident had happened before Henry had gone
undercover. And he was one hundred per cent
sure he had not been followed back from Manchester.

So who was it?

Get in line, he thought. A lot of people bore

grudges against him. Even his ex-boss, Dave Anger – just for sleeping with his wife, for goodness' sake. But Henry was pretty sure it wasn't Anger. In fact, one or two things had happened to him that he couldn't pin on Anger as much as he would have liked to: he'd been assaulted one night outside Blackpool Police Station a few months ago, also outside his local pub, the Tram and Tower. On that occasion Karl Donaldson had intervened to good effect. No one had been caught on either occasion and the attacks remained a puzzle. He wondered if they were connected to the recent incidents.

He pouted.

The prowler was very worrying, though. That brought Kate and the girls into the equation, something he did not like one bit. It meant a line had been crossed. Henry thought he was fair bait, but going for his family was a different matter.

The thought made him utter a deep, primeval growl, and grind his teeth.

He glanced at Kate in the dark.

'My husband,' she had said. A slip of the tongue, no doubt, but maybe it was time to re-pop the question, get everything above board again ... if only he could get an erection ... he'd be a pretty useless hubby if he couldn't get a hard-on ... what the hell was going on down there?

He rolled his eyes, feeling very inadequate, then closed them and visualized the naked Andrea Makin guiding him into the gates of heaven. He shuddered, glad he had not gone there, but appalled at the same time that he couldn't get hard, disgusted he'd even wanted to, scared that there'd been no response from the engine room. Crazy, mixed thoughts.

Had he become impotent? Was that how it happened? Without warning?

The bedside phone rang and made him jump.

'Fuck,' he heard Kate say in her sleep. She rolled over and covered her head with the duvet.

Henry picked up the phone. It was 3.03 a.m. Never a good time to receive a phone call. 'Hello,' he said guardedly.

'Oh, man,' came a spaced-out American-accented voice Henry recognized straight away.

'Karl?'

'Yeah ... were you asleep? ... Sorry to wake you, man,' he said. Henry sat up and touched the base of the bedside lamp, bringing it on to its lowest setting. Kate stirred and pulled the duvet down, opening one eye.

'What is it, Karl?'

'Hey, don' be like that, man,' the American drawled, and Henry could tell, almost smell it down the line, that he had been drinking. The trouble with Karl was that 'been drinking' didn't have to mean by the gallon or litre because it did not take very much alcohol to get him pissed, despite his size. He was a Yank who couldn't hold his liquor. He also had a tendency to revert to his East Coast accent when he drank, losing the mid-Atlantic hybrid he'd picked up from living in England for so long. Drink made him revert to type.

Henry sighed and glanced at Kate, puzzled

108

why his ex-friend was calling at such a godless hour. Henry had had no contact with him since the Akbar shooting because their friendship had suffered a severe, if not fatal blow during the hunt for the terrorist. It would take more than a pissed-up phone call to repair the damage.

'I'm shorry, pal, podna,' Donaldson slurred.

'How much have you had?'

'Full bottle bourbon.'

'Jesus. It's a wonder you can still pick up the phone.'

'Man, oh, man, don' be cruel...'

'What do you want, Karl?'

'She wants us to split ... to leave me, man,' Donaldson sobbed.

'Who? Karen?' Henry could not believe that.

'Yeah, yeah ... it's over, pal ... I screwed up, big style...'

'Hey, I'm sorry.'

'I needed to talk ... to you, H.'

Henry said, 'Hey, first things first – Karen loves you. I know that for sure. Why the hell she does, I don't know, but she does. Secondly, sober up, then we can talk. Get some sleep. OK, pal?' There was no response. 'Karl?'

The line buzzed dead and Henry looked accusingly at the phone in his hand, then replaced it slowly on to the base unit.

Eight

The sound of the en-suite shower woke Henry from his slumber. He looked at the bedside clock and groaned when he saw it was only 8.30 a.m. He dragged the duvet over his head and did not peek out until Kate emerged from the shower, hair dripping and a bath towel wrapped loosely around her body. She went into the walk-in dressing room, left the door open and dropped the towel, then began to attack her hair. Henry could see her from where he lay and enjoyed the sight of a jiggling bum for a few moments before she realized he was ogling her. She twisted around, shouted, 'Oi! Perv!' and closed the door.

'Nice arse,' he shouted, hauling his ageing body out of bed and sitting up. He scratched all those dark, dank places that male members of society felt the need to scrape in a morning, before standing up and lurching towards the shower himself.

'Anything?'

Henry was standing at the far end of the back garden, hands on hips, eyes crossing and re-crossing the area to see if there was something to preserve for a Crime Scene Investigator from the earlier shenanigans. Not that he had any greater pull than a normal member of the public on the services of the CSIs, and a prowler certainly wasn't at the top of their list of priorities for a team already run ragged by Blackpool's high crime rate.

Kate stood at the kitchen door, coffee and toast in hand. She was already late for work, which she did four days a week, 9.30–4.30 at an insurance broker's in town.

There was a raised flower bed next to one part of the back fence and Henry saw a footprint in the soil next to one of his rose bushes. He bent down and inspected it, estimating about a size 8 trainers, maybe. It wasn't his footprint and it was definitely worth preserving from the weather on the off-chance that a CSI might find time to nip around. He placed an upturned seed tray over it and joined Kate back in the kitchen.

'Shoe print,' he explained. 'I'll try and get CSI round, but they'll be busy, I expect.'

'Even if you order them? Is there no benefit in having rank these days?'

'I can't even fiddle expense claim forms anymore, not like in the days of yore when we first met.'

Kate smirked at a memory. 'Those were the days, eh? Sex, sex, sex – oh, and dead bodies.'

'Mm, and your arse isn't that much bigger now,' he teased.

'Nor is your cock,' she responded, punching his shoulder. 'I need to go,' she announced. 'You here tonight?'

'Yeah, back around nine, I guess.'

She looked relieved. 'Good – see you later.'

Henry fixed himself a breakfast of coffee and croissants and sat outside on the patio to eat it, even though the day was chilly, wishing he was on a Paris pavement. He had placed his mobile phones on the garden table in front of him and his business phone, which was set to silent, started to vibrate and flash as a call came through. The display read no number. He coughed to clear his throat, steadied himself and answered it.

'Frank Jagger.'

'Where the hell are you?' growled the voice of Ryan Ingram.

'Out and about.'

'You haven't been at your apartment all night.'

'As I said, out and about.' Ingram had been watching the flat, which was a worry.

'Shaggin'?'

'I wish.'

'I want a meet,' Ingram said. 'I liked what I saw.'

'OK, where, when?'

'You near a landline?'

'I can find one.'

'Find one, quick. I'll give you a call in ten minutes on the mobile, then you give me the number of the landline to ring ... understand why?'

'Can't be too careful?'

'Correct ... ten minutes ... get to it.'

Henry stuffed a croissant down his throat and swallowed it down with a big swill of coffee, then raced out of the house and jumped into the Rover. He realized that if he found a public telephone in Blackpool he would have to give Ingram a number with an 01253 prefix, which would probably start to jingle bells in his suspicious criminal mind. Henry lived only two minutes from the M55, which he joined at Marton Circle, then gunned the Rover east towards Preston. The journey took about twelve minutes, sometimes reaching speeds of 100 mph. He came off at the Broughton junction, near Preston, and drove on to the car park of an Ibis Hotel, screeched to a halt at reception and ran to the public phone just inside the foyer.

Ingram called as he stood breathless by the phone. Henry gave him the number and waited. It rang.

'01772? That's Preston, isn't it?' Ingram asked warily. 'What're you doing there?'

'If I thought it was your business, I'd tell you,' Henry came back harshly, but then thought he'd maybe pushed slightly too hard as a silence came on the line.

'OK,' Ingram said at length, 'but if you want me to bankroll you out of your difficulty, I want answers to my questions, Frank. You see, I'm interested in what you're selling – I like what I saw last night – and I want to help out. But I've been under police investigation for a long time and I don't trust any fucker. You want help, or not?'

Henry licked his lips. 'Yes,' he admitted, needing to keep Ingram on the line – and not just the phone line – the line with the hook and bait

113

on it.

'Once I'm happy with you, things'll be fine.'

'All right,' Frank Jagger said as sullenly as a bollocked teenager.

'So it's like this...' Ingram began.

'He knew I hadn't been in my apartment last night, which is worrying, and means he's already checking me out, which means I need to be on my toes, here.' Henry was talking frantically to Andrea Makin, who he'd met at the pub next to the Ibis, a premises known as the Phantom Winger. She had hurried across from her hotel near Bolton, having told Henry to stay put, which he did. But he was getting increasingly jumpy.

'Do you want to pull out?' she asked. They were in a corner of the pub, which had just opened, drinking coffee, the only beverage that kept Henry going.

He thought seriously about the question, scratching his ear as he did so. 'No,' he said eventually – a decision he would later regret. 'If I do pull out, then it'll be ten times harder for the next U/C, or even impossible. If we can get through this, then I reckon we'll be into him. Keep my nerve and then the cards'll begin to fall.'

'If you're certain.'

'I am.' A surge of adrenalin pulsed through him.

'What does he need?'

Henry scratted his ear even more fervently. 'I told him I'd spent the night with a friend in a hotel, so I need to sort out some hotel receipts. Then, stupidly, I told him something else. I was winging it, like,' he said apologetically.

'What did you tell him?'

'I was just babbling, thinking out loud and I, er, said he could meet the friend if he didn't believe me.'

'Shit.' Andrea slammed down her cup with a clatter of crockery and cutlery. 'So now we've got to find a girlfriend? Bring someone else into this? When does he want to meet you?'

'Lunchtime.'

Andrea frowned, twisted up her face, then looked at the ceiling with despair. She tutted. 'Henry, Henry, Henry ... fucking hell!'

'Sorry. And he wants to spend some time with me today...'

'Doing what, exactly?'

'I told him I was doing some business in the area, offloading some gear, booze, and then he wants to meet the guy I owe the money to.'

She looked squarely at him. 'Fantastic. This just gets worse.'

'But, but' – he held up a finger – 'like all good undercover officers, I have a plan.'

Karl Donaldson awoke feeling dreadful, his mouth clamped tightly shut as though a midnight devil had squeezed a tube of Super Glue into his mouth and sealed it. He had rolled out of his bed and crawled to the toilet, propped his chin on the bowl and heaved into it – a process which prized his mouth open, but replaced the taste of glue with something more abhorrent.

His eldest daughter, Lisa, found him in this position, waiting for the next wave of nausea to strike. Fortunately both her and her younger brother, Liam, were old enough to get themselves up, breakfasted and ready for the school run. When Donaldson crept delicately downstairs, trying not to jar his head, an unshaven, dishevelled wreck, all he had to do was get in the car and drive them.

'I take it you were rat-arsed last night,' Lisa speculated.

Donaldson merely blew out his cheeks and tried to concentrate on the road. He was aware his blood-alcohol level was still dangerously high and if a cop stopped and breathalysed him, he would be done for. One of those sad morning drunk-drivers still over the limit from the night before.

'You don't take alcohol well, do you?' she went on, shaking her head sadly.

In the back seat of the Jeep, Liam was making farting noises by blowing raspberries on to the back of his hand. They were steadily increasing in volume until Donaldson had had enough. He snapped around. 'Shut it, will you?'

Lisa's eyes half-closed. She said, 'Makes you grumpy, too.'

Donaldson exhaled again and eyed her. 'Sorry, darlin', and sorry to you too, pal. Fart away.'

'The thing about undercover cops is that they have real lives,' said Ryan Ingram. 'They live this elaborate double life, scamming the baddies, then going home to their loved ones at the end of the day, which is why I need to check you out good and proper. See if your story has any holes in it and if it has, then I'll sink you.' He smiled – dangerously.

Henry feigned indifference. 'Whatever.'

'Which is why it concerns me that you weren't all tucked up at home last night when Mitch popped around for a brew.'

'I do have a bit of a life,' Henry said. 'What do you want from me?'

'I want to know where you were last night and who you were with and what you'll be doing today ... then, if I'm happy, we'll talk about a way forward with the money. Your choice. A bit of openness and we'll be fine.'

'OK.' Henry, aka Frank Jagger, nodded. 'I spent last night in a hotel with a married woman.'

'Which hotel, what woman?'

'This hotel.' Henry gave Ingram a scrunched up receipt for the Ibis hotel which he peeled flat and read, nodding as he did. He looked at Henry, smiling. 'I take it this is the woman?' He glanced past Henry's shoulder towards the Nissan Micra, in which sat the figure of Andrea Makin. His head bobbed and weaved for a better view.

'Looks a doll.'

'She's here under sufferance ... like I said, she's married and she's got a reputation to pro-tect.'

'Can I have a chat with her?' Ingram took a step towards the Nissan. Henry moved across him. Behind him, Mitch, who was also present, tensed up.

'I don't think so,' Henry said, hardening his voice. If Ingram pushed it, he knew he would have to relent and see if he and Andrea could bluff their way through this. Andrea had assured Henry that she and Ingram had never met, even though she was the detective heading the investigation into him. But they *had* been face to face, because she had been acting out the role of custody officer at Salford police station when Henry had been arrested. She had not dealt with Ingram, but they had been in close proximity when she and Henry had almost come to blows for the benefit of the audience.

What Henry and Andrea had decided to do to appease Ingram involved a big risk, hoping he would not recognize her. If he did, the meeting could turn into something very nasty. On the plus side, with her hair down and make-up on, Andrea now looked nothing like the harsh-faced, harassed custody sergeant.

'She doesn't like being inspected,' Henry said.

He and Ingram were shoulder to shoulder.

They had met on the Bolton motorway services eastbound on the M61 this time. Henry was wary of becoming something of a regular, but he knew such locations were the meeting places of many travelling criminals and their contacts. Ingram and Mitch had come in from the direction of Manchester, then used the service access road to cross the motorway to reach the eastern side.

'She's got to go to work,' Henry insisted.

Ingram sniffed. 'You said your bird had dumped you.'

'She has, but this one isn't my bird. There's a difference between an occasional shag and a regular bird, yeah? I brought her here in good faith just because you wanted to see her and I don't want her to have any further embarrassment, OK?'

'OK, I'll have that.' He bobbed his head for another look. 'Tasty.'

Henry kept his mouth shut.

'OK, then,' Ingram relented.

'I need to take her and drop her off at work, then we can meet up later, if that's all right?'

'And we can join you on your rounds?'

'You can join me – not him.' Henry indicated Mitch.

Ingram waved the hotel receipt Henry had given him. 'I might just go and pay this place a visit in the meantime, see if anyone remembers you.'

'Do what you want,' Henry said. He walked away, trying to stroll casually towards Andrea in the Nissan. Inside he was churning. He dropped into the driver's seat and fumbled for his keys. 'He going to check the hotel,' Henry said through the side of his mouth.

'Shit, we could be stuffed then,' Andrea said.

'More than likely.' Henry fired up the car and headed off down the motorway, not giving Ingram and Mitch a backward glance, but painfully aware that the receipt he had given him was one he'd been lucky to obtain from a real guest at the Ibis who had dropped it whilst packing his car.

'Can I just say something, by the way?'

'Go on.'

'Be careful of Mitch. He's a dangerous bastard.'

Nine

Another car park – this time the one at Botany Bay, the old canal mill standing proud by the M61 that had been renovated and converted into retail outlets – another meet.

Henry sat in the Nissan, drumming his fingers on the steering wheel, wondering whether Ingram would show. And if he did, what would he have discovered at the hotel and what sort of mood would he be in. Henry's face was set hard as he thought about Ingram, a violent, clever man, obviously careful in the extreme, as well as completely ruthless.

He thought back to the evening he had spent with him, sampling Henry's DVD collection, courtesy of the Met. Ingram had taken Henry to the back room of a pub in Cheetham Hill, Manchester, where they would not be disturbed.

But Henry had been disturbed – inside. He had seen Ingram's eyes glued with sick intensity to the pictures on the huge TV screen, almost drooling over the action, whilst Henry, who'd had a little preview of the discs, tried to hide his disgust and discomfort, appalled by the horrendous, graphic content.

Those thoughts made him even more determined to stay with the case. As difficult as it was proving at the moment, he knew if he held his nerve and rode through Ingram's suspicions, he could get under the man's skin and get him to lead him to, or reveal, his grim secrets.

A car drew in behind him.

Henry's eyes rose to the rear-view mirror.

Ingram had arrived – alone.

Henry twisted out of the Nissan, stood to greet him. There was nothing in the man's demeanour that gave Henry cause to be concerned, but that didn't mean he wasn't hiding something. He was a con-artist, amongst his many attributes, and disguising his body language would be something he did well. Henry readied himself for this interaction to go either way.

'Who did you kill, then?' Ingram asked before Henry could say anything.

'What do you mean?'

'Cops were crawling all around the hotel when I got there. Apparently some guy got whacked in one of the rooms last night.'

'Really?' Henry said with disbelief.

'Chambermaid only just found the body. Been knifed a dozen times.'

'Jesus, never heard a thing.'

'Didn't get chance to check on you.' Ingram fished the receipt out of his pocket and gave it back to Henry. 'But I will be doing.'

Henry shrugged. Inside, he was relieved.

'You won't be wanting to go to the cops, then?'

'For what?'

'Because you were at the hotel last night. They'll be wanting to speak to everyone ... possible witnesses.'

'I'll give it a miss. They'll have to come and find me.'

'Not very public spirited.'

'Let 'em whistle.'

'What's the plan for today, then?'

'I'm trying to offload some stolen beer. I'm going to see a guy who's interested.'

'Lead on.' Ingram walked to the passenger side of the Nissan and got in, obviously having got over his fear of being driven by a disqualified driver.

Henry took a breath, relieved that some poor soul had been murdered and saved his hide for the time being.

'It's basically what I do,' Henry, alias Frank, was saying to Ingram as he drove up the steep hill known as Ha'penny Brew, which rose from the M6 towards Preston. 'Usually beer or fags, fence that sort of stuff ... couldn't resist the porn, though, but it went tits up, as it were. What about you?' he asked conversationally.

Henry braked gently as the hill levelled out and he passed through the 30 signs. There was no response from Ingram, who continued to stare dead ahead as though he hadn't heard Henry's question. Henry did not push it. Ingram inhaled a deep breath and sat upright.

'I'm a businessman who gets pleasure from what he does.'

'I take it you're a bit of a porn king? I mean, if you think you can sell on the stuff I've got, you must have some contacts.'

'Some, yeah. I'm very hands-on, too.' He looked into Henry's eyes, his own sparkling with double meaning which churned Henry's stomach.

Henry gave a laugh. 'I like a man who enjoys his work.'

Ingram fell silent again.

They reached a roundabout. Henry drove straight on towards Preston down New Hall Lane. It was a very unprepossessing route into England's newest city, travelling down a long stretch of road with terraced housing either side and a variety of grotty shops, mainly run by members of the Asian community. On the left, behind all this, was Preston's notorious Callum Estate, a hive of fear and violence. Behind the houses on the right was a tight network of terraced streets, populated mainly by ethnic minorities. New Hall Lane ran through the centre of this like the Maginot Line, but Henry knew that whilst racial problems existed, the city generally worked well on that front. It was general lawlessness and youth offenders that caused most of the problems, regardless of ethnic origin.

Henry slowed, turned into a side street that was a dead end. He manoeuvred the Nissan into a tiny parking space.

'Place we're going to is just on the front. You coming?'

Ingram nodded.

Together they walked out of the side street and ambled down the main road, passing a furniture shop, another selling ethnic foods and a boarded-up pub before reaching the front door of a double-fronted second-hand shop called 'Jamil's', which had a pavement display of battered furniture and old bikes for kids. Henry pushed through the door and an old-fashioned bell announced their arrival. The inner display of goods pretty much matched the outer, although it was augmented with an array of electrical goods, boxes of CDs and DVDs. They threaded their way through these wares and arrived at the sales counter behind which sat a young Asian man, mid-twenties, leaning back in an office chair, reading a copy of the *Asian Times*.

He lowered the newspaper and eyed his customers, apparently not recognizing Frank Jagger at first, or so it seemed, but then his slight scowl turned into grin. He folded his newspaper untidily and rocked forwards up on to his feet, extending his hand. 'Hey, pal,' he said, and shook Henry's hand.

Henry felt even more queasy inside, but he gripped the young man's hand and returned the shake.

'Jamil, how you doing?'

'I'm good, Frank, how the shit are you?' He spoke with a broad Preston accent.

'Good, good.' Their hands parted. Henry thumbed at Ingram. 'This is Ryan.'

'Hi, man,' Jamil nodded. He did not shake hands, but gave Henry a suspicious looks which queried Ingram's presence.

'It's OK,' Henry reassured him. 'We're in business.'

Jamil shrugged.

Henry turned to Ingram. 'Let me introduce Jamil Ahmed. This is his business and he's as honest as the day is short.'

'What do you want to sell?' Jamil asked, pleasantries over.

'Back room?' Henry suggested.

Jamil raised the flap on the counter and the three of them retreated to a tiny, cluttered office where the Asian guy dropped into a chair behind a paper-stacked desk and the other two cleared two plastic chairs of rubbish before sitting and facing him.

'How long have you guys known each other?' Ingram asked.

Henry thought, Small talk, big implications.

The two eyed each other uncertainly. Jamil blew out his cheeks as he worked out the answer. 'Four years, give or take.'

Ingram nodded.

Jamil turned his attention to Henry. 'What've you got for me, Frank, mate?'

'Well,' Henry drawled, 'I'm in the process of clearing the decks, so I've got a bit of a sale on...'

'Frank, I'm a busy man, as you can see. Just get to the detail, will you? I'm not interested in your financial probs.'

Henry looked at the ceiling with a squint, then back at Jamil. 'I have in my possession twenty thousand half-litre cans of Stella, which I need to offload PDQ.'

'A cash-flow crisis,' Jamil said with insight, sniggering.

'Not remotely,' Henry said firmly. 'Just offering an old friend a bargain.'

'How much?'

'They cost a quid a tin in the shops.'

'I can get lager for twenty-two pence in ASDA.'

'But this is quality,' Henry said. 'Stella Artois.'

'How much?'

'I need to cover my costs and make some profit.'

'How much, Frank?' Jamil asked irritably.

'Make an offer.'

Jamil emitted an exasperated breath. 'Twenty thousand tins?' His brown nostrils flared.

'You have to collect,' Henry said.

Jamil's head tilted sideways as he considered. 'Five pence a tin.'

Henry almost leapt out of his chair. 'That's just a grand!'

Jamil shrugged. 'Take it, leave it.'

'You robbin', Muslim bastard!'

'Robbing, maybe; Muslim, no way. I'm an atheist, just like you.'

'Robbin' atheist bastard, then,' Henry snarled. He sat back down. 'Ten pence a tin.'

Jamil shook his head. 'Seven pence, final offer.'

Henry worked it out. 'Fourteen hundred quid,' he said despondently. 'Make it a round fifteen and it's a deal.'

'Fifteen hundred it is.' Jamil extended his hand.

'What's the profit margin in that?' Ingram asked.

'Narrow,' Henry said bitterly. 'Very fucking narrow. Pile 'em high, sell 'em cheap.' He shook his head in disbelief as they headed back out of Preston towards the motorway. 'Maybe three-fifty after costs ... doesn't even pay my bloody fine, let alone my creditor.' His voice was purposely hopeless and so immersed was he in his thoughts, he failed to spot the speed camera until it flashed brightly behind him. 'Hell, that's all I need,' he bleated.

'Not as though you're likely to pay it, are you?'

'No. The car's registered to an Asian guy in Rusholme, I think.' Henry put his foot down and sped to the motorway junction, cutting south on to the M6, then east on to the M61 and back to the car park at Botany Bay, parking behind Ingram's car.

Henry waited for him to get out, but the man sat there staring, deep in contemplation for a few tedious moments. He then said, turning to look Henry in the eye, 'So far, so good.'

'Glad you think so.'

'Now I need to speak to your creditor.'

'And why would that be? If you're gonna bail me out, just go ahead and do it. Give me the money I owe, I'll pay him off, then you shift the DVDs. Give me five per cent of that and I'll be happy.'

'I'll bet you will. How do I know this whole thing still isn't a con, just to get me to pay you, then you disappear?'

Henry sighed.

'You are, after all, a bit of a con merchant, aren't you?'

'I'm a businessman. On the wrong side of the tracks, maybe, but still a businessman. I'm trustworthy and that's why I'm so uptight about my creditor – as well as the fact he'll cut my balls off if I don't pay up. I don't welch on deals,' he said forcefully.

'This'll be the last thing, then. Let me meet him, let me talk to him, and then you and me can be partners. How does that sound?'

The London apartments were always in high demand. Donaldson, therefore, was lucky to get one. It was one of six in a converted house in Holland Park, all owned by the American Embassy. Individually they were valued at around the three-quarters of a million pound mark, but Donaldson observed that even for that price, there wasn't enough room to swing a raccoon in it. He felt that he had to squeeze in through the door, down a narrow hallway and into the living room-cum-kitchen. The bedroom and bathroom were off to one side. It was all laminate floors and modern, square furniture. His eyes took in the tiny living space, recently used by an FBI agent on a three-month secondment from LA.

'Is it to your liking?'

Behind him was the young lady from 'Facilities' at the embassy. She had been more than eager to help Donaldson find a pad, especially when he regaled her with his tale of woe. He had bumped into the lady more than once in the corridors and had been aware of her lustful gazes. She wiggled the door keys between her fingers.

'It's good, thanks, Alex,' he said gratefully, dropping his two hefty holdalls on the floor. He took the keys and she ran her forefinger across his palm in a suggestive way. Her eyes shone.

'I know you're going through some really bad shit,' she said, 'but if you need a shoulder or something, you've got my mobile number.'

Donaldson nodded dumbly. 'I have, yeah, that'd be good.' He did not look her in the face.

When she left he sat on the two-seater sofa and began to cry.

'It's very dangerous.'

'Couldn't agree more.' Henry inserted a piece of fried chorizo into his mouth and looked around the restaurant, checking if he'd been followed. His senses were on high alert and his radar tuned in, and he thought he had managed to get into Manchester city centre without a tail, but he could never be one hundred per cent sure. Ingram was very edgy about him still, and Henry was sure the man would not be feeling completely safe until he had chased up every avenue with Frank Jagger. Henry emitted a small groan of pleasure as his bit into the Spanish sausage, his eyes rolling heavenwards.

'Nice,' he said to his dining companion in the tapas bar.

Andrea Makin smiled wickedly. 'I could make you do that.'

Henry started to chew quickly, dropped his

eyes and jabbed his fork into a bowl of mixed olives.

'Sorry, changed the subject there,' she apologized insincerely. 'What you are planning is very dangerous and could blow the whole thing to bits. You've come a long way in a short space of time ... it would be a shame to spoil it.'

'I think it's the best way.'

Andrea sat back. She wiped her lips before taking a sip of her Rioja. 'Convince me.'

'I've had this guy on a rope for over ten years. He owes me a lot and he knows it, even if we have had our run-ins in the past,' he said wistfully. 'He knows what side his bread is buttered on, and at the end of the day, it's a pretty simple ask. All he has to do is remember my name and say he lent me some money that he wants back.'

'Why not use another undercover cop?'

Henry rotated his jaw. 'Because' – he stabbed another chunk of chorizo – 'this guy already has the background, a real background that will withstand any degree of scrutiny, because it *is* real. He's a crim, a known dealer, belongs to a criminal family and is therefore watertight if Ingram goes nosing. We don't have to make anything up, because it's all there. If he gets followed home, it's fine. If he gets followed around, fine. The guy's a lowlife – plus he's been my snout for ever.'

'What's his name?'

'Can't tell you that, can I?'

'You have to.'

'Only if he agrees ... if he doesn't, we'll rethink.' Henry spooned some paella on to his plate. 'It'll work,' he said confidently.

'Your last idea did, I suppose.'

'Oh yes.'

'But what if Ingram goes nosing into that?'

'Jamil's place? No probs. It's been trading for two and a half years now and Jamil is so deep undercover I'm surprised he even remembers he's a cop. That little shop has produced a lot of superb intel for us, and no one knows it's run by the police. It's a dream.'

Henry's personal phone rang. Kate calling.

'Hello, sweetheart.' He glanced across at Andrea, who winced and pulled a face. 'Yeah, yeah, I'm really sorry but I can't come home tonight ... I've arranged for the local cops to keep an eye on the house ... don't worry ... and your mum's there for the night, isn't she? She'd scare the crap out of any prowler ... I wish I could, but ... I know you know ... night. Love you.' He ended the call.

Andrea regarded him, puzzled. 'Something going on?' She nodded to indicate the phone.

'Had a few problems with a prowler.'

'Serious?'

'Who knows?'

There was a beat of silence, then Andrea said, 'So you're in town for another night?'

'I thought it prudent – just in case Mitch checks on me again.'

Andrea pursed her lips. 'Of course, if we get seen together now it's legit, isn't it? Ingram's seen us as a couple.'

Henry shook his head. 'We managed to scam that once and we're lucky he didn't recognize you. If he starts to follow you up, you've no cover to crawl under and then the job would be screwed.'

She pushed herself away from the table. 'I could do wonders for those erection problems of yours.'

Henry blanched and the tortilla in his mouth lost its taste.

'Anyway, room twenty-six, that's on the second floor of the Premier Inn, about two hundred yards down the road, which is where I'm staying now. I'll sneak off.' She stood up slowly. 'If you're not there in half an hour, we'll forget it. Deal?'

'Deal,' Henry murmured.

Ten

With a terrible churning in his guts, telling him this was a huge mistake, Henry Christie made the introductions and prayed that the next phase of the 'mating-up' with Ryan Ingram did not hit the fan and cover him with shit.

In the past Henry had been accused of a lack of judgement and that morning he wondered if the allegations had been correct. *I mean*, he thought, *introducing this idiot to Ingram! What the hell am I thinking? This can only go one way – down the U bend and out to the sewage treatment works.*

But it was too late now.

Henry had laid the ground and the only possible way of pulling out now was to declare he was a cop.

And, to add extra spice to the situation, Henry was again operating on home turf and dangerously near to his home patch of Blackpool, laughing in the face of the accepted practice that undercover cops should not work within sixty miles of their homes.

At least he had arranged the meeting between Ingram and his creditor in the café of a large garden centre about halfway between the resort and Preston, not somewhere Henry would usually be found.

It was Wednesday morning. Henry had picked up Ryan in Manchester, beaten the traffic and arrived at the garden centre at nine thirty.

The man to whom Frank Jagger allegedly owed a hefty wodge of cash was sitting in a window seat in the downstairs café, sipping black coffee and looking uncomfortably out of place.

'Troy, uh, Mr Costain,' Henry said respectfully, 'can I introduce you to Ryan Ingram? Ryan – Troy Costain.'

Costain gave a little sneer, eyeing Henry as if he were a slug, and nodded at Ingram.

'Coffee for me,' Ingram said to Henry. 'You need another?' he asked Costain.

'Yuh.'

Ingram raised his eyebrows at Henry, then his hand appeared from his pocket, a neatly folded tenner between his first and second fingers which he held towards Henry. 'My shout,' he

said, with a supercilious grin. He sat down opposite Costain and shooed Henry away with a flick
of the hand. Henry scuttled off like a cockroach
to the counter, his face set hard, inwardly swearing as he waited for the coffees to be filtered. He
watched the two men in deep conversation about
him.

Suddenly both their faces snapped round to
look at him.

Henry gave them a little wave.

It is often the case in undercover police operations that a well-briefed and trusted source, or
informant, introduces the undercover cop to the
target criminal. It is less usual for an informant
to be brought into the scenario at a later stage,
but this is what was happening that day, and
Henry was finding it just a little on the arse-
twitching side.

He knew the situation was fraught with danger.
As he collected the three coffees and placed
them on a tray, his mind quickly considered
whether this was a good idea or not, especially
with someone as untrustworthy as Troy Costain,
local Blackpool villain, hard man, drug dealer
and, unknown to the population at large, Henry
Christie's snout.

The Costain family ruled life on a Blackpool
council estate called Shoreside. A ragtag bunch
of misfits, proudly boasting they were descended from Romany gypsies, they terrorized, intimidated, robbed, burgled; in fact they did anything that meant a profit came in their direction.
Old man Costain and his grossly fat wife, Trace,

had settled in Spain and Troy, the eldest son, had inherited the family crown, but he had no strategic ideas and couldn't control the youngsters and couldn't even distance himself from the sharp end of criminality. He saw himself as a Godfather, but because it was in his blood to be part of day-to-day thieving and dealing, he would never run a true criminal empire.

Henry had been involved with the Costain clan for many years. He had met Troy when the little crim was no more than a spotty, gangly teenager who, it transpired, despite the boasts and bravado, lived in terror of being thrown into a cell. His claustrophobia was something Henry had used ruthlessly to his advantage ever since.

Troy had provided Henry with a lot of good information since, once resulting in a year when Henry locked up over sixty people on the back of Troy's say-so.

In reality, Henry should have declared Troy as an informant and got him properly registered under the new system. That would have meant Troy being allocated a handler and a controller from the Intelligence Unit and being taken away from Henry for ever. So, wrongly, Henry had kept him under wraps – like a true detective – so he could use all the information for himself. The situation could have backfired, but so far – Henry touched the Formica-topped tray as a wood substitute – other than a few ups and downs, Henry had managed to keep a grip on Troy, but he knew the writing was on the wall.

As he paid for his coffee with Ingram's ten-pound note, he decided that if he got through today's trauma, he would turn Troy over to the intel boys and wipe his hands of the little twat. The only problem with that, though, was Henry knew Troy would dry up as a source, which would be a terrible shame.

Henry glanced across the café. Costain and Ingram talked earnestly, heads close together. They laughed at something.

Henry's mind went back to the previous day when he'd approached Costain.

It was the morning after the night before, the night when he had almost knocked on the door of Premier Inn room 26 and, erection permitting, would have (he imagined) had terrific sex with Andrea Makin. At the last moment he had veered away and returned to the apartment on Salford Quays, ignoring the barrage of texts that landed on his mobile phone from the scorned Andrea Makin. Instead he called up a sleepy Kate, who was ecstatic to hear from him, and told her how much he loved and missed her. Having found out she was safe and sound, he climbed into bed with a superior grin on his face and had a much needed sleep, waking refreshed and ready for action – in every regard.

As expected, his mobile phone, which he had switched to silent, had over a dozen missed calls on it and an equal number of unread texts, but no voice messages left. He deleted all the texts without reading them.

He switched the mobile ring tone back on and immediately it rang. It was a very frosty Andrea Makin.

'You didn't come,' she said flatly.

'No.'

'That's it, then?'

'That was the deal.'

Silence, then, 'Plans for today?'

'Fix up tomorrow's meeting. I need to get back to Blackpool to sort it out.'

'Let me know how it pans out.' Click – call ended, connection cut.

Henry looked at the phone and gave a short chuckle, then decided to forgo breakfast in the flat. He had to get on the road, make sure he wasn't being followed. He picked up the Nissan from the underground garage and meandered his way across Salford on to the A56, found a McDonald's, where he parked up and had a sausage and egg McMuffin breakfast with a cup of coffee. He snaffled a *Daily Express* from the rack and took about twenty minutes over the meal, constantly watching the toing and froing of people and vehicles. Nothing roused his suspicions. He continued the journey up through Prestwich to the big motorway roundabout that was junction 17 of the M60. He circled it twice, then accelerated down the slip road on to the motorway, a plume of oily purple smoke blowing out of the exhaust in a very worrying way. Within a few minutes he was crossing on to the M61, heading west, fumbling with his mobile to make a few calls whilst driving.

Troy Costain laughed uproariously. Henry waited patiently for the mirth to subside.

'You want *me* to help *you*?'

'In a nutshell.'

Costain sneered. 'I don't think so, Henry.'

Henry's face hardened. 'It'll be worth your while.'

'Bollocks, Henry. I've paid my dues to you in spades.'

'Troy,' he said with patience, 'that will never be the case. You did one very bad thing to me and whilst we might have drawn a line under it and you did provide a bit of assistance in clearing up a job, it will always be there emotionally for me.' Henry placed his hand over his heart. 'You robbed my dear old mother, remember?'

Costain gulped. 'We made a deal over it.'

'Maybe so, but what you did still hurts me here and reminds me what a piece of shite you are.'

'I don't think that's fair, Henry.'

'Anyone who goes about conning vulnerable old people is scum, Troy, let's face it.'

'We did a trade for that, and I told you I was sorry. I wouldn't have done it if I'd known it was your mum.'

'You'd have done it to someone else's, though.' Henry took a breath and steadied himself. 'Look, we can go in circles here. Either you give me a chuck up, or you don't, but if you don't, I'll feed you to the wolves. Bottom line.'

'Whaddya mean by that?'

'Work it out, pal. If you don't help me, I've no further use for you.' Henry stared him out.

They had met, reluctantly on Costain's part, on the sea front at Lytham St Annes, near to the windmill on the green. They had walked across to Lowther Gardens where they were now seated in the café. Henry was getting weary of meeting people and he suddenly thought that the sooner this assignment was over, the better. The tediousness of such jobs had been sidelined in his memory, which had selectively recalled the excitement and the danger, not the ennui. He sighed, waiting for Troy's response.

'You always have the upper hand, don't you?'

'I'm a cop, you're a criminal – and a crap one at that. So, yes, obviously, I have.'

'What's the job then?'

Which left Henry with an afternoon free on his home turf after he'd got Costain's signature on the necessary paperwork.

As soon as he had thoroughly briefed Costain and they had parted company, Henry strolled into Lytham town centre and booked a room for the night at the County Arms. This done, he dialled Kate's mobile number from one of the hotel phones.

'Kate Christie,' she answered. Henry knew she would be at work.

'Kate Christie,' he said thoughtfully, 'now listen very carefully...' He heard her stifle a giggle. 'Whether or not you are busy at work, you are now required to take the rest of the day off – no ifs, no buts – then you will immediately drive down to the County Hotel in Lytham and go straight up to room—' Henry fumbled for the key fob and read her the number. 'Here a naked man will be waiting for you to give you some red-hot sex, followed by an evening of delight and further debauchery at the hot spots of

139

Lytham St Annes. Probably followed by more red-hot sex.'

'May I go home first and collect ... certain belongings?'

'Only if they happen to be a change of cloth-ing, a Basque, suspenders and a change of clothing for me, too.'

'One hour.'

'I'll be there with a rose between my teeth.'

Henry hung up slowly, a dirty, crooked smile on his face, and hoped to hell his plumbing would not let him down.

Ingram and Costain watched Henry approach with the drinks. He placed the tray carefully down and slid it on to the table.

'You look worried, Frank,' Ingram observed. Henry shrugged, shook his head and sat down, thinking his nervousness probably added realism to the situation. He wanted Ingram to believe he was on edge about the meeting, but only for the reasons he knew about, not because Troy Costain was unreliable.

'I'm fine,' he croaked.

'Good. I've been having a nice little natter with Troy and it seems you do owe him some money.'

'Like I said.'

'Four and a half big ones,' Costain butted in.

'Four two-fifty,' Henry corrected him.

'That's including interest.'

Henry's right leg began to jerk with annoy-ance. Costain had been given his parameters and told not to go beyond them. Hamming it up was

140

not in the script.

'Question is,' Ingram said, 'do I cover the debt or am I just being set up for a fall here? I'm still very suspicious, see,' he said to Costain. 'Nothing personal.'

'I'm owed money. That's all I care about,' Costain said indifferently.

'Look,' Henry said, as Frank, 'if you want to help me, that's great. If you don't, well that's your choice. If you pay him off you've got the merchandise cheap; if you don't I've still got it and the debt.'

'And me around your throat,' Costain put in helpfully.

'Choice is yours.' Henry looked from one to the other, wishing he was somewhere else.

Ingram sat back.

Costain waited.

Henry stood up. 'I'll be up in the car park.'

As he waited his mind switched to the previous day. He *had* been waiting naked, although sans rose, for Kate to arrive. Within seconds of her coming through the door, she was as naked as he and they were together for a serious bout of love-making. They collapsed exhausted an hour later with Henry having performed to the best of his ability.

'Hell,' Kate said as she rolled off him. 'You on Viagra or something?'

'Nah, just blood and natural He-Man hormones,' he replied, jerking with pleasure as she squeezed his still erect penis gently. He gasped.

'That was fantastic.'

'You were fantastic,' he rejoined. 'How do you fancy a night in a motel?'

'Very much.'

He explained his situation to her, that he would have to be up early to get back to Manchester, and she readily accepted it.

'You can be a bit of a romantic,' she said.

'Aye, that's me, Mr Romantic.' He pulled her tight to him. 'Fancy another shag?'

It was a devastating line he often used to great effect.

Times like this, Henry could see the benefits of being a smoker. Waiting tensely by the car, he tried not to think too deeply about what might be transpiring between the two criminals down in the café.

Costain could easily have blown the whole thing and dropped Henry in it and Ingram could be coming out, all guns blazing.

Trying not to think about it, Henry's mind went back to his time with Kate again, and following another successful sexual union, during which Henry surprised and surpassed himself, they showered together. Then they got dressed and went for a stroll along the sea front before coming back into town for a Chinese meal. After that they went to the Taps, a pub well known for its great beers and atmosphere. They spent the evening there before crashing back to the hotel and into bed where there was no necessity to make love again. They simply fell asleep in each other's arms...

Henry jerked out of his reverie.

Ingram and Costain were coming out of the garden centre.

Other than being off work sick because he had been shot, Karl Donaldson was proud of his record that, whatever the knocks, however ill he felt, he had never had a day of sick leave in all his working life. But when he woke up that morning, alone in the FBI owned apartment, he did not feel he had the ability to drag himself into the office.

He was feeling sorry for himself, depressed and angry, desperately missing Karen, the kids, his home.

There had been a brief, frosty conversation with Karen when she made it clear he was not wanted at home and it would be better for all concerned if he just kept away, at least for the short term.

She put the kids on the phone and they seemed completely unfazed by the situation, which had clearly not sunk in. Daddy was often away. It was a fact of life, so there was nothing different today. When he asked for the phone to be handed back to their mother, it went dead. Message received, loud, clear and understood.

He sat on the edge of the bed, naked, for a long time after that, his brain full of thoughts, yet empty of anything at the same time.

Eventually he picked up his mobile phone and tabbed through to the number of Alex, the young lady from Facilities who had made her intentions quite clear. It was a number he had looked at a few times, his thumb hovering over the call button. He pressed it this time – then immediately panicked and cancelled the call.

'That will achieve nothing.' He tossed the phone away.

He slapped his muscular thighs and stood up. He had thought of punishing Karen by cheating on her, but that wasn't what their separation was about. He was the one who had done bad things to her in the first place, but it had been the job that was his mistress.

He needed to sort his life out.

He found his running gear scrunched up in one of his holdalls, pulled it on and decided there were things he needed to put right in his life, get his priorities right.

As he jogged out on the pavement to begin a three-mile jog around London, he thought he would try and tackle one thing at a time. The first of those was 250 miles north. Then he would return in a few days, when the dust had settled, and take on the most important challenge – his family.

He settled into an easy pace, just on the edge of pain.

They seemed pleased with themselves, chatting and laughing like old mates.

'OK, Frank?' Costain winked, grinning like a fool.

Henry nodded doubtfully.

Ingram slapped Costain on the back. 'See you around, then.'

'Sooner rather than later, I hope.'

'Absolutely.'

Costain gave them a short wave and crossed to where his BMW was parked up. It had smoked glass windows, racing stripes, fat wheels. All that was missing was a huge hand hovering over it with a sign saying, 'Drug Dealer on Board'.

Ingram watched him through narrowed eyes, then turned to Henry.

'I think we're in business, Frank.'

'What exactly have you worked out?'

Ingram sniffed. 'Not your concern ... all you need to know is that you can forget the debt.' He leaned towards Henry, aggressively invading his personal space. 'And I now own you.'

Eleven

'I'll be in touch, day or two at most. Got something to set up and I might be able to use you on it.' Ingram was saying this whilst leaning through the passenger door of Henry's Nissan. They were back in Manchester and Henry had been instructed to drive to the NCP car park at the bottom end of Deansgate where Ingram had arranged to meet Mitch, the heavy, heavy.

'OK.'

'And don't go getting into more debt,' he admonished Henry with a wag of his finger.

'I won't,' he said, like a chastised child.

Mitch drew in behind the Nissan, seated at the wheel of the Peugeot 607. Ingram slammed the door without another word and jumped in beside his henchman who screeched away, leaving Henry behind. Henry waited a few minutes to allow them to disappear, did a U-turn, drove under the railway bridge, did a left then headed towards Salford Quays, his hands dithering on the wheel as he exhaled the tension out of his body. His grimace turned to an expression of satisfaction, then his head began to nod to a beat only he could hear.

'Got you, you bastard,' he said gleefully.

Unsettlingly, a police car followed him for about a quarter of a mile along Trinity Way. He thought he was about to get pulled over when the car suddenly veered off up a side street, allowing him a sigh of relief. That could have put a spanner in the works, because he wouldn't have been able to claim to be who he really was and, under the guise of Frank Jagger, he would have ended up in court, in custody and probably in prison.

Fifteen minutes later he was in the Salford Quays apartment, kettle on, relaxing. His own mobile phone had been hidden away, taped behind a radiator just on the off-chance someone might have broken in. He peeled it free and switched it on.

Two texts were waiting to be read and there were several missed calls logged.

The first text was from Andrea Makin, who he hadn't seen since her last proposition to him. She was telling him she had to go back to London, but would be back later that day.

The second text sent him cold.

'Hi – nice shag at County? Kate enjoy it?'

He gasped, not realizing he had been holding his breath. He tabbed quickly to the number of the sender, but it wasn't one he recognized. He dialled it immediately but it went through to voice mail. Next he phoned Kate, who would be at work.

'Hello, lover,' she giggled in a whisper.

'Hi, sweetie.' His voice was clipped.

'What's the matter, love?' she asked, instantly picking up on his tone.

'Are you OK?'

'Fine ... why?' she asked.

'Oh, nothing...' He was almost going to say nothing about the text, but changed his mind. It was probably better she knew. 'Look, I've had a strange text...' He explained it to her and heard her intake of breath.

'Someone's following you,' she said.

'I'm pretty sure I wasn't followed.'

'That means...'

'Someone followed you.'

The door buzzer sounded. 'I'll call you back shortly,' he said, and crossed to the door. Through the spyhole he saw Andrea Makin on the other side.

'Shit,' he breathed, and opened the door for her.

'Henry,' she said in a crisp, businesslike manner. He stepped aside and she brushed past him, no eye contact, just a chill factor. She was carrying a briefcase which she heaved on to the coffee table, before peeling off her jacket and draping it over the back of the couch and facing him.

'I thought you were in London.'

'Been there and back,' she said. 'Progress?'

'He's taken the bait. It went well with Costain, and I'm in if I want to be, I reckon. But he wants to own me.'

A smile cracked across her face. 'Seriously?'

He nodded. 'But the question of the debt is a problem.' He moved into the kitchen, separated from the living area by a drawer unit. He flicked the kettle to re-boil, took out a coffee jug and placed a filter on it, spooning some fresh ground coffee into it, which smelled wonderful. 'Where do we stand if he pays the money over? It could be looked on as fraud on our part – a very grey area.'

She screwed up her face. Henry came back and handed her a mug of coffee. 'Let's just put it on hold for a moment and see what happens. Tell me in detail how today went.'

He filled her in.

'So Costain did a good job?'

'On the face of it. I've yet to speak to him. He needs a proper debrief.'

Andrea perched on the edge of the sofa, cupping her mug in two hands, contemplating things.

'Ingram said he might be able to use you?'

'Un-huh.'

'Wonder what that means.'

Henry shrugged. 'Hate to think.'

He looked at her and experienced a twinge of sexual regret. He'd had the chance – two chances, actually, the first blown because of mechanical reasons, the second because of guilt.

He thought he had probably taken the best course of action, even if he hadn't actually had a choice on the first occasion when Mr Stiffy had failed to materialize.

'However,' Henry began slowly, 'I want to pull out.'

The words seemed to fell Andrea like a tree. Stunned, she stared at Henry, completely lost for words. Her lips popped soundlessly. She placed her mug on the table, then found her voice.

'You are fucking joking?'

'No.' Henry set hard. 'Something's come up.'

'And...?' she said with a sneer. 'Like what? You can't just drop out when you feel like it. Has Kate got something to do with this?' she demanded. 'Does she know about us?'

'Us? There is no "us", Andrea.'

She glared at him, then deflated ever so slightly. 'What is it then?'

'Remember I mentioned the prowler? It's kind of moved up a gear, got really scary, and I think it might compromise this job, so I'd rather bow out before there's anything to be spoiled. The fact is, I need to be at home, or at least within striking distance.'

'Why, what's changed?'

'I think Kate may be in danger.' He then went on to reveal all – the ex-car and the road rage, the prowler and the text message. 'I'm a hundred per cent it's not connected with Ingram ... but I'm sorry,' he concluded weakly.

A deep, thoughtful sigh racked her body, her chest rising and falling quite mesmerizingly. 'I'm very, very disappointed.'

'Me, too.'

She consulted her nails.

'You have to understand that it's my place to be at home.'

'Yeah, I do ... but I need to explain something about Ingram, too.' She raised her face again. This time the aura of the good-looking, brusque, professional woman was replaced by a moist-eyed, vulnerable one. At first Henry thought she had dropped into another role, one designed to manipulate his heart strings. This view changed dramatically when she spoke.

'I have a sister,' she said, almost inaudibly. 'She lives in London, married to a doctor, two daughters. She's a midwife, by the way. Her daughters are ten and twelve, Laura and Shona.' She broke off, chin quivering.

She slithered down on to the sofa and Henry sat next to her. He took her hands and held them on his knee.

'Which one?' he probed gently.

'Laura, the ten-year-old.' Andrea swallowed. Her chin continued to shake. 'Same old story, disappears on a trip to the local shop, less than two hundred yards from home. Not been seen since. That's six months ago, six fucking months!' she said furiously. She pulled her hands away from Henry's grip and rubbed her eyes with the palms. When they came away, the mascara had been completely spoiled. 'Ingram was, is, the only suspect, but can I prove it? Like hell, the snivelling, slimy bastard. A car belonging to him was seen in the vicinity. A man fitting his description, too.' She made eye contact and a genuine tear rolled down her cheek, which she wiped away with the back of her hand. 'Nothing else.'

'I'm sorry.'

'She was an angel,' Andrea said, choking back further sobs. 'I was very close to her and she was like the daughter I never had, nor will have ... the whole family is devastated.'

Henry nodded sagely. He had seen and lived with families affected by similar tragedies.

'I promised my sister I would get him one way or the other.' She looked squarely at Henry. 'Then he moved north with his running mate and I thought that would be the best chance of getting someone undercover whilst he was meeting new faces ... that's where you came in.'

Henry stood up, took his coffee, crossed to the window and looked at the building that was the Imperial War Museum. He had two daughters and, thankfully, touch wood, no harm had ever befallen them. They were now young ladies on the verge of adulthood, both on the cusp of moving away and forging their own lives, something Laura would never have the opportunity of doing. He turned back to Andrea after a little consideration.

She waited expectantly.

'It doesn't change anything,' he said. 'I'm worried about what's going on at home. I don't understand where it's coming from and I need to find out...' Andrea opened her mouth to protest. 'However, I'll give it a few more days with Ingram, see what he wants me to do, see if I can worm anything out of him, or uncover some evidence and then I hand it back and pull out.'

A big sigh of relief rose and fell in her.

'Thank you,' she said gratefully. 'Er, now I need to clean myself up. I must look a terrible mess.' She got to her feet and they found themselves standing close to each other. Henry was holding his mug in front of his chest, a barrier. Andrea took it from him and placed it on the coffee table, stepped in close, slid a hand around the back of his neck and drew him towards her. They kissed, then abruptly she pulled him away and gave him a sad look.

'It'll never be, will it?'

He shook his head. 'I'm trying to go straight.'

'Then good luck.'

She went into the bathroom, leaving Henry at the window, deep in thought and knowing he needed to phone Kate back. It would have to wait until Andrea had departed.

A few minutes later a freshened version of Andrea Makin emerged, make-up – eyeliner and mascara – back in immaculate place. She opened her briefcase and took out a thick file which she laid on the coffee table. Henry sat beside her, leaving a gap of a couple of inches.

'This is why I went to London,' she said. 'I know you don't want to know too much about Ingram, lest you drop yourself in it by giving something away you shouldn't know...'

'True.'

'However, I thought this might be of interest. I have an intelligence cell constantly working on him and we've found out that he's actually sold, or is selling, all the property we know he owned in and around London. He had lots – houses, flats, warehouses, a farm – all owned indirectly by him through third parties. The estimate is that he's got about three million sloshing about somewhere by now...'

'And he's living in a bloody Travelodge.'

'That's all we know about. It wouldn't surprise me if he's already bought something up here.'

'He hasn't mentioned anything yet.'

The intercom buzzed, making both of them jump. They looked at each other, puzzled.

'Who's this?' Andrea said.

Henry didn't speak, but crossed to the wall by the door and spoke into the intercom which was linked to the main door of the building. 'Yep?'

'Ingram.'

Henry mouthed 'Shit!' to Makin, who quickly shoved the file back into her briefcase and snapped it shut.

'Not a good moment,' Henry said into the intercom.

'Open the fuckin' door.'

'Come up.' Henry pressed the door release button and turned in a slight panic to Andrea, then had a thought. 'Rub your eyes,' he said quickly. 'We've just had a barney and you're storming out, with your briefcase ... lover,' he added ironically.

She nodded, going with the flow immediately. She hitched her jacket on, then scrunched the palms of her hands into her eyes, mussing up the newly applied make-up, making her look like a panda again.

There was a knock on the door: Ingram.

153

'As far as I'm concerned, you can just get stuffed,' Henry raised his voice as he made his way to the door.

'You bastard!' she shouted, storming up behind him and, just as he unlocked the door, pushing past him on to the landing. 'You can stick it.' She turned like a vixen and snarled, ignoring the presence of Ingram and Mitch. 'You make me want to vomit!' Her eyes blazed through the black smudges that surrounded them. She swivelled to face Ingram, who she sneered at. He looked askance at her, stepping back. 'You can fuck off, too,' she told him with a snarl, then gave Henry the middle finger and stalked haughtily away without a backward glance.

Ingram and Mitch regarded Henry with knowing smiles.

'Touchy bitch. You fallen out?' Ingram said.

'Told her to fuck off, basically,' Henry said, 'then she gets all catty and accuses me of using her.' He grinned. 'Which I was,' he added conspiratorially, like blokes together.

'Are you lettin' me in?' Ingram asked, now bored with the domestic chit-chat.

'Aye, come on.' Henry stood aside.

They sauntered into the apartment, hands in pockets, both making to the window to admire the view, which was pretty stunning.

'Wouldn't mind one of these pads myself,' Ingram ruminated, appraising the interior.

Henry's eyes did a worried rove, too. Was anything out of place? Was there anything here not belonging to Frank Jagger?

154

He was feeling OK about things up to the point where he spotted his own, not Frank's, mobile phone on the coffee table. His own personal property, the one he'd used to call Kate only minutes before. Mitch slobbed down on to the sofa and plonked a foot on the table, his ankle right next to the offending device.

Henry's mouth dried up. 'Coffee?' he croaked. 'Just brewed.'

It had been Mitch who had downloaded the SIM card information from Frank Jagger's phone, and the one only inches away from his foot was a completely different make and model. Frank Jagger's phone was in his jacket at that moment.

'I'll have one.' Mitch twisted to look at Henry.

The mobile phone seemed to grow in size to that of a brick. Henry expected it to ring at any moment.

'Sugar, milk?'

'Black, no sugar.'

'How about you?' Henry asked Ingram, who turned from the window, hands thrust deep in his pockets. 'Sugar, no milk.' His sharp eyes scanned the room continually.

Henry hesitated. Going into the kitchen meant putting a little bit of distance between him and them, something he was loath to do. But, with trepidation, he went in.

'I thought you said a day or two?' he said, finding a couple of mugs.

'I did.'

Henry looked up. Ingram was leaning against a kitchen cupboard, scrutinizing Henry.

'What?' Henry asked.

'Just looking at you ... you're a bit familiar, which is always slightly worrying.'

Henry shook his head. 'I thought you were, too, but I've wracked my brains and ... nothing.' He looked squarely at Ingram, unfazed by him. 'Milk, you say?'

'Just sugar.'

Henry handed a mug to him and he moved back into the living area. Henry came in with Mitch's coffee.

The big man had not moved. Still slouched on the couch, feet on the coffee table, mobile phone still there.

How would it look if I moved it? Henry thought. Can't do anything too unusual or obvious. If I give him his coffee, then pick up the phone and pocket it, how would that come across? Henry agonized as Mitch sat up and took the mug in his big, chubby hands.

He decided to leave it, take the chance.

His visitors sipped their drinks.

'Nice,' murmured Mitch appreciatively, sitting back and putting a leg on the table again, resting his coffee on his chest below his ample neck.

'Something I can do for you, then?' Henry faced Ingram. He *was* familiar, Henry had to admit. He prided himself on never forgetting a face or a name, one of his greatest gifts as a detective, yet he could not quite place Ingram and he cursed himself for not having delved into the guy's antecedents a little more deeply – but that was part of the balancing act with under-cover knowledge. Too much could be too dangerous. Not enough could be fatal.

It was also obvious that Ingram thought he knew Frank Jagger from somewhere. Henry's worry was that if he did make the connection – if there was one to be made – things could get very hirsute for Henry.

Maybe he didn't know. Maybe he just thought he did.

Such were the ambiguities and dangers of working U/C. You could never tell when it might all come crashing down around your ears.

'How are you fixed for a bit of travel?'

'Depends what, where, when, how long ... stuff like that.'

'Let me rephrase that. You're going on a journey.'

'And if I don't want to?'

'Your wishes don't come into it, Frank, mate. I fuckin' own you now, so don't forget it.'

A horrible creeping sensation tightened Henry's skin.

His bag was packed. He threw it into the back of the Jeep, then reversed the big car out of the narrow parking bay in the underground lot beneath the apartment building. He manoeuvred his way out of central London, always heading north, until he joined the M1, which was mercifully clear of traffic. He stepped on the gas and moved the vehicle up to eighty, set the cruise control and sat back to enjoy the drive. He had a full tank of gas, a cool car, a pair of shades, Otis Redding on the CD player and just for once in a long time, he felt chilled and relaxed. The bullet wound ached, probably would for ever, but that was all.

He was on the road now, about to right some wrongs, about to reset his whole life, make some positive decisions.

It felt good.

He flicked off the cruise control and pushed the car up to ninety.

'My name is Karl,' he said to himself.

'Just fancy.' Her voice was cynical, pissed off.

Henry flounced back in the chair and folded his arms, face set like a rock.

Back home that evening, he had told Kate more than he should ever have done: about Ingram, about Andrea Makin, about the job he was involved in. He knew that cops were reluctant to discuss their work with their partners at the best of times and it was a complete no-no to say anything about U/C work to anyone not involved, but Henry had made an exception. The hope was that Kate would understand his reasons for staying at it a few more days.

She was not convinced.

He felt as though he was in a TV cop drama, one of those telling the tale of the dedicated cop who gave his all to the job at the expense of his family.

Ironically, that *was* the position he was in.

Something he had done all his working life, put his family second even though he had resolved on many occasions to do otherwise. It was just that the job ensnared him, had him in its grip, seduced him. But he *was* trying to break

158

free from its shackles, but by saying yes to an undercover operation it would not have taken the brain of Britain to tell him it was decision he'd come to regret, because it was bound to tear him in all directions.

'I knew this would happen,' Kate confirmed it all. 'I always come second.'

'Listen, I promise I'll do this one thing,' said Henry, well on the back foot now, 'then I will pull out and come home, work nine-to-five in the office and be there for you ... how does that sound?'

It must have sounded reasonably OK because that evening they jumped on the sexual bandwagon again. Kate, a couple of glasses of Blossom Hill red inside her, very much took charge, whilst Henry lay back and took it like a man. They drifted off afterwards in each other's arms, his mind already moving on to what the next few days might bring.

He was asleep soon ... until a flickering brightness slowly played over his closed eyelids. Unable to believe it was dawn already, Henry opened his eyes and looked across at the curtains, puzzled by what he was seeing for a few moments – until it hit him.

'Shit!' He leapt out of bed and ran to the window, pulling back the curtain.

'What is it?' Kate asked blearily.

Henry was right.

It was a fire.

And burning brightly on his front lawn was a blue Ford Mondeo – his old car – flames gush-ing out of the window, rising high into the night sky. There was a loud crack and the rear window exploded.

Kate joined him at the window, pulling her dressing gown tightly around her, horrified at the sight.

'That's your old car,' she exclaimed.

'Yeah,' he said sourly, 'better call the fire service just in case no one else has.'

Twelve

Henry was feeling dithery and tired when he dropped off his slightly singed Rover 75 and picked up the Nissan from the unit, then headed for Manchester, desperately trying to get himself into the role of Frank Jagger.

His mind, understandably, was elsewhere, and even though Karl Donaldson had turned up out of the blue in the middle of the night – why, Henry did not have time to find out – and assured Henry he would keep watch over Kate, Henry knew it was his job, not someone else's, to watch over his loved ones.

He thought that if Ingram or anyone else commented on his vagueness, he could always use the excuse of being distracted by the break-up with his 'lover', Andrea Makin.

Thinking of whom, Henry stopped at Bolton West services and called her from his mobile.

She answered immediately.

'Hi, Henry, how're you feeling? Up for this?'

He hesitated before telling her about the incident of the Ford in the night-time.

'Shit,' she said tightly. Then, 'You can pull out if you want to.'

'No, I said I'll see it through, and anyway, an old friend turned up out of the blue last night and he'll be keeping an eye on Kate for me. Karl Donaldson – remember him?'

'Yeah, do I!' She had met Donaldson at the same time as she had first met Henry, in Black-pool, hunting down a bomber linked in with the white supremacist movement. 'You're a good one, Henry,' she said.

'Kate isn't that impressed.'

'She's luckier than she thinks.'

'I doubt that's a point of view she shares ... anyway, she's got protection, so she should be OK.'

'You can pull if you need to.'

'No, let's crack on.'

'Still no inkling what the day will bring?'

'Not a clue.'

'You still going in without back-up?'

'That's the general idea.'

'Is that wise?'

'Who knows? At the first sign of trouble, I'll do a Jesse Owens. I've got a hell of a sprint on me when the chips're down.'

Andrea laughed. 'I appreciate this – really.'

'My pleasure.'

'Just keep in touch.'

'I will.'

Henry deleted all the details of the call from his mobile, then screwed the little Nissan down the motorway, blue smoke all the way. Half an hour later he was back on Salford Quays in the apartment, showering and doing his best to freshen up, get his brain into gear. He changed into clean jeans, tee-shirt and trainers, then made a strong coffee, flicked on the CD player and let Amy Winehouse perform a bit of rehab on him. He had only just picked up on her, after seeing her take the stage with the Rolling Stones at the Isle of Wight festival, viewed on YouTube. He was now deeply in love with her gravelly voice and superb music. He hoped she wouldn't main-line her talent away and destroy herself.

The door intercom buzzed.

Henry shot to his feet, switched off the music and looked around the room. This time there were no stray mobile phones to give him palpitations. He had hidden his personal one and there was nothing else to indicate there was any-one else who lived here other than Frank Jagger, bits 'n' bobs scallywag.

'Yep?'

'It's Mitch – you ready?'

'You coming up?'

'Why, d'you wanna screw me?'

'Not especially.'

'Then get your arse down here, pillock face.'

'Fuck you, too,' Henry said, but only after he had released the speak button. Obviously Mitch had not particularly taken to him.

He shrugged on a leather jacket, patted down his pockets, took a breath and went for it.

Mitch was in the underground car park leaning against the Peugeot 607. Two fat things together, Henry mused.

'Where's Ingram?'

Mitch put a finger to his lips. 'No names, nothing,' he said, narrowing his porky eyes. 'Get in.' His stubby thumb jerked at the car and Henry climbed into the passenger seat whilst Mitch eased himself behind the wheel, giving Henry a grin as he got comfortable.

He held out his left hand, palm up. 'Phone,' he said.

'What?'

'I want your mobile.'

'Why would that be?'

'This is one of those incognito journeys.' He shifted his bulk and faced Henry, who noticed a wafting smell of body odour mixed in with that of soap and cheap deodorant. Obviously BO was an ongoing problem for Mitch that even a shower could not overcome. The smell reminded Henry of a dead man on a mortuary slab.

Henry made a show of annoyance and disgust at the inconvenience of having to give Mitch the phone, which he slapped down into his hand.

Mitch immediately checked it, tabbing through it, checking numbers dialled and received, sent and received texts.

He found nothing and looked curiously at Henry, whose inside curdled.

'It's empty. All the files are empty.'

'So?'

'Who empties files, other then someone who's trying to hide something?'

'Force of habit,' Henry quipped. 'And that silly bitch I just binned,' he ad-libbed, 'has been firing me loads of calls and texts. I just deleted 'em all and all the others, too.'

Mitch's fat jaw edged from side to side. 'Oh, right.' He wasn't convinced. He sniffed and looked at the phone itself, slightly puzzled. The furrows in his brow were deep. Something nagged at him, something he could not quite fathom. He tossed the phone on to the dashboard.

'I wonder if she'll keep sending you texts today?'

'Hopefully she's got the message – not interested.'

'Got the message in what, twenty-four hours? Women don't get messages that quickly, mate,' Mitch said knowledgeably. 'Not in my experience.'

Henry looked at him levelly. 'What would your experience be?'

'More than you'd fuckin' imagine.' He started the car and reversed out of the parking bay. Henry sat back. Suddenly he felt very vulnerable.

'What's today about, then?'

'Collection and delivery.'

'What's that supposed to mean?'

'What it says on the tin ... you'll find out in due course. First things first, though.'

Henry decided to keep quiet for a while and let things pan out. Maybe Mitch would start to fill in some of the pregnant pauses, start blabbing a few titbits which would be useful for Henry to pass on.

He was driven across Manchester in the direction of the Trafford Centre retail park, a place Henry avoided like the plague. Kate and his daughters seemed to be at home there, though. Henry only went under sufferance, letting them free whilst he went to a bookshop, bought a thriller and then found a coffee house. The Trafford Centre itself was bordered by various qualities of industrial areas and Mitch found one under the shadow of the newly erected indoor ski slope which dominated the skyline. He turned in to a massive area which was a warren of roads with big, medium and small units lining them.

The car turned in to a cul-de-sac and pulled up outside the sliding door of a small unit. Mitch pressed a button on a fob and the door began to clatter open. When it was high enough he drove the Peugeot inside and parked alongside a Hyundai Sonata. Henry clocked and stored the route to the premises in his memory.

'Transport for the day,' Mitch announced, heaving his bulk out of the driver's seat.

The Sonata was a grey colour, as big and sloppy as the Peugeot, obviously with enough room in it to house Mitch in comfort. He needed big cars. Henry glanced around the interior of the unit, but it was virtually bare, apart from a couple of Tesco carrier bags next to the Sonata.

Picking up one of the bags, Mitch handed it to him. 'Here, change of clothing.'

'What for?' Henry peered inside the bag to see a pair of jeans, tee-shirt, a zip-up jacket, socks and underpants, all still with price tags still attached.

'I reckon they'll be your size,' Mitch said, as though he hadn't heard Henry's question.

'I said, what for?'

Mitch looked critically at him. 'Use your noggin.' He tapped his head.

It dawned on Henry, like being struck by a demolition ball.

Forensics.

Replacement clothing was so cheap these days – Henry estimated he was probably holding about £30 worth of goods in his hand, max – that most savvy crims went shopping at places like Tesco or ASDA before they went on any jobs. They then did the job in new clothing, disposed of it after, showered, got dressed in their own gear and whey-hey! – no forensic links.

'We're going on a job?' he asked incredulously.

'It's just in case ... can't be too careful these days.' Mitch winked. 'Now, don't be a shy boy – get fucking changed!' he ordered Henry. He himself was already pulling his shirt off over his fat head, revealing a chest bearing very saggy man-boobs and great rolls of gut fat. Henry wanted to retch, but retreated so he was partially hidden by the back wing of the Sonata and quickly got changed. The clothes, all XXL in size, and size ten trainers, fitted perfectly.

He folded up his own clothing and held it in his arms.

'Leave it in the back of the Peugeot' – Mitch hitched up a pair of super-sized jeans, which

166

fastened tightly under the folds of his belly –
'then get in here.' He nodded at the Sonata.

'Cat got your tongue?'

Henry glanced sideways at Mitch. They were
on the M6, heading south, Mitch at the wheel.
They'd had little conversation on the journey.
They were now approaching the outskirts of
Birmingham.

'I thought you were going to tell me what was
happening?'

'Suppose I can, now.'

'How generous,' Henry quipped.

'Basically we're gonna meet a couple of guys
who are gonna give us something ... that's about
it.'

'What are they going to give us?'

'Use your imagination. You thick or something?'

Henry sighed. 'Why two of us?'

'Necessity.' Mitch did not expand.

The car sped on to the Midlands Expressway,
the new M6 toll road which cut out the requirement to travel through Birmingham.

'Not much further to go, but I need a brew, and
some breakfast.'

Henry guessed what sort of breakfast Mitch
would prefer and wasn't wrong when he sat
down opposite Henry at the services on the
Expressway and tucked into the largest all-day
breakfast they did. Henry contented himself
with more coffee.

The food seemed to have a euphoric effect on
Mitch, relaxed him, made him more garrulous.

Henry picked up on his mood and thought he'd try a few questions. He knew from experience that given the right environment, criminals liked to boast about their exploits and Henry hoped that a few innocently put, chatty questions would start to prisc him open.

'How long've you been with Ingram, then?'

'Ages, years.' He folded the white of an egg into his mouth.

'You seem to have a pretty big' – Henry almost said appetite, but refrained – 'operation.' Criminals, he also knew, liked to bask in praise.

'You could say that.'

'Porn's pretty big business.'

'Phenomenal, worth millions.' Now a fork full of fried mushrooms disappeared with obvious relish.

'Only if you know the business,' Henry suggested.

'True enough.'

'You and Ingram obviously do.'

Mitch's eyes sparkled. 'That we do.'

'What, like just selling DVDs?'

Mitch chortled. 'That's just a tiny part of it.'

'Oh, right,' Henry said, leaning forward. 'Tell me more.'

Mitch shrugged. 'DVDs, sex shops, strip clubs, hookers...' He shrugged again.

'You mean you've got a sex shop? What, dildos and all that?'

'*A* sex shop?'

'Yeah, a sex shop.'

Mitch ran the back of his hand across his chin to catch some fat dribble. 'He's got twenty.'

'Fuckin' hell!' Henry pretended to almost choke on his coffee.

'Twelve clubs, runs prostitutes all over the county, does porn movies, too.'

'Bloody hell!' Henry said in continuing amazement.

'And on top of that, guess what?' Mitch picked up a sachet of white sugar, which he tapped on the edge of the table, tore open and shook into his coffee, the white crystals disappearing into the black liquid. 'Not that I take sugar, but does that give you a clue?'

'What do you mean?' Henry asked stupidly, but knew what Mitch was alluding to.

He picked up another sachet and waved it in front of Henry's nose, tore it open and added it to his drink. 'White powder?' he said, eyeballs rising.

'You mean...?'

'Drugs.' He stirred the coffee. 'Oh, aye, drugs. We have a distribution network from London to Manchester,' he boasted.

'You must be worth tons.'

'Add a property portfolio – legit – on top of that. Student flats, maybe two hundred of them ... small shopping arcades ... in fact, that might be where you come in, Frank.'

Henry leaned forwards eagerly.

'We're always after people who can work for us and keep their gobs shut, especially since we relocated.'

'Relocated?'

'Yeah, we just moved up from London. Didn't he tell you?'

'Told me nowt.'

'Well, anyway, that's why we checked you out.' Mitch regarded him as he sliced his fried bread. 'We need some help on the property side of things – management, like.'

'I could do that. Sounds interesting.'

'Anyway' – Mitch crunched the hard bread – 'said too much already.'

'So, what's this collection and delivery thing? A test or something?'

'Frank, it's a job. If you do it competently, back me up, then all well and good. A test? Ha!' He scooped up a big circle of black pudding and shovelled it into his mouth.

Henry watched him, repulsed.

Back on the motorway, Mitch looped off the M6 on to the M42, then the M40, picking up the signs for London.

'If we're going to the Smoke, wouldn't it be easier to have stayed on the M6?' Henry commented.

'Don't make assumptions.'

'So it's not London?'

'Nah.'

'Isn't it about time you told me? There's only so much being fed shit I can stand. I don't do ambiguity well.'

'OK, OK, we're picking up some packages off a couple of gents, then taking them home with us, that's all the job is.'

'Drugs?'

'Cocaine.'

'Big packages?'

'Try half a million quid's worth big.'

Henry/Frank blew out a whistle. 'Bugger.'
'Bugger indeed.'

'These guys think they're brainy, a cut above,' Mitch complained as he came off the M40, junction 16, and cut south to Stratford-upon-Avon.

'Which guys?'

'You don't need to know their names. A and B, say. They think they're arty-farty, which is why we're going to Stratford ... know who was born there?'

'Shakespeare?' Henry offered hopefully, hoping he didn't come across as too arty-farty himself.

'Bang on! Well, these guys purport to be into Shakespeare, but it's all bollocks to me. Hey nonny-no and all that shit.' Mitch raised a cheek of his backside and revealed his contempt for the arts by breaking wind and filling the car with a terrible smell. 'Anyway, they're down here tonight to watch a play.'

Henry opened his window. 'Which one?'

'How the fuck should I know? You're not arty-farty, are you?' Mitch asked suspiciously.

In real life Henry quite enjoyed a bit of the bard. However, he didn't think that Frank Jagger would. 'Not my cuppa,' he said. 'Only thing I like to see on stage is live sex and strippers.'

'Me, too,' Mitch agreed sagely. 'Anyway, we are meeting them in Stratford so they can go to the theatre after.'

Henry shook his head. Drug dealers into Shakespeare.

171

'But it's not that simple,' Mitch added. 'Thing is, as is so often the case, these guys have got greedy.'

A cramp of the stomach made Henry wince at these words. 'How d'you mean?'

'They've got greedy. Greed leads to theft. Theft is skimming' – Mitch's words hung in the air – 'and Ingram doesn't like skimmers.'

He turned to face Henry, gave him a knowing look.

Although Henry, as Frank Jagger, denied having ever been to Stratford, he had actually been, as Henry, a handful of times. Firstly when studying English Literature at sixth form college in the 1970s when he was forced to go down and watch the Shakespeare play he was studying; since then he had been on a voluntary basis to watch plays occasionally with Kate. He had always enjoyed the experience and spectacle, even though he only had a passing interest in Shakespeare. He also enjoyed the ambience of the town, which he found quite laid back and civilized. Even the yobs spoke with posh accents, he once observed.

It was about 4 p.m. when Mitch drove into town and parked the Sonata in a car park behind a hotel by the river.

'These guys are staying here,' he explained, nodding in the direction of the hotel, 'but I don't think they've landed yet. They're due about six, they said, and are having a pre-theatre meal at a place in town. Fuckin' jessies,' Mitch spat derisively. 'Pre-fucking-theatre meal! Jesus.'

Sounded quite nice to Henry, who'd done the same thing once or twice, but he went along with the façade with nods of agreement and concurring facial expressions.

'What's the plan?'

'We kill time.' Mitch checked his watch. 'Ten past four ... we meet them in their hotel room, get the stuff and head home. Simple,' he said, but Henry did notice there seemed to be a fatal omission in the running order: no mention of the 'skimming' issue.

'In that case I'm going to stretch my legs and have a wander around town, maybe get a bite ... if that's OK with you?'

'Time's your own, just be back here at half five.'

'No worries.' Henry was out of the car in a shot, striding out before Mitch could decide to tag along. He cut through the car park, found himself near a footbridge which spanned the Avon that he crossed quickly towards town, the Royal Shakespeare Theatre over to his left. Mitch, he was glad to note when he shoulder-checked, was not in sight as he crossed Waterside and turned up Bridge Street, the main shopping thoroughfare, and went in search of a mobile phone shop.

His own phone was still on the dashboard of the Peugeot in Manchester and he needed a replacement, charged up and ready to go. He found a Carphone Warehouse and bought the cheapest pay-as-you-go he could find, and with further cajoling and a palm crossed with silver, he also bought a charged-up battery for it from a member of staff's own phone.

Thus armed he almost stepped out of the shop right into Mitch's arms.

Henry spotted him at the last moment and was lucky that the big man was looking in the opposite direction. Henry dropped quickly back into the shop and attempted to secrete himself behind one of the cardboard displays as Mitch rolled past – and did not look inside the shop.

Aware of the curious looks from the staff, he stood upright and walked slowly to the door and saw that Mitch had continued his journey up the street. Henry twisted away in the opposite direction, then turned into British Home Stores and went to the first floor. Between racks of clothing he switched on and registered the phone. There wasn't a great signal, but good enough to put in a call to Andrea Makin, raking up her number from memory.

'Where the hell are you, Henry?'

'Shakespeare country.'

'What?'

He told her.

'What are you doing there?'

'Drugs deal, I think.' He glanced at a lady who was inspecting a rack of clothing. She eyed him uncertainly. He gave her a wan smile and turned his back to her and filled in Andrea on what had happened since he'd last seen her, and gave her all the new information he had got on Ingram from Mitch over breakfast.

'You be bloody careful,' she warned him.

'It's my middle name.'

'What is?'

'U-be.'

She giggled. 'And what the hell is this number?' He filled her in on that, too, then ended the call, switched off the phone and wondered where best to hide it. It could be a lifeline and he didn't want to lose it, or let Mitch get his grubby mitts on it. He had an idea on that score which entailed a short visit to WH Smith's on the opposite side of the street.

Next he found a café – not difficult in Stratford – and bought a lasagne and a bottle of mineral water, which he consumed heartily. He then killed more time with a coffee and a discarded newspaper before going into the men's room, locking himself in a cubicle and taking down his trousers.

It was just after five when he emerged into the end-of-the-day throng in the street, then made his way back across Clopton Bridge to join Mitch who was back in the Sonata, seat reclined, having been asleep. He looked groggy and puffy-eyed.

'Hi, sleepyhead.'

'Where've you been?'

'Moochin', eatin',' Henry said.

'I couldn't find you.'

'Why were you looking?'

Mitch did not answer. Using the steering wheel he heaved himself upright, put his seat back up and declared he needed to piss. He was about to get out of the car when a big Audi saloon rolled into the car park and pulled up close to the back door of the hotel, marked, 'To Reception'.

'Here they are.'

Instinctively Henry lowered himself in the seat and watched two young men get out of the Audi, and each carry a holdall from the boot into the hotel. They looked relaxed and confident, had 'the walk'.

'Let 'em check in, then give 'em a call.'

'OK.' Henry's heart stepped up more than a beat. 'What's going to happen?'

'We go in, get the packages, leave.'

'Why the change of clothing?'

'Just in case.'

'Of what?' Henry was getting annoyed by the conversation and feeling jumpy. He didn't mind a drugs deal going down. That sort of thing was bread and butter for an undercover cop. You just went with the flow and no one got hurt. Things changed seriously when there was the possibility of harm coming to someone. Then duty had to kick in. Whilst Mitch hadn't actually said anything concrete about causing harm to either of these men, he had less than subtly hinted at something and Henry believed Mitch was capable of going the whole nine yards if he had to. There was an undercurrent of violence running through him, underneath all that flab. Henry guessed he would be no slouch when it came to crunch time.

'I thought you needed a piss?'

'I'm holding it.' Mitch squirmed, kneading his privates.

They sat back and waited, giving the men, A and B, fifteen minutes to get settled in their rooms.

Then Mitch called one on his mobile.

'Hey, it's me ... yeah, thought you would've ... look, can we proceed? I know you've got places to go.' Mitch listened a moment. 'Yep, good ... room two-one-six ... be there in minutes.' He ended the call, turned to Henry. 'All you need to do is carry the merchandise, OK, Frank? That's all you need to do,' he stressed. Mitch's breathing became shallow. Henry saw he was suddenly wound up: licking his lips, sweat on the forehead. Or maybe he just needed to get to that toilet. 'Let's do it.'

The pair walked nonchalantly through the hotel, bypassing reception and seeing no one else in the corridors. Room 216 was on the first floor, in a wing a long way from the front of the hotel. There was a painting of some sort of wading bird on the door.

'Hey, a redshank,' Mitch said, then knocked.

The door opened.

Behind it stood Man A, so named by Henry, who saw he was of Asian origin. He was the smaller of the two men, but looked strong and muscled as though he worked out and wasn't averse to a steroid or two. He smiled, flashing bright, unnaturally white teeth with an inlaid diamond in a front one, which twinkled in the light.

He was dressed in a tight-fitting vest and tracksuit bottoms.

'Mitch, hi,' he said. His eyes took in Henry. They narrowed. 'Who's this?'

'New member of staff.'

'CRB checked and everything,' Henry quipped.

Both men gave him a withering look.

'OK,' Man A said. He trusted Mitch. They'd done business in the past. He jerked his head and all three retreated into the room, passing the bathroom on the left, wardrobe on the right, opening out into a double bedroom where Man B lounged indolently on the bed, still dressed in his suit. Henry guessed the room was probably Man A's, because he'd had a change of clothing.

'How do, Mitch,' Man B said amiably. He was a white man, well tanned, with slicked-back hair. He was a good-looking fellow, something along the lines of Pierce Brosnan in his James Bond days, but younger, fitter, alert and more dangerous.

As opposed to the Honey Monster with Henry.

Man B did not even look at Henry.

The two holdalls they had brought in were on the suitcase shelf next to the dressing table.

'No probs?' Mitch asked.

'None.' Man A was standing by his side, Henry was behind Mitch, but he could also see a couple of hand guns on the dressing table.

Mitch picked one up.

Both A and B suddenly became rigid.

'No probs, good to hear.' Mitch inspected the gun, turning it to the light. To their relief, and Henry's, he replaced it. 'Look guys,' he started to say. 'Jeez, need a piss ... mind if I...?' He sort of pointed to the bathroom.

'Help yourself.'

Mitch disappeared into the bathroom, closed and locked the door. The sound of him urinating filled the silence, a long, sustained function.

Henry gave A and B a forced smile. 'Big bladder.'

'You a new employee, eh?' Man A asked.

'That's right.'

'In what capacity?'

'Uh, cultural director,' Henry said, off the cuff.

Both men regarded him with screwed up faces as though he were nuts.

Mitch's peeing continued behind the close doors. He even groaned in relief.

'Motorway coffee,' Henry explained.

The toilet flushed. A tap ran. Mitch hummed noisily, happy now.

Man A perched on the edge of the bed. Henry's eyes moved from the men, to the holdalls, to the guns. He even found himself estimating how long it would take him to reach the firepower. It would be a tight-run thing, that was for sure.

A relieved Mitch emerged from the bathroom, smiling. He stood behind Henry.

'Right guys,' he said, rubbing his wet hands together. 'Is it all there?'

'As ever,' Man B said defensively.

'Mm, as ever,' Mitch ruminated. 'Frank...' He touched Henry in the middle of the back. 'Grab the bags.'

Henry took a step.

'Do we need to check it?' he asked.

'No, these guys're sound.'

Henry saw the faintest glimmer of relief in A and B. Their skimming, so they thought, had gone unnoticed ... at least that is what they believed as Henry grabbed a holdall in each hand and lifted them up. They were pretty weighty, but then half a million's worth of coke, less the skim, would be, he thought.

Mitch stood aside as Henry passed him and went to the room door. He turned and Mitch was still facing the two delivery men. Just then Henry noticed the handle of a pistol sticking out of his waistband at the small of his back.

'By the way, guys, this'll be the last drop-off for you.'

The men tensed up. Their eyes immediately became wary, flicking between their weapons and Mitch, sensing something was now very wrong.

With a speed which Henry would have thought him incapable of, Mitch suddenly grabbed one of the guns from the dressing table and pointed it somewhere between the men.

'What the fuck's going on, Mitch?'

'Game over, fellas. Mr Ingram don't like cheats. He pays you well and you still wanted more.'

'Hey, hey, don't know what you're talking about,' Man A said quickly. 'We don't rip any cunt off.' His hands were up submissively, palms forward, in a gesture of innocence.

Mitch switched hands. The gun went from right to left, then his free arm snaked round his back and he slid the pistol out of his waistband. It had a slim silencer screwed on to it. It was a .22 calibre, an assassin's gun.

'We *know*,' Mitch said, emphasizing the second word. 'Enquiries have been done.'

He didn't waste any more time, which is the way things are done in real life. Killers did not spend a great deal of time chatting to their victims, discussing the psychological aspects of their crimes. They just killed.

The first shot, no more than a 'phtt' went into Man A's face, smacked into his left eyeball at an angle which meant it spun out through his temple, jerking him around and showering the wall and bedside cabinet with blood, brain and eyeball.

Man B started a frantic scramble away up the bed, a squeal of terror starting to form in his mouth.

Mitch shot him in the throat, then in the right shoulder, the impact of the bullets throwing him off the bed. He landed with a thump on the carpet between the bed and the window. Splashes of blood flicked across the net curtain. He gurgled and writhed where he lay, his hands clawing at his throat.

Mitch 'humphed' and turned his attention back to Man A.

He was dead, half on, half off the bed, a quarter of his face missing. For good measure Mitch put another in his head, one in his chest. He then walked around the bed and finished off Man B.

This done, he stood upright and looked at Henry, grinning with satisfaction.

Henry had frozen, transfixed.

He had been more than right about Mitch. Big and fat though he was, he was also fast and deadly.

Henry was stunned, looking accusingly at Mitch, who said, 'What, Frank? Had to be done.'

Henry opened his mouth, but words would not come.

Mitch checked his watch. 'I reckon if we put the "do not disturb" sign on the door, we've a good sixteen or eighteen hours before these idiots are found.' His tone was matter-of-fact and businesslike. 'Let's just get their phones off them, first.' Henry did not move. 'Get their phones!'

'Me?' Henry found a tiny voice.

'Yeah – there's one on the bedside cabinet there, the other'll probably be in a pocket. Can't have the cops finding any incriminating numbers, can we?'

Henry dropped the holdalls and sidled past Mitch, picked up the phone and pocketed it, his eyes always on the dead man.

'Now get the one from him,' Mitch ordered, jerking his index finger at Man B on the opposite side of the bed. Henry did as he was told and knelt down next to dead man number two, he of the gaping throat wound, one in the head, one in the chest, one in the shoulder.

'Shit,' he said under his breath. 'Shit, shit, shit!'

'Oh, just fucking get on with it,' Mitch whined impatiently.

Henry got on with the task, Mitch overseeing his work. He found a mobile phone in Man B's pocket and fished it out, unable to prevent himself getting blood on his jacket at the wrist. 'Done,' he said, shakily standing up.

'Here, give them to me.' Henry passed both phones to Mitch. In his left hand, Mitch was still

182

holding the gun belonging to one of the dead men. He looked at it, then at Henry, who felt his legs quake. But Mitch shook his head angrily. 'Why did I pick this bloody thing up? Now I'll have to take it as it's got my finger-prints all over it. What was I thinking? Stupid boy ... should've just blasted the fuckers ... still...' He looked around the room. 'Don't think we've left anything in the way of DNA and shit, have we?'

'Did you wipe the toilet and the sink?'

'Good point. I pissed on the rim.' He went back to the bathroom. Henry heard him hum-ming whilst he cleaned the toilet with loo paper, then flushed it away. He came out, slid the gun he had been foolish enough to pick up into one of the holdalls. His own gun had disappeared and Henry wondered where it had gone, but he could have hidden it anywhere under all that fat.

'OK, grab the bags, pal ... plan is' – he bent to peer through the security spy hole in the door – 'you mosey out through the hotel by yourself and get into the car, which is open. Put the bags in the boot. Then wait for me. Best if we're not seen together. I'll be with you in five.'

'OK,' Henry said numbly. He heaved up the bags, Mitch let him out of the room and he walked stiffly down the corridor.

In the car, Henry's mind started to whirr as he gasped for air. What was the next step here? He had just witnessed a double murder and all his instincts told him to arrest Mitch – now! But there was still the chance of implicating

Ingram and as Mitch had pointed out, there was a window of time ahead, maybe sixteen hours, which might be used to good advantage – if he played it right. The trouble was, Henry wasn't the player here. He wasn't making the moves. He was just caught up in the whole heap of shit.

Mitch yanked the driver's door open and dropped his bulk into the seat, his body venting a contented groan.

'A good piece of work, well done,' he said, chuffed with himself. 'Two pieces of shit dealt with, half a mill still in the bank, we're on the road and I'm going to stop for a huge burger at the first motorway services we come to. I feel like the Blues Brothers. And,' he added, 'to cap it all, I've got this.' He held something up between his finger and thumb, which glinted in the light. 'Couldn't resist – and can you blame me? He reckoned it cost three grand.'

It was the diamond that had been inset in Man A's front tooth.

Thirteen

Henry Christie was in a toilet cubicle at the northbound Stafford motorway services on the M6. Mitch was stuffing his face in one of the restaurants and Henry had little time to compose his thoughts, but one recurring theme he was unable to quash was 'Henry Christie and the judgement call'.

This, he thought sourly, could all go very, very wrong.

He knew if he didn't get it right, there would be no forgiveness anywhere, from anyone. *I will be for the high jump and all those other clichéd phrases and sayings that go with police discipline, sacking, court appearances and loss of pension rights – and a chief inspector's pension at that.*

He swallowed drily.

The fact was he had witnessed someone kill two other men and undercover though he may have been, there was a forceful argument he should have emerged from the shell that was Frank Jagger, morphed into Henry Christie and laid hands on Mitch's collar, nicked him, sod the rest of it. Go after Ingram when Mitch was banged up and screwed to the floor, unable to wriggle out of anything.

If Henry got this wrong and, for whatever reason, lost Mitch, then he was very definitely up the Swannee without any form of propulsion at all ... but ... but ... Henry wanted Ingram now. Hell, society wanted Ingram, and if he had arrested Mitch there and then, the chances were that Ingram would remain untouchable. But if Mitch stayed free, at least for another sixteen hours, then maybe he could drop Ingram in it either through his own verbosity or though conversations with his boss which were overheard and recorded by Henry...

...the judgement call of Henry Christie questioned once again.

He pulled down his jeans. Sticky-taped to his inner right thigh was the mobile phone he had bought in Stratford. He pulled it free carefully, wincing as his hairs were ripped from their roots, switched it on and waited an interminable length of time for it to pick up a signal.

Ever expecting Mitch to tear the toilet door from its hinges, followed by his head from his shoulders, Henry dialled Andrea Makin's number from memory again. The phone rang, but there was no reply and it went straight to voice-mail.

Henry chunnered a curse, then composed a short text which named the hotel and room number in Stratford and added, 'Protect and preserve the scene'. Then he scnt it, deleted all traces of it and his unsuccessful phone call before strapping the mobile back between his legs.

Mitch was still eating, hadn't moved from the table.

Henry sat down, still pale as a sick ghost. 'You seem pretty relaxed about all this.' His hands flew around in exasperated gestures.

'I am. Why shouldn't I be?'

Henry eyed him, shocked.

Mitch shrugged. 'They deserved to die, thieving bastards.'

'Look, Mitch, I'm a businessmen, not a killer. I don't do killing.'

'You do now. You're one of us – or didn't Ingram make that clear? I think he did, yeah.'

Henry shook his head. 'I'm a bits 'n' bats man.'

'Well, you'd better get your head round it, pal. You're in with us, big style, even down to the blood on your sleeve. Good link to a crime scene, I'd say.' Mitch winked evilly.

Henry glanced at his cuff.

Mitch pushed himself away from the table, stood up, wiping his greasy hands on a napkin. Henry had a fleeting hope that the grease he had just consumed would enter his bloodstream immediately and slam his ventricles shut with a deadly clang.

No such luck.

'Don't do anything silly, Frank. Just go with the flow and you'll be OK. Promise.' He leaned forward and patted Henry on the cheek. 'I wonder how the boss is doing?'

'What do you mean?'

'Didn't I mention?'

'Mention what?'

'He's paying a visit to the guy you owe all that cash to, to end the debt. What's his name?'

'Costain.'

'That's the fella. Yes, he's going to sort out your debt, which, incidentally, he doesn't intend to pay.' Mitch tapped his nose. 'Need a dump.' He walked to the toilets.

Henry stared after him.

'It's good of you to stay.'

Kate Christie and Karl Donaldson were walking arm in arm along the pavement, having decided that a nice trip to the Tram and Tower would be a splendid idea for two people in their situations. They were also good friends and the arm linkage had no sexual connotation to it.

'I had nowhere else, if you want the truth.'

'I know, but even so.'

'Free board and lodgings, gorgeous landlady ... pure gold for a separated man, never to be refused.'

'But that isn't the reason you stayed, or turned up in the first place?'

Donaldson shook his head. 'Nah, complicated...'

They reached the front door of the pub, stopped and turned to talk. 'It's between Henry and me,' Donaldson said.

'Something happened, I know. He wouldn't tell me.'

'Something major. We need to clear the air.' He sounded unsure. 'I hope we can. I'm sorry he had to go to work.'

'Is this "something" linked to what's happened

with you and Karen, too?'

'It has connections, I guess.'

'Mm.' Kate pursed her lips. 'Let's get a drink.'

Mitch and Frank Jagger were back at Ingram's unit near the Trafford Centre by 10.30 p.m., Mitch driving the Sonata in and parking next to the Peugeot.

'What now?' Henry asked.

'Get changed and wait for Ingram to call or show up.'

'OK.'

Henry got out and retrieved the bag containing his own clothing from the Peugeot, whilst Mitch opened the boot of the Sonata and heaved the two holdalls out and carried them to an office in the corner of the unit. Henry waited until he had disappeared before quickly stripping and changing into his own clothing. As he pulled his own jeans on, he heard Mitch's mobile ring, reminding him that his own was still on the dash of the Peugeot.

Henry reached in and grabbed it, pocketed it, just as Mitch emerged from the office, doing a sort of disco jig and singing, *'Celebrate good times, come on, doo doo doo doo doo dah dah dah...'* His whole body wobbled obscenely as he danced towards Henry as though he thought he was an exotic dancer.

'Happy today,' Henry remarked, as opposed to 'Happy Michelin Man', which was the phrase on his lips.

'Party time,' Mitch announced. He stopped dancing and began to divest his clothes in front of Henry, who turned away for the sake of modesty and disgust.

'Party – why's that?'

'Good day's work, good night's play,' Mitch answered, jeans falling. 'We're off to Marco's,' he said. 'Ingram wants to see us there, pat on the back time – you in particular,' he said.

Marco's was in Manchester on the edge of Chinatown. It was close to a club where Henry, as a rookie cop on a course held in GMP, had once been given the eye by a beautiful trans-vestite. If he had not been held back by a more savvy colleague, he would have made an error of judgement that would have scarred him for life. That had been almost thirty years ago. And still, he thought bitterly, his judgement was not as honed as it could be.

Mitch walked straight to the head of the queue at Marco's and was immediately waved in by the bouncers.

'Does Ingram have something to do with this place?'

'He's made himself a sleeping partner.' Mitch had to shout as the doors opened and a blast of music slammed into both of them.

Henry guessed this meant he'd made the owner an offer he couldn't refuse.

They dropped down a dog-leg set of stairs into the club in the basement of the building. It was tight, compact, hot, sweaty and overpoweringly noisy. It had no appeal for Henry whatsoever.

He followed Mitch as the big man boogied his way around a tiny, packed dance floor towards a raised area by one of the bars. This was roped off and guarded by a bouncer, but as soon as Mitch was spotted – which was immediately, because he couldn't be missed – the bouncer unlatched the rope and allowed him and Henry through to a tiny seating area reserved for the great and bad, from which there was a good view across the club. Mitch slumped on to a wide, low chair. Henry sat on a low leather one, which revolved.

'He's a partner?' Henry shouted into Mitch's ear.

'Yep – first step in Manchester. Good one, too.'

A bartender came and took their drinks order. Henry sat back and surveyed the dancing throng and the people crushed up to the bar, wondering how little the police actually knew about Ingram and the scale of his operation. Maybe they did and weren't letting on to Henry, which was fine because it was up to Ingram to reveal stuff to him. But he got the impression that Andrea Makin hardly knew anything at all. He guessed she didn't know about Marco's. And if she didn't know very much, it meant that Ingram was more canny and careful than she could ever have imagined.

Henry's lager arrived. Mitch had ordered a cocktail of some sort, a green and orange con-coction with a little umbrella and a parrot on a stick that looked ridiculous in his hands. Henry would have expected him to have ordered a pint of beer, not a girlie cocktail.

He watched Mitch surreptitiously, hoping the contempt he showed for him did not show on his face, then quickly ran through his predicament and made some crucial decisions.

Firstly, he would not allow the U/C charade to go on much longer. The further removed Mitch was from the scene of the double murder in terms of time and distance the weaker the case against him was, evidentially.

Henry also wondered where he had hidden the gun he'd used. He guessed it was in the industrial unit with the drugs.

Secondly, he somehow needed to implicate Ingram in the murder by getting him to admit his 'managerial' role in it. But if that didn't happen tonight, tough shit. Henry would get them both arrested and do it the hard way ... not that any method used against these two gangsters would be easy, but if he could just get Ingram to say something silly, it would make the whole thing much smoother.

And thirdly, he was getting far too old for this shit, as the elderly cop often said in films.

Witnessing the murders had shaken him to the core.

The stress of being U/C was taking its toll on him and his family. Ten years ago, it was fine, and he realized now that jumping at the chance to get out from behind his desk had been another error of judgement...

He shook his head involuntarily.

'Still thinking about it?' Mitch said.

'Yep.'

'Don't worry, it'll be fine. Get some booze down your gullet.'

Henry nodded, his face strained. He swigged

his beer and it tasted sour. He pulled his face and feigned illness. 'I got to go to the bog, feel sick.'

He stood up and received a hefty pat on the back from Mitch, sending him staggering out of the seating area in the direction of the toilets. He threaded his way through the dancers, his eyes catching several pairs of heaving young bosoms and rotating backsides, none of which made him feel any better at all.

Inside the toilets he found himself alone, the music from the club muted. He washed his face and considered using one of the mobile phones now in his possession, but decided it would be too dangerous. He'd already taken a chance on the motorway services and he needed his luck to hold, at least for the next few hours.

They had a nice, companionable evening in the pub, Kate listening mostly to Karl Donaldson as he gradually opened up, his verbosity fuelled by an intake of lager and a whisky chaser. He did not drink much and it did not take too much to affect him, so whilst he was nowhere near as inebriated as he had been when he'd drunkenly called Henry in the middle of the night, he was very loose-tongued.

He told Kate some of the things that Henry had never divulged to her. Some of it was deeply shocking, too.

He gave a fairly long, rambling explanation, fuelled by emotion, sometimes cold and matter-of-fact. He ended up by bringing Kate up to speed with himself and Karen.

'An' I gotta admit, I was tempted by the lady

from Facilities,' Donaldson admitted. 'I was lying there, all alone, with my cell phone in my hand and my thumb hovering over the call button. She has the hots for me, y'know? Just one press and I'd've committed adultery...' His slurred voice trailed off wistfully.

'But you didn't,' Kate said.

'Nah.' He rubbed his face. He was exhausted. His insides were hurting along the track of the bullet and his brain was scrambled from his emotional turmoil. 'I love her an' I've never come close to cheating on her.'

'Other than with your job,' Kate suggested.

Donaldson sniffed up, considered her remark. 'You're right. I lost sight of what was important.'

'Work–life balance.'

'Hm,' he muttered darkly, 'not much balance there.'

They drank and had a few moments of silent contemplation.

'And it's destroyed my friendship with Henry, too,' he admitted. 'I got so focused on something and y'know, it was screw him or what he thinks, and I think I lost a pal, too.'

'I don't think you have,' Kate said. 'He can be as brick-headed as you.'

'That's a fact.' He looked her in the eye. 'But I want to right the wrong I did to him, if I can.'

'You don't really need to. He'll come around.'

'Oh yes I do, and, I dunno, something in me says that by doing it, it'll be the start of getting the rest of my life back on track, a sort of building block: sort out Henry, then sort out Karen

194

and me. Put work where it should be, maybe even think about early retirement.'

'You! Retire?'

'It's an approaching option. I've had an offer from the private sector already ... bit of a shady one, but an offer nevertheless. I've been doing this FBI shit for twenty-five years now.'

'What's the offer?' Kate was intrigued.

'Private security.'

'Maybe you should set up with Henry. I'm hoping he'll retire when he can, which is soon.'

Donaldson laughed at the thought. 'DC Investigations.' He pouted. 'Who knows?' But it wasn't a serious thought. He stretched and yawned.

'How about a night cap?' Kate asked.

'Back at your place?'

She gave him a dirty smile. 'Where else?'

'I suppose I'll have to be good?'

'In that you'll be sleeping in Leanne's bed, you mean?'

'Yup.' He stood up and helped Kate to her feet. Outside the pub they linked arms again and began the half-mile stroll back to the house. 'So when are you and Henry tying the knot again?'

That brought a guffaw from her. 'Sometimes I think he's about to ask me, then he bottles out ... but I'm not so fussed, really. If he asks, I'll say yes, but I'm not going to push the issue.'

'I like being married,' Donaldson proclaimed. Then, sadly, added, 'I don't want to lose it.'

Kate pulled herself tighter to him. 'I'm sure Karen doesn't want to, either.'

'Mm.' It was a doubtful noise.

They walked on in silence, both deep in thought.

As Kate inserted her key into the front door, she said, 'I'll be opening the Glenfiddich for you.'

'Lovely.'

He was standing behind her. He glanced over his shoulder. The estate was quiet, but then he heard the sound of a car being driven fast, the noise increasing. Then it screamed around the corner and accelerated in their direction.

'Get in,' Donaldson said, his senses suddenly sharp. He reached inside his jacket – a conditioned reflex from all those years as an agent – but there was no firearm there.

The car raced down the avenue and skidded to a halt at the end of the driveway.

Donaldson relaxed slightly when he saw the driver was a female who jumped out and quickly strode up the drive.

'Kate Christie?' the woman asked sharply.

Donaldson recognized her now, but she had not even looked at him.

'Yes?'

'I'm Detective Superintendent Makin.' She flashed her warrant card.

'Hello, Andrea. Remember me?' Donaldson cut in.

Recognition dawned on her face. 'FBI Agent Karl Donaldson ... nice to meet you again.' Her eyes flicked once over his features, but her attention turned back to Kate. 'Kate,' she said worriedly, 'I need to know ... have you heard anything from Henry in the last couple of hours?'

When Henry returned from the toilets, Ingram had arrived at the club. He was sitting with Mitch in the raised area, speaking into Mitch's ear, a serious expression on the fat man's face which Henry did not like very much.

He rejoined them, Ingram nodding at him.

'Frank.'

'Hello.'

'Been in the wars?'

'Something like that ... I may look cool, but I'm freaked out.'

'Don't be, it'll be fine ... hey, what say we get some booze in and head off for a bit of a celebration?'

'Celebrating what?'

'Well, for one thing, I've taken care of your debt, so that's a weight off your shoulders.'

Henry squinted at him.

'Now you owe me,' he added.

'So I'm still in debt?'

'Kinda, yes, but in a good way. I'll sell on your goods, then you won't owe a thing, mate, but you'll work for me.'

'OK – what else is there to celebrate?'

'You were there, you should know.'

'That's a cause for celebration?'

'Is from where I'm sitting,' Ingram said.

'They must have really been screwing you.'

'You don't know the half of it ... let's get some booze and get out of here.'

Fourteen

His face was battered to beyond a pulp. His eyes were purple and swollen, his cheekbones crushed, jaw broken, mangled and distorted, as was his nose. Both forearms had been stamped on and shattered, his knees smashed and his lower right leg broken. His ribs had multiple fractures, one of them had split and ruptured a lung and there was other, extensive internal damage not yet fully assessed. He was going for a brain scan because his skull had probably been fractured and it was possible there was a blood clot on the brain.

He had been left for dead.

But he was still alive.

Just.

'If he hadn't been found, he would be dead.'

Andrea Makin spoke these words to Karl Donaldson whilst striding through the corridors of Blackpool Victoria Hospital towards the intensive care unit.

She had taken a lot of convincing to open up to Donaldson, but had finally relented because she knew him of old.

'Where was he found?'

'Roadside ditch, near a place called Out Rawcliffe, out in the sticks. He'd obviously been dumped from a car or van and rolled into a rat-piss-infested dyke.' Andrea turned to him and gave him a 'you dare' look which prevented any smart remark. He just raised his eyebrows. 'He may have swallowed the ditch water.'

'Weil's Disease, y'mean?'

She raised her eyebrows, impressed by his knowledge. 'It's something that needs to be checked out.'

'Who found him?'

'Passing motorist stopping for a pee, ironically.'

They carried on walking, Andrea purposeful in her stride.

'Tell me about Henry's last message again?'

She reached into her shoulder bag, thumbed through her mobile phone and handed it to Donaldson, who, as the excitement of the moment rushed through him, seemed to have purged all traces of alcohol from his system and replaced it with adrenalin.

'A hotel and room number?'

'With two dead bodies in it.'

'Identified?'

'Not yet.'

'Suspicions?'

'Dealers from London,' she said, snatching the phone back. 'Look, I've told you all this, Karl.'

'And I'm trying to get my head round it. He is my friend, you know and if he's in danger, I want to help.'

'You're just a guest at the moment, so don't get uninvited ... I need to think.'

Donaldson was undeterred, but for the moment

he decided that silence was the best course of action.

They marched on down the corridor, following the coloured lines on the floor to the ICU, eventually arriving there.

Two uniformed constables hovered outside the entrance, accompanied by Dave Anger, the officer in charge of FMIT, who turned and watched them arrive.

'Andrea,' he said formally. He pointed at the American. 'Karl Donaldson, right?' They had met before and clashed and Anger knew of his relationship with Henry. 'What are you...?'

'Where are we up to?' Andrea said firmly, hurriedly, no time to enter any debate as to why Donaldson was here.

Anger's eyes came back to her and Donaldson could see he was smitten by her as his face softened – although hers just became harder. 'It's not looking good.'

'Where is he?'

'In there.' He jerked his head at the double swing doors leading to the ICU.

'Let's look.'

The uniforms stood aside to allow the detectives through. The ICU was divided into several cubicles on either side of the unit. Anger led them to the nearest one and drew back the curtain.

The sight made Andrea recoil.

Donaldson stifled a gasp, too.

Troy Costain was a terrible, terrible mess. His swollen face, one side of it ballooning out horribly, was unrecognizable. Banks of monitors,

IV drips and oxygen tanks, all attached, clipped on or inserted as necessary, surrounded him. His lips were cut, gashed, skewed out of shape. His breathing was shallow and difficult.

'Hell fire!' Andrea said, shocked. 'Has he regained consciousness at all?'

Anger shook his head. 'He's going into theatre in minutes. It's touch and go,' he said dramatically. 'This could soon be a murder investigation.'

A team of porters, nurses and doctors came in moments later, shooing the detectives aside as they wheeled Costain out to theatre, leaving an empty space where the bed once was.

'We need to talk,' Anger said to Andrea, glancing at Donaldson who clearly got the message.

'I want to be part of this,' he said quickly.

'I don't think so,' Anger said.

The two men traded looks. Anger's eyes were magnified behind his round glasses.

'There's no time for this,' Andrea cut across the male posturing. 'Karl's an experienced law enforcement officer, and a good one as you damn well know, and that's good enough for me.'

'Look at me as being on secondment,' Donaldson suggested.

Anger gave a snort, but he did know about Donaldson and, inwardly, had an immense, albeit grudging, respect for him. He nodded reluctantly and Donaldson guessed he was only assenting to his presence in the hope that in the near future Andrea Makin's lips would be wrapped around Anger's cock.

'Let's get coffee and talk,' she said.

Words which were honey to Donaldson, whose mouth was bone dry from the alcohol.

They found a drinks dispenser in a corridor and grouped around it, the money going in and hot black liquid coming out. To describe it as coffee, though, was an insult to all coffee bean growers the world over. However, it did the trick for Donaldson, grim though it was.

Andrea cleared her throat, began a summary.

'Henry texted me earlier,' she began, realizing the ball was very definitely in her court, 'as a result of which two bodies were found in a hotel room in Stratford-upon-Avon. Then you contacted me, Dave' – she nodded at Anger – 'telling me that Troy Costain had been found in a ditch, beaten, left for dead. You're aware of the role Costain played in the operation Henry is engaged in.' Anger nodded. 'Now I cannot contact Henry and, to put it in a nutshell, I'm frantic with worry,' she admitted. 'If Costain's beating had something to do with his involvement in this operation, which is the hypothesis I would like to continue with, then I can only assume that Henry might have been compromised.' Bleakly, she said, 'Add to that the bodies in the hotel, and I do know Henry was down in Stratford with Mitch Percy, earlier today ... I have a very bad feeling about it all.'

Anger released a long breath. He pursed his lips. 'There's something else, too, which may or may not be connected ... a young girl was abducted in Poulton-le-Fylde earlier this evening, quite close to Out Rawcliffe. Straight off the street into the back of a van. I know that Ingram is suspected of crimes similar to this and if he has been in the area and assaulted Costain, then he could be tied in with this. My colleagues on FMIT are dealing with the abduction.' He looked at them. 'I'm not one for coincidences, so I'd rather treat these things as a whole rather than separately until we know otherwise.'

'I'll go with that,' Donaldson seconded him. Andrea nodded.

'I'm going to pull together a linked investigation team as regards Costain and the missing girl ... re. the job in Stratford, I'll get someone down there within the next three hours to liaise. On top of that, let's locate Henry. Much as we do not get along, his safety is paramount and at the very least he knows something about the murders...'

'I just hope he's alive, that's all,' Andrea said gravely.

And indeed, Henry Christie was very much alive and kicking, sitting in the back of an old Ford Granada, Ingram and Mitch up front, passenger and driver respectively. They were both quiet as Mitch drove the old car out of Manchester, out towards Rochdale. Henry tried to keep track of his whereabouts, knowing the area reasonably well, but he did lose track of the route for a brief period when they reached Rochdale. As they began to rise out of the town, he realized they were on the A680 which cut across the moors between that town and Rossendale. The knowledge made him feel a little more comfortable, as did the feel of the mobile phone strapped to his inner thigh, a bit like having a derringer tucked away for emergencies, even though he did have his own phone in his pocket.

Mitch drove well, racing quickly on to the moors. It was hard to believe he had shot two people dead only hours before. Henry knew this was the difference between most members of the public and bad bastards: *conscience*.

'What's the crack?' Henry asked. He leaned forwards between the front seats. 'Where are we going? Where the hell are we, in fact?' he asked, playing dumb.

Suddenly a smack of heavy rain battered down, drenching the car. Mitch flicked on the wipers.

'You'll see,' Ingram said.

Henry sat back, feeling that the mood of celebration seemed to have dissipated.

Two miles farther on, Mitch slowed, peering through the downpour, then turned right on to a farm track which, pitted and rutted though it was, did not cause any problems for the car, even in the bad weather.

'Where are we?' Henry asked brightly.

Neither one replied.

Henry's right hand reached slyly to the door handle, which he tried and found, with a rushing feeling rising inside him, to be child-locked.

The track continued up the moor. The car bounced down a particularly deep rut that threw Henry up and across the seat.

'Jeez!'

He strained to see into the dark. He twisted

around and saw the lights of Rochdale in the distance.

Mitch turned in through some stone gates and drove up to a farmhouse, security lights coming on as the car stopped. From what Henry could see, it looked as though it was no longer a real farmhouse, but had been converted into a des res with a wide gravel drive.

'Looks nice, this,' he said admiringly.

'My new pad,' Ingram said. 'Ops centre.'

The rain lashed down as they climbed out of the car, Mitch opening the door for Henry, and dashed to the front door, Ingram ahead.

Henry took in as much as possible, noticing a scruffy white van parked to one side of the drive, no other vehicles. They had left the Peugeot in Manchester.

Then they were in, the lights on, out of the rain. Even as Henry stood in the entrance hall and removed his jacket, he saw the place had been superbly modernized.

'Nice, nice,' he said. There was a grandfather clock in the entrance hall which looked like a genuine antique, which struck two, making Henry jump and realize he was in the middle of nowhere with a man who was a murderer and another who, possibly, was far worse. And no one knew where he was.

His anus contracted.

Donaldson's mobile rang: it was Kate Christie.

'What's happening, Karl?' Her voice cracked.

'Nothing concrete yet.'

'Do you think Henry's in trouble?'

205

He sighed, impatient with his own lack of knowledge. 'Knowing Henry, he'll be fine,' he said, pulling himself together for Kate's sake.

'I trust you,' Kate said simply. She did not need to add anything more and terminated the call.

Donaldson looked squarely at Andrea Makin.

Their eyes interlocked until they could no longer look at each other.

'How do we take this forward?' Donaldson asked.

She shrugged helplessly.

'You know the number Henry called from, the new mobile number, don't you?'

Andrea nodded.

'Well, let's get in a position to track the signal if the mobile comes back on ... we can be ready for that, can't we?'

'Yeah.'

Donaldson and Andrea were still at BVH. Costain was under the knife and the drill. The police in Poulton were searching the area for a lost child. The cops in Stratford were working on a murder scene. Henry Christie had not been heard of for hours.

'Do it,' Donaldson said.

'OK.' She punched a number in her phone and called Dave Anger. He was the one who could get the necessary authorization to locate mobile phone signals. She turned away from Donaldson as she made her request to Anger.

Donaldson paced the corridor, waiting for her to finish.

'Done,' she said, closing her phone.

They regarded each other again.

'If Costain was attacked by Ingram, or by his cronies, and he did blab, then Henry could well be dead,' Andrea said. 'Ingram doesn't take prisoners.'

'I get the picture.'

'So what the fuck do we do?'

'Has anyone checked Ingram's address?'

'He's been living in a Travelodge in Manchester. He checked out last evening.'

'No other addresses?'

Andrea looked blankly at him. 'He's only recently come north and kept a very low profile ... started from scratch, covering his tracks all the way.'

'What about associates?'

Andrea told him about Mitch Percy and that he, too, had come north with Ingram and started from scratch.

'What about their mobile phones? Do you have their numbers, their service providers?'

'They use and dispose of pay-as-you-go ones all the time. Impossible to keep track of.'

'Basically, you don't know very much about Ingram.'

She shook her head.

'So we're fucked?'

'Looks that way.'

The lounge was spacious and high-ceilinged, beautifully furnished, big screen TV, wooden beams, the whole *Lancashire Life* touch.

Henry lounged in one of the leather armchairs, sinking into its soft cushions, whisky glass in

hand, a shot of Grouse in it which he had water-
ed down. Ingram was on the settee, Mitch tight
in another armchair, both with drinks in their
hands.

A pornographic DVD was playing on the TV,
which was affixed to the chimney breast, like a
cinema screen. Its images and dialogue were just
background and Henry had no trouble ignoring
it. Mitch was riveted, engrossed, and Henry
hoped to hell he didn't feel the need to whip out
his cock and start masturbating.

'Mitch said you did good today,' Ingram told
Henry.

'More by luck than judgement,' Henry agreed
reluctantly. 'My first double murder, you know.'

'It needed doing.'

'I would've appreciated some warning.'

'Best to go in at the deep end.'

Henry shook his head. 'I prefer short, simple
steps.'

'Mitch mentioned property management to
you?'

'In passing.' Henry was astonished by the subject change, as though the murder of two men
was just another business thing. But that, terrify-
ingly, was exactly how these men were. Killing
meant nothing. Just another tool in their day-to-
day life. Something that 'needed doing'.

Henry felt nauseous. He sipped his drink, sensing something in the atmosphere, something
dark and scary. He knew he needed to keep
his wits about him. He glanced at Mitch, who
moved uncomfortably in the chair, pushing
his hand down over his crotch as he watched

the DVD.

'I'll have a lot of property soon. It'll need looking after. I need someone trustworthy to run it.'

'And that's me?'

'Very definitely.'

'So you went to see Troy Costain today.'

'Uh-huh – debt taken care of.'

'You paid him?'

'You could say that ... now all you need to worry about is me, but there'll be plenty of ways to repay me.'

Mitch was now kneading his cock, which, thankfully, was still inside his trousers.

Ingram said, 'Do you like the house?'

'Very smart.'

'Knock-down price, real bargain. The previous owner was only too glad to sell to me.'

Henry shivered wondering what that meant.

'It's mostly renovated, but there's barns and outbuildings not yet touched. Lots of possibilities. Want to see them?'

'Now?' Outside, the rain continued to hammer remorselessly.

'Yeah, now.' Ingram glanced at his henchman. 'Oi, let go of it, will you? Time for a guided tour.'

Mitch reluctantly removed his hand.

On the big screen a sexual act was taking place between two men and a little girl who, to Henry, looked no more than twelve years old.

'I need to be getting home,' Henry whined.

'Nah – tour first, then I'll call you a taxi,' Ingram said.

'No, really, I need to get gone.'

'No, like I said: tour first.'

Andrea and Donaldson had moved to the hastily commandeered incident room at Poulton Police Station. She pinched the bridge of her nose, a severe headache cutting through her skull like an axe. Donaldson, still fighting the residue of earlier alcohol, watched her, feeling helpless and foolish.

'There's nothing to say that Troy Costain was assaulted by Ingram, nor that he abducted the girl,' Donaldson said.

Andrea just shook her head.

The room they were in was nothing more than a former games room where there had once been a three-quarter size snooker table, now removed. A dartboard hung lonely on the wall, two darts shoved into the bull, their feathered flights broken. The third dart was nowhere to be seen.

The hanging lights that had once lit up the baize illuminated an old desk that stood where the snooker table had once been.

It was not a good incident room.

In the morning they would transfer to the newly built incident room at Blackpool.

'I hate undercover work,' Andrea admitted.

Donaldson nodded. He knew she had once lost an undercover cop. He had also lost agents and it was a terrible experience.

'Henry knows what he's doing. He'll be fine,' Donaldson said.

Her face twisted desperately. 'God, I hope so.'

The door opened and Dave Anger came into

the room. They raised their faces expectantly; however, he did not exude confidence in his manner.

'Nothing from the hospital yet,' he reported. 'Nothing on the missing girl and nothing from the mobile phone company.'

'The guy who owned this was into cars, doing them up, restoring them,' Ingram explained. They had toured the residential area of the farm – six bedrooms, three bathrooms, etc. – and Ingram had sounded like an estate agent. Now they had stepped outside into the wild night, a blast of cold moorland air and rain hitting then hard.

Henry checked his watch. It was going on three, not a time to be being shown around any-one's property, he thought. They stood at the front door and looked across at the outbuildings, a series of low barns and middens and one stand-alone building with a sliding door.

He wondered why Ingram was feeling the need to show him around. The boasting criminal?

However, something felt terribly wrong.

'Hell,' Ingram hissed at the weather.

'You want to give this a miss, boss?' Henry said.

'Hey, I like that. You called me boss.'

'That's what you are, isn't it?' Henry said, buttering him up.

'Yeah, suppose I am ... let me just show you something across in that building.' He pointed to the one with the sliding door. 'It used to be the owner's garage and workshop. Won't take long. It's brill.' He put his head down and trudged against the weather across the yard.

Mitch gave Henry a shove, propelling him on.

After a moment of fumbling with the big lock, Ingram slid back the ten-foot-high door, reached in for the light switch, found it, then stepped into the garage. Henry and Mitch clustered in behind him, glad to get somewhere dry. Even the short dash across the yard had drenched them.

It was a huge building, probably had once been a hay barn. Steps up one side led on to a separate, suspended first floor which was fitted like a gallery, reminding Henry of a duplex apartment.

'Impressive,' Henry said, though the thought of a workshop/garage didn't appeal to him. God wouldn't have given the world mechanics if he'd meant us to fix our own cars, he'd once pointed out to Kate. He wasn't a practical man in that sense ... now maybe if this had been a home cinema...

'Come here,' Ingram said, crooking a finger for Henry to follow. He led Henry across the concrete floor towards a big, rectangular sheet of metal that covered a vehicle inspection pit. This was hinged on one side, with a steel handle on the other and was secured to the floor by a heavy padlock. It was like the doorway to hell ... a few moments later Henry realized it was the pit of hell.

'Just have a look at this.'

Ingram indicated for Mitch to move. He bent down with difficulty, his fat legs not built for squatting. He produced a key with which he unfastened the padlock, then heaved up the metal cover, which creaked on its rusting hinges, then let it drop away, revealing the inspection pit. It was about five feet deep, three feet across, eight feet long and lined with concrete.

As the light from the barn illuminated it, Henry immediately saw the girl. Maybe ten, maybe twelve years old, sitting huddled in one corner of the pit, knees drawn up to her chin. Her hands were bound with parcel tape that also gagged her mouth. Frightened eyes peered up at the three men towering over her and she sank further back into the corner of the pit. A muffled sound of fear was trapped in her throat.

Henry stepped back, shocked. 'What the hell is this?' he spluttered, but his voice was cut short as Mitch's left arms wrapped around his neck and tightened with a powerful jerk, choking him. Mitch yanked Henry backwards, taking him off balance, and thrust a gun into his face.

Ingram stepped in front of Henry.

'You've become a problem,' Ingram said. With that he punched Henry in the stomach. Hard. Driving the air out of him. He could not double over, as Mitch was holding him tight with his arm, arching him backwards. The gun remained skewered into his cheek, the muzzle cold. 'Down,' Ingram said to Mitch, who lowered Henry on to his knees right at the edge of the inspection pit. When Henry was in position, Mitch growled, 'Do not move,' then released his grip, stepped away. His hand went into Henry's jacket pocket and found his mobile phone. He took it out and threw it on the floor, crushing it with his heel.

Henry groaned and held his guts.

Then the muzzle of the gun was rammed into the back of his neck at the point where his head balanced on the backbone. Ingram grabbed his arms and tied them behind his back using the same parcel tape the girl had been trussed up with.

It happened quickly, expertly, frighteningly, and within moments Henry was kneeling on the edge of the pit, hands bound, a gun pressed into his neck, looking down into the blackness at a kidnapped girl.

'What the fuck...?' he tried to say. Mitch silenced him by slamming the butt of the gun across his head, knocking him on to his left side.

The gun was forced into his face again.

Mitch's face was close to his ear.

'First thing I noticed was a change of mobiles,' Mitch hissed. 'One day I checked one; the next day it was a different one; then it was back to the original.'

'But people often have several mobiles,' Ingram said. He was standing somewhere behind Henry, out of his peripheral vision. 'But today I found out for sure.'

'Found out what?' Henry demanded. 'What's going on?'

'You really had us fooled, I'll give you that,' Ingram said with respect. 'I should've realized when I got locked up for a warrant that didn't exist and I got banged up with a drunk. Good set-up, really was, Frank.'

'I don't know what the hell you're talking

about.' There was no way under any circumstances Henry would admit to being a cop. Bitterly, he thought, Troy Costain, you are a dead man.

'Frank Jagger, my arse,' Ingram snorted. 'Henry Christie, I think.'

Mitch dragged Henry back up to his knees, stood behind him and screwed the muzzle of the gun into his neck again. It was the gun he'd used to kill the two drug dealers, the .22. He held it at such an angle that when he fired, the slug would travel up into Henry's brain diagonally and exit at the point to where his thin hair had receded.

Then there was a ripping sound – parcel tape being stripped from a roll – and Henry's head was jerked back as Ingram wound the tape around Henry's face, covering his mouth and nose.

Mitch then kicked Henry in the back, sending him pitching headlong into the inspection pit with no way of cushioning his fall with his hands tied behind his back. His head hit the opposite wall of the pit with a hollow, sick thud, then crashed on to the pit floor with his shoulder, and then there was blackness.

Fifteen

He needed to vomit. There was something revoltingly horrible in his throat, lumpy, tasting of blood and alcohol and it had to be ejected otherwise he would choke to death. Only problem was that parcel tape was wrapped tightly around his face, covering his mouth, and there was nowhere for the sick to go, except into his mouth and back down his gullet until it choked him.

His head hurt badly. He had landed hard. He recalled the crash, the sound of it, then the darkness and then waking up and knowing immediately he had to throw up and realizing he couldn't.

He lay there fighting it back, his insides making their own noises behind the tape as he gagged for breath and tried to swallow something that did not want to be swallowed, that shouldn't be swallowed.

And still he hadn't opened his eyes.

Then he did.

And he was still in darkness.

The memory flooded back. The situation he was in.

He closed his eyes, fought back the nausea, the fear.

216

Then another memory: the girl, bound and gagged in the pit.

His eyes flicked open again and he took stock of where he was lying – on the inspection pit floor on his front, his arms taped behind his back, his legs twisted at some strange angle. The metal lid of the pit had been closed and no doubt locked, so the world, initially, was pitch black, no apparent chinks of light. But his eyes had not yet become accustomed to the darkness.

He moved gingerly, still swallowing.

His knee hurt. He'd banged it on the way down. Also his elbow and his chest. He had basically bellyflopped into the pit when Mitch had kicked him, but he didn't think anything was broken.

'Are you awake?'

A voice. Tiny, unsure, hesitant, female – the girl. Hadn't she been gagged?

She was behind him, still tucked up in her corner.

'Hello?'

Henry swallowed his vomit. He groaned and moved, making a noise in his throat meant to be as close a proximation as possible to 'hello'.

'Oh, you're alive!'

He groaned a response, then shifted agonizingly on to his side. A sheet of excruciating pain whammed through his chest. Maybe he had broken something – ribs. When he moved it felt like they'd snapped and the ends were poking into his heart and lungs.

He managed to twist his legs up so he was in a fetal position, then he was aware that the girl had moved and she was leaning over him. She breathed into his ear and he could smell her, a mix of light, girlish perfume and sweat.

'I'm Gina,' she whispered.

Henry groaned again, swallowed urgently.

'My hands are still tied behind my back,' she said.

'Un-huh,' Henry strained to say.

'Are you hurt?'

'Un-huh.'

He could now feel his breathing start to quicken. He was suddenly hot and clammy and it was only a matter of time before he was unable to swallow back his vomit and then drown in it. Panic surged through him.

The girl's face was even nearer. Her hair fell on his face and he tensed. Next, her mouth was at his chin and he thought she was going to kiss him. He went totally rigid, not understanding what she was doing to him. Her mouth moved across to his ear, crawling across his face like an insect, then it opened and she bared her teeth.

'It's OK. I'm going to try and pull the tape off with my teeth.'

'Un-huh.' He relaxed.

Her face came down again, lips searching for the edge of the tape. She found it, opened her mouth again and scraped her teeth down his face until she bit the top edge of the tape. She clamped her teeth along it, then lost it, found it again and tugged gently, easing it away from his skin as he lay there inert, feeling her do this thing for him. She, whoever she was, this Gina, already amazed him. She certainly had some resilience

218

left in her.

She nibbled away at the tape until she could get a proper bite on it with her upper and lower teeth, then she pulled away and said, 'This will hurt.' She bent forward again, found the bit she had loosened, eased her teeth into position, gritted them. Henry heard them grate together, felt her steel herself, then pull hard, ripping the tape off with agonizing slowness, ripping up his skin and hair as she did.

The tape came away, bit by bit until she had pulled it away from the front of his face, but because of her position and his, she could go no further, though Henry's mouth was still covered.

'I'll need to climb over you,' she said. She rolled over him, crushing his ribs, drawing a muted howl of pain from him, and she fell in front of him, now face to face. 'Sorry about hurting you.'

'It's OK,' he would have liked to say.

She adjusted her position, using her elbows to steady herself, then got her teeth on the tape again and did not stand on ceremony. She ripped it off.

Air rushed in.

Henry gagged, managed to say, 'Sorry,' and was then sick, trying his best not to do it in her face, but he knew he had spewed on to her front and down himself. He heard her chirp with disgust.

'Sorry, love, I was choking on it. You saved my life.'

'It's OK,' she said, adding, 'Yuck!'

Henry spat out the remnants of the sick and tried to clear the taste of it away using saliva, but the petrol tang remained.

He breathed out.

'Christ,' he said, and tried to roll himself up into a sitting position, something he achieved with much huffing and puffing and effort and much sweat. It was uncomfortable with his hands behind his back. His eyes had properly adjusted to the darkness now, his pupils expanding to take in all available light. He saw there were a few slivers of light grey where the metal door covering the pit did not fit flush with the floor of the garage. It was obvious that the lights in the garage had been switched off and what light there was out there must be coming through the windows.

Henry was aware of the girl, could just make out her slim shape in one corner of the pit, cowering away from him, he guessed. Now and again, when her eyes moved, he caught a glint of white.

'Thanks, Gina,' Henry said.

'That's OK.'

'When I saw you at first I thought you had tape around your face.'

'I did, but I scraped it off against the wall of the pit. It's quite rough concrete. I've scratched my face and I'm bleeding.' She stifled a sob.

'Wow, you're very clever,' Henry said.

'Not clever enough,' she said bleakly.

'I'm Frank Jagger, by the way.'

'I thought that man called you Henry something?'

'He was wrong.'

'I'm Gina Weyers.'

'I think we're in a bit of a pickle, Gina.'

The greyness filtering through the cracks became slightly brighter: dawn, although still a long way off, was approaching.

Henry pushed himself to his feet, having to bow to stand upright, the back of his neck against the metal door of the pit. He pushed upwards, testing any give in the door. It moved slightly on its hinges, but would not open.

'It's well secure,' he said, and slid back down on to his backside.

'Are we going to die?' Gina's voice was thin, scared.

'Good lord, no,' he guffawed reassuringly, trying to keep hysteria out of his voice.

'What do they want from me?'

He had a good idea, but said, 'I don't know.'

'What are they going to do with you?'

'Don't know that, either.'

'Kill you?'

'Let's hope not.'

'You seem to have upset them.'

'So it would appear.'

'I thought the fat man was going to blow your brains out.'

'Thanks for that.'

Gina began to sob softly.

'Hey, come on. We'll be OK.'

'I'm scared.'

'So am I, but that doesn't mean we won't get out of here ... in fact, being scared is good. It makes you think and act quickly when necessary.' Gina stayed silent, unconvinced. 'How did you get here?' Henry asked her.

'The man, the thinner one ... I was going to the shop for my mum and he stopped and asked for directions ... he got out with a map and then grabbed me really quickly, punched me on the side of the head. I went all woozy and next thing I was in the back of a van, all tied up. It happened so quickly.'

'You poor mite. Where was this?'

'Poulton-le-Fylde.'

'Really?' Henry said, then thought, Could fit in with Ingram seeing that bastard Costain, the one who dropped me right in the shit. Henry stiffened. Now he had a very good reason to get out of this – to beat the living crap out of Troy Costain, then punch him some more. 'Hey,' he said, 'do you think there's any chance of us getting back to back and getting our hands free? I'll try and pull the tape from your wrists, OK?'

'We can try.'

They shuffled around until they were back to back and Henry fumbled for the girl's wrists. 'By the way, Gina,' he said, 'I think you're very brave and handling this really well.'

'Thanks, but I don't feel brave. I want my mum.' Once more she began to sob. 'And anyway,' she blubbered, 'what's the point of getting our hands free if they've got guns?'

He pulled and tugged, tried to get his fingertips behind the tape as Gina used all the strength in her thin arms to stretch and weaken it. It came apart thread by thread until she could waggle her hands, then slowly eased one hand out.

All the while they listened for the return of their captors.

Once her hands were free, Gina spun around and got to work releasing Henry's.

'Good girl,' he said as his right, then left wrist came free. 'Well done.'

'Now what?' she said, kneeling up and tearing the last of the tape off her arms.

Henry turned to face her, rubbing his wrists, 'oohing' with the pain from his chest. He could quite clearly see her face now. She was a bonny girl.

'I've got something up my sleeve, so to speak.' He didn't say he had it down his pants for fear of scaring the life out of her.

'Shit,' he said under his breath, 'no signal.'

He was holding the phone he'd bought under-handedly in Stratford, the one he'd secreted down his pants, taped to the inside of his leg. He had switched it on, had jumped and cringed when the phone had sung its welcome jingle which sounded incredibly loud within the confines of the pit, then watched the screen as the battery indicator showed two bars of charge and zero signal. He tried phoning anyway. Nothing. He tried many times, moving into different positions, even holding the phone up to one of the gaps between the door and the floor. Nothing.

'Send a text,' Gina suggested. 'On New Year's Eve I remember trying to text my mate, but all the networks were busy and my phone said "text failed", but she still got it.'

'I'll try,' Henry said. He thumbed a message, giving his approximate location and added the words, 'Urgent help reqd. Am with Gina Weyers', hoping that meant something to Andrea Makin, if she got it. The message, according to the phone, went nowhere.

'Send it a few times,' Gina said.

Henry sent it a few times more, conscious that the battery might run out of charge if he did too much.

Then there was the sound of the garage door opening.

Ingram and Mitch were back.

The alcohol he had consumed was making him groggy. He was only glad he hadn't drunk more. That would have completely wrecked his chances of being useful, even though as he sat on his backside in the incident room he felt about as useful as a fart in a spacesuit.

He took a long drink from a glass of cold water, feeling its icy tentacles seep through his system.

Andrea was on her mobile phone talking to some detective down in Stratford.

Ending the call, she turned to Donaldson, a look of despair on her face. 'Two men shot dead in a hotel room, not yet identified, as you know.' She closed her fists in frustration. 'All the hallmarks of a drugs deal gone wrong or a straightforward gangland execution.'

'And the question is, where does Henry fit into all this?'

'Who the fuck knows?' She shook her head, pursed her lips tightly. 'I don't think I've ever been so scared or felt so utterly incapable in my life...' A thought struck her. 'Well, maybe that's not entirely true, but I hate this inaction, this not knowing ... hell! Where is he? Fuck him!'

Dave Anger walked in, businesslike.

'Update,' he said briskly. 'We've had a house-to-house going on out there despite the late hour and all we've managed to uncover so far is the sighting of a white van in the vicinity the girl was abducted. No registered number.' He paused. 'It's a start.'

'Anything else?'

'Costain is out of surgery, but not out of danger. Critical and still unconscious. I've informed Mr Fanshaw-Bayley, the chief constable, of the situation, too.'

Donaldson and Andrea eyed each other wordlessly.

'We're doing all we can,' Anger said. 'Henry might not be on my Christmas card list, but...' Donaldson's mobile phone rang, interrupting him. He answered without checking the caller, just pressed a random button.

'Karl, it's Kate.'

'Hiya darlin', we haven't—'

'Karl, there's someone outside the house,' came her whispering, petrified voice. 'I think they're trying to get in, or something.'

Henry blinked as the pit door was lifted and light flooded in. The two menacing, backlit figures of Ingram and Mitch leered over the edge. Henry

225

and Gina were huddled together in a corner, his right arm around her shoulders. She was tucked into him and he could feel her quaking.

'Don't be scared,' he whispered.

'Can't help it.'

'Well, well, well,' Ingram said, 'or should I say, "'Ello, 'ello, 'ello, what's going on 'ere then?" What a pretty picture. Hm, I see you managed to get your hands free, the least I would have expected from a cop. Doesn't matter, though.' He had a gun in his hand, waving it loosely at the two captives.

Shielding his eyes with his left hand, Henry said, 'I'm not a cop and whoever told you I am is lying.'

'Makes no odds to me,' Ingram said. 'No smoke without fire, is what I say, and if I suspect something I always act on it.'

'What're you going to do?'

'Kill you.'

'And if I am a cop, then you'll be up the shitter, won't you?'

'And if you're not, you'll be dead anyway ... if you are, so be it. I don't take chances.'

'You need to let us both go.'

Ingram hee-hawed and looked at Mitch, then back at Henry. 'Nah, she's an asset, you're a liability ... I'm just going to balance the books, is all.'

Mitch said, 'Shall we?' with glee.

Ingram nodded.

'OK, Frank, or whatever your name is' – he too held a handgun pointed directly at Henry – 'up you get. You too, missy.'

'What's going to happen?'

'Er, you're gonna get dead and she's gonna get fucked.'

Gina emitted a moan of terror. Henry held her tightly. She gripped him in return.

Mitch moved to the head of the inspection pit steps.

'You first, Frank. Up here.'

A jerk of pain shot up through Henry's rib cage as he shifted even slightly. He wanted to say something reassuring to Gina, but couldn't find the words. He was feeling helpless and impotent. He raised himself slowly, wincing as he came upright, and wondered how he was going to deal with this, maybe his last few minutes on planet Earth.

He guessed there would be little opportunity for anything. Having seen Mitch in action, he doubted whether either he or Ingram would wish to spend much time discussing their holiday plans with him. These two men were ruthless operators, murderous individuals who killed without remorse, not feeling any reason to explain anything to their victims, as Henry had witnessed in Stratford, a town, he guessed, which would reel in the aftermath of the double murder.

But Henry knew that any time he could wangle out of them would give him a chance – and somehow he had to make time. If they were going to march him out of here and double tap his head without any formalities, then that was that, game over. He had to stall them, buy some time, look for a chance.

He glanced at Gina. She stared up at him, open-mouthed, trusting. He gave her a discreet wink.

'What're you going to do with her?' He raised his face at the two men.

'Indulge ourselves,' Ingram said, so matter-of-fact it scared the daylights out of Henry. A shadow crossed the man's face, the look of lust and perversion. 'After we've killed you, that is.'

Henry's insides did a quick roll-over. He gasped. It was an emission of fear, but he hoped Ingram would interpret it as something else, along the lines his depraved mind was working.

'Can I watch?' Henry blurted.

'You-fucking-what?' Mitch laughed with disbelief.

'Whatever happens, whatever you believe about me, I'm going to die, yeah? So just let me watch the girl being fucked, then do me and at least I'll die happy.'

'You want me to let you watch as I fist fuck her?'

'Last request and all that. I won't cause problems, just sit, watch, maybe pull my plug.'

Ingram and Mitch exchanged glances again. Henry had touched a perverted nerve.

Ingram smiled in a twisted, contorted way.

'Up her arse, everything,' Henry encouraged him. He did not allow himself to look at Gina, but he knew she was right down in the corner of the pit, sobbing, knees drawn up tight, her head hidden, her hands covering her ears, mortified by this betrayal.

'I quite like that idea,' Ingram said.

Henry knew he would, Sex. Power. Life. Death. Ingram thought he controlled everything.

'You're more of a perv than I am, Henry.'

'My name is Frank.'

'Whatever.'

But then Henry had a sudden, dreadful premonition.

This idea might buy him some time, but if it could do nothing to change his destiny, he would go to his death having witnessed the rape, torture and molestation of this wonderful, brave girl – and at his instigation.

He would die with that on his mind.

Sixteen

Donaldson powered his Jeep out of Poulton-le-Fylde and accelerated towards Blackpool, his mobile phone cradled to his ear.

'The local cops have been told and they're on their way. I'm ten minutes away.'

'Thank God,' Kate breathed.

'What's happening now?' Donaldson swerved and overtook a slower moving car and floored the accelerator and did not even flinch when a speed camera flashed behind him, though he did glance at his speedo, which was registering seventy-two. He had enough faith in British justice to believe that, under the circumstances, this demeanour would be scrubbed.

'I don't know.'

'Have you seen anyone? Have you looked outside?'

'Not for a few minutes. It's all gone quiet.'

'Maybe he's gone ... where are you in the house?'

'Our bedroom. I'm frightened to move.'

'OK, stay put. Cops'll be there soon, then me.'

'Thank God,' Kate reiterated. 'Hang on, there's something ... just a second...'

'Kate, what's going on?' Donaldson slowed for some red lights, but they changed to green as he hit them.

'I heard something. I'm going on to the landing.'

'What did you hear?'

'Something at the front door, sounded like a letter coming through.'

Donaldson could hear a shuffling noise, Kate walking perhaps, a door opening, then there was a loud crashing noise, maybe a window breaking, and then Kate screaming dreadfully into the phone.

'Kate! Kate!' Donaldson yelled as he almost rear-ended another car, but managed to brake and overtake.

The line went dead.

Mitch forced Henry down on to his knees as he came out of the pit, and whilst Ingram shoved the muzzle of his gun into the soft flesh at Henry's windpipe, Mitch rebound his wrists in front of him, palm to palm, as though he was praying.

Ingram bent close to Henry's face.

'You are a cop, aren't you?' He screwed the gun painfully into his flesh.

'No.'

'I don't believe you.'

He could smell Ingram's breath – garlic – and body odour – sweat.

'I'm Frank Jagger, a fucking good-for-nothing Jack the Lad, that's all I am.' Henry was looking at Ingram through the corner of his eye, his chin raised, his whole body twitching nervously.

'Actually, I don't give a shit.'

'I—' Henry began, but stopped before he'd started as he felt his mobile phone vibrating against the inside of his thigh. It was working. There was a signal now. Had his messages got through?

'I, what, Frank, Henry?' Ingram asked. He shoved the barrel in hard against his Adam's apple.

'Nothing.'

'Done.' Mitch stepped away from Henry's tethered hands. Henry tensed his wrists, testing the strength of the fastening.

Ingram stood up.

The feel, the impression of the gun was still in Henry's neck even though Ingram had removed it.

Mitch pulled Henry roughly to his feet, obviously not caring too deeply about any injury he might have incurred. The phone between his legs dropped a quarter of an inch and Henry quickly drew his legs together. Too quickly. It was a movement noted by Ingram.

'Problem?'

'Need a piss,' Henry lied.

'Do it in your pants, then.' Ingram looked down at the girl. 'Come on.' She looked at him in fear, biting her lips, shaking her head. 'You don't come, I drag you,' he warned her.

'Fuck off,' she said.

Henry hid an inner smile. She really had some bottle, this kid.

Ingram tutted, went down the steps and dragged her to her feet with ease, and though she kicked and punched him, he held her with his left hand, his right still holding his gun, and seemed to enjoy her writhings.

Sex, power, Henry thought.

After a few moments, though, Ingram had had enough.

He got rough.

He smacked the butt of his gun across her face, then punched her down with a left jab, then began to pound on her.

Henry jerked towards him, his protective instinct cutting in.

Mitch grabbed his upper arm in a vice-like grip and gave him a warning look.

Then Henry settled back. He knew he had to keep a grip on himself. He was still Frank Jagger and if necessary it was the identity he would take to the grave with him. The same Frank Jagger who had just made the most perverted last request ever – so the girl getting a pre-rape battering wasn't something that should have bothered him in the slightest.

Ingram screwed his left hand into Gina's hair

and balled his fingers into a fist, then heaved her up and shoved his face into hers.

'I like that,' he breathed.

Despite himself, Henry could not control his heartbeat, nor the flaring of his nostrils, nor the surge deep within him.

Gina, God bless her, spat a mouthful of phlegm and blood into Ingram's face, which drove him into a paroxysm of undiluted rage. He threw his gun down and started to beat Gina about the head, pummelling her repeatedly with his fists, driving his knees into her lithe body.

Henry caught Mitch watching this display of manliness with the expression of a salivating dog. No doubt he would get the leftovers.

Just for a moment, the big man's guard was down.

Henry now had to make his judgement. Was this the moment he had been seeking? Or was it doomed to failure?

Both villains were now diverted by the suffering of a little girl, their minds focused on that and nothing else.

Henry's moment had arrived.

Donaldson pressed the redial button, could hear Kate's phone ringing out.

'Come on, girl,' he intoned, negotiating a roundabout one-handed, the Jeep lurching, tyres squealing. He was in Blackpool now, on the back roads, almost at the junction of the A587, having just passed the hospital in which Troy Costain had undergone emergency surgery, and the zoo. Once on the 587, he was about three minutes from Henry's house – if he ran all the speed cameras along that road – which he fully intended to do.

The phone was answered.

Kate was hysterical.

'He's pouring petrol in through the letter box!'

Donaldson almost swerved off the road.

Other than surprise, Henry had no weapons at his disposal. His hands were tied in front of him; Mitch, standing two feet away from him at the edge of the pit, was armed, as was Ingram down in the pit itself, beating up the girl – although he had thrown his gun down when he'd decided to attack her with two fists.

Between his legs, Henry's phone vibrated.

At least they would be able to triangulate his position, he thought disconnectedly at the back of his mind. Find my body, maybe.

Henry interlinked his fingers rather like a volley ball player about to make a dig.

God, he was hurting, too. Every small movement made him wince. The pain was incredible.

There would be no second chance with Mitch.

It had to be right.

It had to be now.

He tensed his whole being, fought off all thoughts of pain. Mind over matter: it was not going to hurt him.

Mitch looked at him, a faraway look of pleasure in his eyes.

In the pit, Ingram pounded Gina mercilessly. Kicked, punched, engrossed like a demon.

Henry caught Mitch's expression, reflected it

back. Two guys, same wavelength. Two sick guys.

It needed to be an upward swing, executed perfectly, almost like a golf stroke.

His body twisted at the hip. His right shoulder rose, his left dipped and his bunched hands drew back and then he pivoted. He swung round and ignoring the ribs and everything else, he cobbled together all his strength and went for the hole in one. The punch he hoped would be enough to floor the big man.

It came up under Mitch's chin and connected with the sound of knuckles rapping a door as Henry's fists smacked up into the jaw. There was even more pain for Henry as he felt one of the bones in his hand crack. He hit him as hard as possible and knew from the impact that shock waves must have been sent up through the big man's cranium like an earthquake.

His head snapped back and he staggered away a few steps, but even then, Henry knew he had to keep going, pound in his advantage and make it pay, otherwise Mitch would just shake his head like a grizzly bear, then shoot Henry dead.

No hesitation, no second thoughts.

Henry went in hard, following Mitch as he went backwards.

With his hands still interlocked into one powerful fist, he charged at the man, holding his arms outstretched and locked into place, and like a lance held by a medieval knight, he slammed into Mitch's chest. On impact, Henry twisted slightly and managed to get his right foot behind Mitch's right ankle and tipped him over.

Still stunned by the chin blow, Mitch's legs gave way and he crumbled backwards on to the concrete floor. The gun was still in his hand and this was Henry's next target. He jumped on Mitch's right forearm, then stamped down hard on it, again and again. But the fingers wouldn't open and Henry knew he was running out of time and advantage, even though the assault had lasted only a matter of seconds so far.

And all Ingram had to do was raise his head from his own assault, then Henry's little episode would be over.

That thought made Henry jump on to Mitch's head with both feet, then step back and continue to stamp on it with one foot repeatedly.

The first blow to the underside of the chin had obviously been even better than Henry could have hoped for, because after the fifth stamp of Henry's foot on his head, he became still, his countenance a bloody mass. Not bloody enough in Henry's opinion, but he had more to do yet. He dropped to his knees and wrestled the gun from Mitch's grip, which for some unaccountable reason, he still held on tight to. Henry prized the fat, sausage-like fingers open, expecting Mitch to jump to life and crush him to death in a bear hug, but he didn't.

He just gagged for breath and Henry wished he'd stamped on the fat ugly head one more time for luck.

Now, with the gun clasped between his bound hands, Henry stood up, crouched and turned towards the pit.

* * *

236

The Jeep skittered into the cul-de-sac. Donaldson righted it, corrected the swerve and accelerated toward the house which was directly ahead – with not one cop car in sight.

For a moment he was confused by what he saw: orange and yellow lights dancing behind the front door.

'Fuck!'

Flames.

The house was on fire, confirmed spectacularly as the window in the panel next to the door blew out with a booming explosion, sending glass shattering in a million directions, and then the fire licked upwards.

He brought the jeep to a halt at an angle to the road and leapt out.

That's when he saw Kate's face at the bedroom window above the garage door.

She opened a window, leaned out and screamed, 'Karl! Karl!'

The garage was to the left of the front door and for a moment the fire raged directly up to the first-floor window above it, which Karl knew belonged to the en-suite adjoining the main bedroom in which Kate now was, seemingly trapped.

Donaldson ran up to the house and stood underneath the window Kate leaned from, his strong arms wide as though he expected her to jump down into them. The flames were immensely hot, even though he was standing two metres away from the front door. Already the fire had taken hold of the downstairs hallway. The flames crackled nastily, like bones being snapped.

The adrenalin surge through the American acted like a painkiller on his bullet wound.

'You have to climb out, Kate.'

Unbelievably there was a whoosh to his right. The flames roared with more intensity and suddenly there was a 'boom' and the UPVC front door was blasted by a back draft from its hinges, and a ball of fire, like a meteor, soared out of the house, then immediately licked upwards. The flames fanned wider, causing Kate to duck out of their way, screaming in terror as she did.

Donaldson had to hurl himself sideways to avoid being roasted by the burst.

He picked himself up from the ground.

The cul-de-sac was coming to life now, lights going on, people appearing at doors and windows. A couple of pyjama-clad men pulling on dressing gowns and slippers rushed towards the house.

'Kate! Kate!' Donaldson cupped his hands around his mouth into a loudspeaker.

In the distance came the sound of sirens.

The flames from the door died back, but through the space where the door had once been, the new inrush of oxygen had fuelled them even more and Donaldson could see the fire spreading up the stairs, quickly, relentlessly, like an army intent on massacre.

'Kate!' he screamed once more. She did not reappear. 'Shit.'

His mind raced.

The fire raged.

He ran back to his Jeep and leapt into the

driving seat. The engine was still running. He slammed it into reverse, yanked down the steering wheel and slammed down the accelerator. The vehicle lurched backwards in a sweeping 'U'. He braked, forced the gearstick into Drive and mounted the pavement, crossing the charred front lawn, twisted the wheel down again and stopped with a lurching judder parallel to the house, in front of the garage, underneath the bedroom window. He leapt out, clambered via the bonnet of the Jeep on to its roof and threw himself across on to the roof of the front porch, which jutted out below the open window.

Slipping and sliding, always in danger of falling, he climbed across the tiles and dragged himself up through the open window, then dropped into an untidy heap on the floor next to Henry's bed.

The bedroom door was closed, but even so, he could feel the terrific heat from the fire which was fiercely taking over the house. Smoke was creeping frighteningly underneath the door.

He knew there was little time.

But Kate wasn't in the bedroom.

He shouted her name as he strode to the door. Surely she hadn't gone on to the landing?

'Kate!' he bellowed again.

Then the door of the walk-in dressing room opened slightly. She had retreated in there for safety.

'Karl,' she uttered, throwing open the door when she saw him. She raced toward him.

'C'mon,' he said, his big arms encircling her slim waist and urging her in the direction of the window.

'How did you get in?' she began.

'You'll see.'

They reached the window. Behind them was the sound like a dragon breathing. Flames now licked under the bedroom door.

'There's no one else in the house?' he asked. She shook her head.

A police car tore down the cul-de-sac.

A lumbering fire engine came behind it.

Donaldson checked over his shoulder again. There was no time to wait for ladders. Somehow he had to get Kate out and on to the roof of the Jeep, then he had to follow, quickly.

'How?' she said, looking down at the Jeep, which seemed a long way away, but was perhaps only three feet from the wall of the house and directly under the window.

'I'll hold you ... we've no choice.'

The dragon was now at the door, roaring angrily, trying to burst through.

Both turned and looked at the same time, horror on their faces.

'No time, either,' Donaldson added.

Kate peered out of the window. It seemed so far.

'I don't know if I can,' she pleaded.

Outside, two cops were on the front lawn. The fire engine had stopped, its occupants disgorging, equipment being deployed.

'Sit on the window frame, twist, hold on to my arms and I'll ease you down. You have to do it.'

'I'm scared.'

'I'm in that club, too.'

Below, one of the cops climbed on to the roof of the Jeep, steadied himself and opened his arms. Kate clambered on to the window and sat, legs dangling. She twisted her body around, then began to lower herself towards the Jeep. Donaldson clamped his big, powerful fingers around her forearms, held tight, eased her down.

'I can't do it,' she screamed.

Donaldson, his face muscles straining like steel rope with the effort, steadied himself, then swung her out towards the waiting policeman. She dropped out of Donaldson's hands with a scream and fell backwards the last few feet, arms flailing.

The cop grabbed her, then lost his footing, but somehow righted himself, held on to Kate, then both lost their balance and fell backwards off the roof of the Jeep – but into the massed, waiting clutches of the other policeman and three fire fighters, who caught them raggedly, but safely.

Donaldson watched it all helplessly.

Behind him, with a roar of contempt, the dragon that was the fire blew out the bedroom door with a heave of power and burst into the bedroom.

There was a moment of silence. Only a moment, though it felt like a lifetime.

Henry took a breath, steadying himself.

Suddenly Ingram's head popped up from the pit as though he was taking a quick peek over a wall.

He saw Henry with the gun, ducked quickly back down.

Henry ran across the six feet or so to the edge of the pit, but did not reach it quickly enough. By the time he got there, Ingram had grabbed Gina, twisted her round and held her against him like a shield. His left forearm was slotted across her neck, making her gurgle and struggle, and his right hand held his gun to her face, pushing into her cheek.

The gun in Henry's hand was raised, aimed at both of them.

Ingram laughed.

'You're at one big fuckin' disadvantage,' Ingram cackled maniacally. 'Drop the gun or I blow her fuckin' head right off.'

Henry's eyes took in the girl. Her face was a ghastly mess, but her eyes were still open, appealing for help and defiant.

Ingram tightened his grip across her throat. His forearm must have been like an iron bar. She gagged, fighting for breath, her fingers pulling at the limb. She kicked out pathetically, but Ingram held her securely, not giving one inch.

Henry kept the gun aimed at least for the moment but he wasn't sure of his ability with a firearm these days, so having a go was out of the question.

Ingram's feral eyes looked beyond Henry at the prostrate figure of his partner in crime.

'You took Mitch down.'

'He was easy – glass jaw.'

'You won't get me, cop.'

'I'm not a cop,' Henry insisted. 'You're wrong...'

'Then we can talk.'

242

'Sure we can, but only when the girl goes ... I don't mind a bit of porn, but not like you like it. She goes,' he insisted.

'Nah,' Ingram sneered. 'Not a chance.' He moved his left arm down across her chest. 'Fuckin' ripe for the picking.'

Henry went sick with disgust. 'Let her go, you perverted bastard.' His gun wavered.

Ingram jammed the muzzle of his gun further into Gina's cheek, forcing a squeal of pain to be emitted. 'Drop the gun, Frank, or whatever you're called. I will kill her,' he finished simply.

'And how many more have you killed?'

'Plenty.'

On the floor behind Henry, Mitch groaned.

Shit, Henry thought. He knew he would have to put his weapon down, knew that his chance had passed unsuccessfully. Although Ingram was standing in the pit, he had the power. What would Frank Jagger do? he thought.

But maybe that wasn't the burning question.

Maybe the question was, What is Ingram going to do?

Henry knew the answer – carry on as before. He would kill Frank Jagger because he didn't trust him, kill the girl, and run.

Even if Henry gave up his weapon, he would still be a dead man.

A win–lose situation, in Ingram's favour. 'You'll kill me, whatever,' he said.

'Didn't take you long to figure that one out.' Ingram took the gun out of Gina's face and levelled it at Henry

Gina went completely still, almost relaxed.

She looked imploringly at Henry. *Save me. Please.*

Henry tensed.

Suddenly, as if poleaxed, Gina's knees gave way and she collapsed purposely. Ingram's arm wasn't at her throat, it was still across her chest, and her movement caught him by surprise and she slid out of his grasp as though she had been greased, exposing Ingram's upper body above the edge of the pit. His gun wavered unsteadily as he tried to grab her, but he'd lost his hold.

Henry could not hesitate.

Now, less than six feet away from him was an easy target.

He double-tapped him, the slugs driving into Ingram's chest and chucking him back against the pit wall with their force. His arms flew upwards and his right hand released the gun, which went skittering across the garage floor. He slithered down on to his arse, his eyes never once leaving Henry's.

Gina was on her feet instantly, scrambling out of the pit. She raced to Henry and clamped her arms around him, clinging tightly, his wrists still taped together and the gun in his hands, pointing down at the floor.

Henry's breathing was harsh, rasping. 'It's OK, it's OK ... let's get my wrists undone.'

'I don't think there's anything more we can do for him,' Henry said. He stood up and looked at his bloodstained hands, then at the body of Ryan Ingram, who, despite two holes in the upper right quadrant of his chest, was still alive –

244

barely. He was on the floor of the inspection pit with kitchen towels stacked on to the wounds, which were clogged with blood.

Henry raised his eyes and looked floor level across to Mitch who, with a big, swollen head, drifted in and out of consciousness. Even so, just to be on the safe side, Henry had taped up his hands and ankles. The last thing he wanted was to have to deal with that raging monster again.

Gina sat with her legs dangling over the edge of the pit. She was very battered and sore, her head a real mess from the pistol-whipping Ingram had vested on her. Henry admired her spirit. She was unputdownable, a real fighter.

'How you doing?' he asked her.

'Not good, been better.'

He gave a short laugh. 'You are bloody fantastic,' he told her, coming up the steps out of the pit and parking his backside next to hers. He put an arm around her shoulders.

'When will they be here?'

'Not long, now.'

Outside it was daylight.

'Why have you looked after him?' she asked, confused.

'Good question ... I don't like people dying, I suppose.'

She turned her smashed-up face to him. 'You are a policeman, aren't you?'

He gave her a sardonic look. 'Yeah,' he said tiredly, 'I guess I am.'

Seventeen

'What the hell do you think I'm going to do, leave the country?' Henry glared at the SS-bespectacled Dave Anger in disbelief. 'Some things are more important than effing crime scenes!'

'Listen you, you ... fucker, despite me not liking you one jot, I've pulled out my tripe on your behalf and I expect a bit of cooperation in return.'

It had degenerated into a contest to see who could insert the 'f' word in as many places as possible in the dialogue, from which no one was going to emerge smelling of roses. This, however, did not stop Henry from ranting.

'My fucking house has been burned down by a maniac, my wife's in hospital and you expect me to stay here and then go to a nick with you to be questioned? Not a fucking chance in hell, you fucking, unfeeling twat.'

Anger adjusted his glasses. His face was scarlet with the argument.

'Henry' – he coughed to clear his throat – 'Henry, there's a guy been double-tapped in the chest, by you; there's another been kicked unconscious, by you,' he pointed out, not unreasonably.

'Hey – stop right there, right now,' Henry commanded.

The altercation between the two fractious officers was taking place very publicly at the front door of the farmhouse owned by Ingram.

Andrea Makin watched, agog.

Other cops, medics, gathered and ogled from a respectful distance.

'I'll give you the gist again. They were going to kill me and they were going to rape that little girl Ingram had abducted.' His eyes were wide, mad looking, lots of white showing. 'I acted in self-defence, end of story, details to follow later. That's all you need to know. The crime scene itself is pure, too.'

He stared threateningly at Anger.

'Someone let Ingram know I was a cop,' he then added, not for the first time, either. It was like a steel wire was constricting his chest, being pulled tighter, like some medieval form of torture. His teeth ground together. He leaned towards Anger. 'Either fucking arrest me, or let me go home.'

The fucking contest was over.

'OK, love?'

Gina nodded, took hold of Henry's hand. Together they walked towards the Lancashire force helicopter, India 99, the mode of transport scrambled to enable Makin and Anger and two armed officers to make the journey right across Lancashire once Henry's position had been triangulated by means of the mobile phone pulse.

An air ambulance had also been, and gone, having conveyed the two casualties, plus armed officers to guard them, to hospital.

She squeezed his hand, making him feel like the weak one.

'Was that your boss?' she asked.

'Sort of.'

'He doesn't like you much,' she said. 'Have you done something to upset him?'

'Not recently,' Henry reflected.

The helicopter had landed in a field in front of the farmhouse. As he and Gina walked to it, he glanced back at the police/ambulance activity. It was frantic, but he was curiously detached from it. What had happened there was, for the moment, strange and unreal.

'I've never been in a helicopter,' Gina said. 'Have you?'

'Once or twice,' he responded absently, but didn't add that it wasn't his most favourite form of transport. It gave him the willies. 'How are you feeling?'

'Sore and still scared,' she answered.

'Me too.'

'Henry!'

Andrea Makin was running towards him. She braked as she got close. 'Can we have a quick word?'

Henry detached himself from Gina's grip and walked a few steps away.

'Can't it wait?' he asked irritably.

'Look,' she said apologetically, 'sorry for getting you into this mess.'

'It was my choice. I could've refused, but no,

I wanted action and adventure and ended up with ... shit!'

'I'm sorry, but we do need to have a talk sooner rather than later.'

'I know ... but...' He gestured towards the helicopter.

'You need to get back to Kate. I understand.'

'And to get this little lass back to Mum and Dad.'

Arrangements had already been made to kill two birds with one stone. Although the paramedics at the scene had treated Gina for the injuries she'd sustained from Ingram's beating, they had still insisted she needed to go to hospital to be thoroughly checked over. The compromise reached, with Gina's consent, was that the police helicopter would take her back across the country to be reunited with her parents at Blackpool Victoria Hospital. That also meant Henry could link up with Kate and Karl Donaldson who were there, too, and get checked over himself. A double reunion.

'I promise I won't go on the run.'

'I know.' Makin touched Henry's face tenderly with the palm of her hand and tiptoed up to him, brushing her lips across his cheek. She whispered, 'I wish you'd killed him.'

'Dead men tell no tales ... and I expect you'd rather get the story out of him than bury him without knowing the truth about your niece and other girls.'

'In my heart I know the truth.'

Henry walked back to Gina, took her hand and they jogged to the helicopter, ducking down under the rotor blades, then climbing in to the passenger seats behind the pilot and observer.

Immediately the blades began to whump around.

The observer handed them both helmets, which they fitted after strapping themselves in. Henry's was tight, crushing his ears and cheeks; Gina's rattled loosely on her small head.

They held each other's hands as the ungainly machine defied all the laws of physics, built up power and lifted from the ground, tilted forwards, then was up in the sky.

The overnight rain had cleared. It was a fine day for flying.

Fifteen minutes later they landed on the helipad at BVH, a small crowd there to receive them. As Henry and Gina dismounted, her parents broke free from the throng and rushed towards their little girl, arms outstretched, overcome with relief. Gina walked coolly towards them and Henry smiled at her. She had remained so composed, yet he wondered what would happen to her when the reality of the situation struck, which he knew it would.

She was whisked away by her parents, a nurse and a policewoman, leaving Henry to walk away from the helicopter, acknowledging the pilot and observer with a nod of grateful thanks for getting him back alive.

He ducked under the blades and walked towards the big figure of Karl Donaldson, who stood waiting for him, hands on hips and a crooked smile playing on his mouth.

Henry approached him cautiously, squinting at his bulk.

'H, you look like shit.'

'And you're a big, good-looking mother, which really annoys me.'

Pleasantries over, something moved inside each of them and they shared a manly hug with lots of shoulder patting. Henry squeaked in pain.

'I believe I need to thank you.'

Donaldson shrugged modestly. They headed to the hospital, as behind them the helicopter rose into the sky, banked and returned to base at Warton Aerodrome.

Henry limped and groaned. Suddenly, all the adrenalin left him. He sagged down and reached out to grasp Donaldson's sleeve. The American caught him.

'Whoa, there.'

'Sorry, sorry, pal.' Then he went slightly dizzy. 'Hell.'

The American slid his arm around Henry's back, held him upright and assisted him all the way to A&E whilst telling him what had gone on at the house, the fire, Kate, the rescue.

After what seemed like a five-mile trek, they entered the hospital, by which time Henry had regained some of his macho dignity and was walking without aid.

'I need to see Kate first. She is OK, isn't she?'

'She's fine,' Donaldson reassured him, and not for the first time. 'Breathed in some smoke and twisted her ankle when I threw her out of the bedroom window – joke ... In fact, she did more damage to my car, dented the goddamned roof,

251

man,' he mock-whined.

He led Henry through the department to a cubicle in which Kate sat up on a bed with an oxygen mask over her face. Their daughters, Leanne and Jenny, were at her bedside.

As soon as they saw Henry, they all burst into tears as if on cue.

As did Henry.

Karl Donaldson looked away and hid his own tears.

Discharged after a fairly perfunctory examination, Henry sat in the waiting room of the A&E department six hours after having presented himself to the triage nurse. He had a polystyrene cup of coffee in his hands, which tasted just like the material of the cup it was in, and was staring unblinkingly at the tiled floor, still trying to come down.

The pains in his body were great, but now under control with the assistance of good quality analgesics, and though his breathing was uncomfortable – two cracked ribs confirmed by an X-ray – he was feeling better physically, but mentally still fuzzed-up and cracked-out.

'DCI Christie?'

Henry raised his eyes to see a man standing in front of him. He recognized Gina's father, an amiable looking gent around the thirty mark. He looked exhausted as he extended his right hand. Henry sat creakily upright and they shook.

'I need to thank you. You saved Gina's life.'

'How is she?'

The father blew out his cheeks. 'OK,' he said

cautiously, 'but I expect that may change.'

'She's a brave kid, but she has seen and experienced some bad things. I'm sorry she had to go through it and I'm sorry I couldn't prevent her getting a battering.'

'The physical scars will heal.'

Henry nodded. 'I'll come and see her soon.'

'Look forward to it.' He touched Henry's shoulder, his chin wobbling, then left. Henry sat back, closed his eyes, resting his cup on his knee.

'She'll be out in a few minutes.' Henry came to with a start. In front of him now was Karl Donaldson. 'Don't fall asleep – you'll spill. I'll go and bring the car around.'

'Thanks, Karl.'

'No big deal.'

'Yeah it is – very big deal.'

'Hey, asshole! That's what friends are for.' He spun away. Henry watched his departure, as did several google-eyed nurses, including a male one.

'Good-looking bastard,' Henry said, sotto voce.

He was now desperately exhausted, but there was still much to do, not least to go and inspect the house and arrange alternative accommodation, two tasks he was dreading. But something else came to mind.

Henry hobbled through the hospital corridors, suddenly driven, ignoring the pain.

'Bastard, bastard,' he kept mouthing through gritted teeth.

He walked, unchallenged, into the intensive care unit, moved from bed to bed until he found the one he was looking for – but he did not find the patient he was looking for.

He went back to the office at the top of the ward and knocked gently, pushing his tender head through. A nurse glanced up from some forms he was completing. 'Can I help you?'

'Hello, I'm ... er...' he began, still a little befuddled. 'Troy Costain ... I'm after Troy Costain ... he was brought here last evening following an assault. He had surgery?'

'Are you a relative?'

'I'm a police officer ... and a friend of his.'

'Do you have some ID?'

'No, I'm afraid not,' he jerked helplessly. 'I just want to know how he is.'

'You don't look like a police officer.'

'It's been a long night.'

She considered him thoughtfully, then her eyes softened. She blew a little breath out of her nose. 'I'm afraid I have some bad news. Mr Costain had to be taken urgently to surgery to remove a blood clot from his brain ... unfortunately he suffered a heart attack on the operating table and died.'

Eighteen

'I very much doubt he'll say a dicky bird.'

Andrea Makin linked an arm though Henry Christie's. The two of them were on a three-mile stroll from the front entrance of the headquarters building, through a posh housing estate built on a site which was once an agricultural college, then looping back along a country lane to HQ. Three miles, a distance and route Henry often ran at lunch times from his Special Projects office.

It was a pleasant, warm day, no breeze. Good walking weather.

She pulled herself tighter to him and looked up into his face.

'This is non-sexual, by the way.'

'Damn! OK,' he said, feigning disappointment.

'I can see you love Kate ... isn't it about time you did the honourable thing?'

'We're pretty comfortable,' he said, uncomfortably clearing his throat. 'You were saying about Ingram?'

'He's still being cared for in hospital, now on a private ward, surrounded by briefs, but guarded by cops. He's going to live, unfortunately. As soon as he's well enough, he'll be in custody.'

'And Mitch?'

'Very much alive, but with a sore head. He's about to be charged. Your statement, plus the gun, plus the tooth-diamond we found on him, and the drugs, have pretty much sewn him up. He's in Stratford and once they've finished with him, I'll move in.'

Henry took a deep breath.

It was one week later. His physical injuries were still hurting, but improving daily. Mentally he was still a mess, all tangled up. He had taken sick leave and, for the first time in his career, was in no hurry to return to work.

He'd done what needed to be done in terms of being debriefed and providing statements, even had a session with the police psychologist just to appease the powers that be, in case they got sued later for using an undercover cop who wasn't fully capable of doing the role. Beyond that, the days had been spent sorting out his private life.

Kate was a wreck, needing constant reassurance, and his daughters were much the same. He knew he had to be there for them.

The house had been gutted by the fire and they were now living in a rented house, courtesy of the insurance company. An early estimate to restore the house to its former glory was two hundred grand, give or take.

'You OK, Henry?'

He screwed up his face and looked at Andrea. He had come in at her request to discuss how things would move forwards.

'If you don't feel up to it, we can take a rain check.'

'I don't want to procrastinate, but I do feel like shit.'

The idea for the walk had come from him. He had thought it might help clear his head and channel his thoughts, but he was still having problems putting everything into a logical, coherent sequence. 'Let's see, I went undercover to get information about Ryan Ingram, ended up witnessing a double murder, somehow how had my cover blown, presumably by Troy Costain, got threatened with execution and then shot Ingram. Meanwhile my family home is being torched by a madman who we cannot find and my ex-wife is almost killed. Then to cap it all, Troy Costain actually died because I got him involved in it. I mean, shit! I screwed up.'

'Hold on!' She snapped at Henry, swinging him around to face her. 'You did a brilliant job, Henry. You saved a young girl's life and you've gathered enough evidence to put Ingram and Mitch away for a long time – which was the whole idea.'

'I've known Troy since he was a teenager,' he said simply. 'I used and abused him and finally got him killed.'

Andrea's eyes searched Henry's expression desperately. 'Not your fault.'

'Bad, bad judgement – again,' Henry spat bitterly. 'Dave Anger's going to have a field day with me.'

'You are so wrong. He thinks you did a great job. Begrudgingly, of course. But everyone does, even the chief constable.'

'Fanshaw-Bayley?'

'Yes, he's right behind you. You'll be supported every inch of the way, here.'

Henry shook his head. 'I'm feeling very rocky
about this, Andrea. The shit'll hit the fan.
They'll find out that Troy was my informant –
unofficially – for years and that I put him in a
dangerous situation.'

'One that he agreed to. He knew the risks,
lived by them, died by them ... and anyway,
we've yet to get Ingram to admit to killing him.
Could be a tricky one.'

They reached a particularly pleasant section of
the walk, about halfway around, on a path
through a wooded area.

'Henry? Just ruminating here ... but do you
think there's a connection between who ever it is
causing you personal grief and Ingram?'

'I wonder about it constantly, but it doesn't
add up, so I'm sure there isn't. I've been through
the reasons before.' Henry suddenly had a
jarring thought: something he had not followed
up.

'You've just had a brainstorm,' Andrea said.

'I wouldn't put it that way, just something I
need to do.'

It was cooler under the trees, the sunshine
dappling through the leaf canopy. Lots of insects
buzzed, but it was quiet, felt like a million miles
away from real life.

Two HQ joggers on their lunch break came up
behind them at an easy pace. Henry and Andrea
sidestepped to allow them through.

'Has anything come from the scene of the fire

yet?' Andrea asked as they resumed their stroll, still linked to him.

He shook his head. 'The police in Blackpool have worked hard on it, but nothing's come yet, other than a foot impression on a flowerbed, the same trainer sole as the one who'd terrorized Kate before, the one I chased.'

'Perhaps this is aimed at Kate?'

'It did cross my mind and we have discussed it, but I don't think so. She's led a pretty blameless existence.'

'What an angel,' Andrea quipped.

Henry let it ride. 'Whoever it is, though, has stepped things up a gear and seems determined to cause real harm, death even. She could easily have been killed.' His voice faded bleakly. 'It's just whether or not he's finished, satisfied with what he's done – or is there more to come?'

Two hours later he was in the DI's office in Blackpool nick, looking across the desk at Rik Dean, an old friend, who, years before, Henry had been instrumental in getting on to the CID. Rik's subsequent rise from DC to DI had been all his own doing. He was now proving to be a good manager, too. Secretly, Henry was proud of him, thought of him as a protégé.

'As ever, Henry, you look disgusting.'

'You should see the other guys.'

'So I believe.'

'I've come for an update.'

'On what in particular?'

'Oh, y'know, the fact that some bastard tried to burn down my house and fry Kate.'

Henry knew that Rik had taken a personal interest in the investigation. It was being treated as attempted murder and a detective super-intendent from FMIT, Henry's old team, was overseeing the whole thing. The reality, though, was that just two DCs had been put on to it full time, all the resources the force could manage.

Rik leaned back, but not uncomfortably. 'Nothing to report, I'm afraid.'

Henry gave him a blank look. 'Run that past me again.'

Rik shook his head, bit his top lip. 'There's two good jacks on it,' he said brightly. 'Maybe if you came up with a list of names of scrotes that bear you grudges it might help.'

Henry pretended to belly laugh, holding his sides. 'Have you investigated the whereabouts of Dave Anger?' he suggested, then saw Rik's expression. 'It could be anyone I've dealt with over the last twenty-eight years, mate. They all hate me.'

'How about a list of the favourites?'

The house they were renting, a four bedroom detached, was on an estate in Kirkham, a town about halfway between Blackpool and Preston. This meant that Henry, on leaving Blackpool Police Station to get home had, more or less, to drive past the estate on which his own fire-dam-aged house was situated, close to the motorway junction at Marton Circle. A feeling of morbid curiosity made him turn down his cul-de-sac to see how it was all looking.

It was a strange, unsettling journey, driving

along those familiar avenues until he reached his house.

Then he wished he hadn't come.

He parked up and sat looking at the sorry state of it. Now boarded up, the brickwork extensively charred, it looked more like something from a sink council estate. Still on the lawn outside were the remains of all the burned furniture and carpets, dragged out and dumped by the fire service and not yet collected and disposed of a week later.

'Two hundred grand,' he breathed, but wasn't sure if that was enough to get the family back there. He knew he didn't want to return. Kate hadn't said anything, but he sensed her reluctance. She would never settle again, Henry knew that. The work would take months and months, anyway, so there was adequate time to decide on their future. Sitting there, he could feel his breathing becoming laboured, that tightness across his chest returning with the stress.

Who? he thought. Who? Who? Who? Dammit!

Henry was about to slam the car into gear and move off when there was a sharp tap on the driver's door window. Henry opened it and cricked his face upwards to look at the man standing on the footpath.

'Mr Christie.' He was an oldish man, mid-seventies, and lived on the edge of the estate in one of the two-bedroomed semis with his invalid wife. The man, Mr Jackson, could often be seen out walking with his dog, a West Highland White terrier that looked about as old as him.

The dog was down by his heels now, looking up at Henry, pink tongue lolling.

'Hello, Mr Jackson.' Henry tried to sound bright.

'This is a very nasty business.'

'Oh, yeah.'

'I'm sorry for you, it must be scary.'

'It is, but thanks for your words.' Henry laid his hands on the steering wheel in a gesture that meant, 'must get on'.

'I was wondering...' Mr Jackson bent to look in his car, his lined, grey face only inches from Henry's. The dog jumped up the side of the car, its claws scraping on the metal.

'Wondering what?' Henry eyed the dog distastefully.

'Why the police haven't come knocking on my door. They've been doing house-to-house, haven't they?'

'Yes. Why, do you have something for them?'

'Might have ... my house, as you know, has to be driven past in order to get on to the estate, or walked past, come to that – unless one uses the public footpath off the main road...'

Henry suppressed a shimmer of excitement. 'Would it be worth the police calling?'

Mr Jackson pouted. 'Might be.'

'Would it be worth me calling?'

Jackson nodded. 'I need to take Trevor for a poo on the back field and I'll be home in ten minutes. Meet me there.'

Trevor, the Westie, had had a rather messy poo which meant he had to be placed on a plastic sheet whilst his whole back end was washed off with a flannel, kept just for that purpose, Mr Jackson assured Henry.

The operation took place in the kitchen, Henry hovering in the hallway, confirming his reasons for never getting a dog.

'He's got a delicate tum,' Mr Jackson explained, 'and therefore shits, mostly, like a flock of sparrows, if you'll pardon the description. Very runny indeed.'

Henry went just a little queasy.

Mr Jackson held up Trevor's tail and dabbed the flannel on the dirty arse.

'Anyway, one of my hobbies is watching the comings and goings on the estate. I've often seen you and Mrs Christie – although I know she's not your wife – on the way to the Tram and Tower, then on the way back,' he said dubiously. 'I also know you owned a blue Ford Mondeo, didn't you?'

'I did.'

'But I didn't immediately pick up, to my chagrin, that you'd exchanged it for that Rover 75 ... I'm nosy, but not that nosy.'

'Quite.'

Mrs Jackson, who Henry knew was bedridden in the front room, coughed and spluttered. Mr Jackson waited a moment before carrying on. 'And when I put two and two together, I didn't think anything of it at first, but then I did.'

'How d'you mean?'

Mr Jackson dried the dog's bottom on a tea towel, again retained exclusively for the purpose. At least, Henry hoped that, as he was holding a cup of tea in his hand.

'At first I thought you'd passed the car on to a member of your family, but then it didn't seem to fit.'

'Why?' seemed the obvious question.

'Because the occupant of the car parked it up on several occasions on the cul-de-sac opposite and walked away from it, towards your house. Then I saw it cruise by on a few occasions, but only after you'd gone out to work, though. Then I saw the man who had been driving it walk past a few times, but I didn't see the car anywhere. I presumed he had parked it off the estate, somewhere. Then, of course, the car was set on fire outside your house ... then your house was burned down.' He looked at Henry. 'Coincidence, or what?'

'No, I don't think so.' Henry sounded tired. 'I don't suppose you...?'

'Kept notes? No, I'm not a Neighbourhood Watch person ... but I did take some pictures.'

'Shame, but they're not much use even blown-up and enhanced. Back of the head, side of the head, no real way of identifying the guy.' Henry was explaining this to Karl Donaldson that evening as they sat in a pub in the middle of Kirkham. It was Henry's new local now that he was living in the town and was rather nice, slightly olde worlde with a bit more character than the Tram and Tower. He had almost snatched Mr Jackson's digital camera from his hand and tear-arsed to the Scientific Support department at HQ, but the journey had been less than

264

fruitful. 'But at least it gives us something ... male, white, five-eight, mid-to-late thirties.'

'And you've no idea who it is?'

'I've stared and stared: nothing.'

'Has Kate looked at them?'

'Yeah, nothing.' He had shown the photographs to Donaldson, now he gathered them together, slid them back into an envelope.

Donaldson had been in London for the last few days, immersed in paperwork and visiting the children. There had been no visible thaw in Karen, who had remained aloof, not wanting to talk. He had not pushed her. Now, with the blessing of his boss, he was back in Lancashire for a few days, ostensibly in his FBI liaison role, but really there to link up with Henry and also take time to get himself together.

'Let me put a possibility to you,' Donaldson said. 'Supposing that Troy Costain didn't blab to Ingram...'

'Troy was a tough guy, except when the tables were turned against him, then he was pathetic.'

'I know that, but he was pretty loyal to you in a screwy sort of way, wasn't he?'

'In a very screwy sort of way.' Henry took a sip of his Stella.

'But just supposin' he held out and said nothing to Ingram ... no!' – Donaldson held up a cautioning finger to Henry as he started to protest – 'If that was the case, who blew your cover?'

The question stumped Henry. 'I always assumed—'

'Yeah, and we all know what assumption did.'

'In which case, who did blow me out?'

'What about that guy?' Donaldson pointed at the envelope containing the photos. 'What if he knew what you were doing, y'know, working undercover?'

'No one did, except Makin and Anger.'

'Listen, H' – Donaldson leaned on the table, over his mineral water – 'this is not a criticism of you, pal, but there's every chance you could have been your own worst enemy here.'

Henry balked inwardly.

'Then again, let me be ruthless. How long is it since you worked under cover?'

Henry shrugged irritably. 'You know the answer to that.'

'OK then, after being a pen-pushing asshole for a number of years, you get chance to dive back into it ... man, are you gonna be one rusty son of a B.'

Henry sunk lower.

'How long do you think this guy's been stalking you? Days, weeks, months, years?'

'Dunno.'

'Exactly, you don't know. You do not know how closely your life has been watched by some mad freak, because you didn't have to know. People do not expect to be watched and followed, unless they're specifically in the game. And that includes cops. Unless you're an undercover cop, you do not expect to be followed, do you? You don't carry out anti-surveillance moves on your way to work, or back home again, do you?'

'No.' It was bitterly said.

'And a few things have happened to you, assaults that were unexplained, yeah? I was

266

there for one.'

'There hasn't been anything for a while, though.'

'Maybe the guy was plotting, maybe he was in prison, maybe he was building up the courage ... who knows? But what I'm saying is—'

'That I got sloppy?'

Donaldson breathed a sigh down his nose. 'It's possible this guy might have tailed you right to Ingram, or the apartment in Salford, and maybe he saw an opportunity to fuck you up, put your life in peril without putting himself at risk, and then going for the soft option – Kate, alone at home.'

Henry sat back, thoughts brimming.

'But whatever,' Donaldson warned, 'there's one sicko out there and he needs to be caught before he comes back and succeeds where he failed. The way I see it is, this guy wants your family dead and he hasn't succeeded yet.'

He sat back, point made – but he couldn't resist going on.

'How long before he discovers where you live now?'

'Probably not long ... might even know now.' Henry chewed the inside of his cheek, then downed the remainder of his lager.

'I think you need to know what Ingram knows, get that out the way, then see how the land lies.'

'But first I need to go home and protect my family.' Henry was having bad feelings about things.

'OK, I understand.' Donaldson emptied his water down his throat. The two men left the pub and began the walk back home.

'Trouble is,' Henry postulated, 'we can't talk to Ingram, not yet. Doctors say he's still too ill to be interviewed, arrested, et cetera.'

'But he can talk?'

'Apparently.'

Donaldson exchanged a glance with Henry. 'Look, pal, I know you disapprove of some of my methods, and we had a heated discussion about that earlier and cleared the air between us, I hope ... but sometimes things have to be done for the greater good.'

'We cannot speak to him, if that's what you're thinking.'

'I know that.'

'And he's being guarded twenty-four–seven by two cops. And his solicitor is watching us like a hawk.'

'I know that, too.'

'And I couldn't even contemplate an off-the-record interview. If that happened and it was discovered, it might jeopardize the whole case against him.'

'I know that, too.'

'So where does that leave me?'

They crossed the main street in Kirkham.

'You don't have to be involved in anything.'

'Go on.'

'Under the right, unofficial pressure, Ingram might tell you the name of the person who ratted on you, which could well lead to the arrest of your stalker, and save you and Kate and the girls a lot of grief.' Donaldson liked the word, grief, used it often.

Henry's hands stuffed deep into his jeans' pockets. His head was bowed low as he walked.

'I'm good at this sort of thing,' Donaldson said. 'I have no moral qualms whatsoever, whether I'm dealing with a terrorist, gangster, whatever – especially when I could save a friend's life.'

To all intents and purposes the friendship between these two men had ended when Henry violently disagreed with the tactics used by Donaldson to extract a confession from a suspected terrorist. They were back on course now, but Donaldson was obviously now suggesting something which made Henry feel queasy again, something which went against his sense of decency ... but for the sake of the safety of his family, Henry knew he would have to surmount it and fuck the ethics.

'And anyway,' Donaldson wittered on, 'all I want to do is have a chat with the guy and also, as I'm not a British cop, I'm not actually bound by your police procedural stuff, am I?'

'You probably are,' Henry said.

'Does that mean yes?'

Henry nodded glumly.

'Hey, don't worry, pal.' Donaldson slapped him hard on the back, causing Henry to hiss with pain. 'I'll just squeeze a few of his tubes, that's all.'

Nineteen

Henry considered making a phone call, but as it was his wont to turn up unexpectedly and catch people on the back foot, he jumped into the Rover next day and headed out of Kirkham to the M55. Donaldson had been up early, having crashed for the night in a sleeping bag in the spare bedroom, and his Jeep was conspicuous in its absence. Henry shivered when he speculated what Karl might be up to.

But Henry was on his own mission, which might or might not help ID the man who attempted to murder Kate.

The journey had been prompted by the thought he'd had on yesterday's stroll with Andrea Makin, something he knew he needed to follow up.

He went east on the motorway, M55 – M6 – M61 – M60, then off on the A56 and towards Manchester through Prestwich until about two miles short of the city centre he drew on to the forecourt of the car sales dealership specializing in MGs and Rovers. He slotted into a space on the customer parking lot and entered the plush showroom. He couldn't see Ken, the boozy-breathed salesman with whom he had previously dealt. He approached the counter, behind which

270

sat an extremely pretty young lady, unnecessarily layered in make-up.

'Hello, sir, may I help?'

'I'm looking for Ken, salesman Ken. I don't recall his surname.'

The young lady's name badge said she was called Sandy. 'Ken Connolly?'

'That'd be the one,' Henry guessed. 'Many Kens here?'

'There have been a few – a lot of our salesmen seem to be called Ken' – she giggled – 'but he was the most recent.'

'Be him, then.'

'I'm afraid he's left.'

'For the day, for breakfast?'

'For ever ... he resigned. One minute here, next gone.'

'Oh.'

'Can anyone else help?'

'Why did he leave?'

'I don't know. It was very sudden, unexpected.'

'Could I see the manager, then?' Henry fished out and flashed his warrant card. 'Cop,' he said, smiling.

'I'll give Mr Lennox a ring.' Sandy picked up the phone with a finely manicured hand and dialled a short number. Henry glanced towards a glass-fronted office at the back of the showroom where a desk-bound individual in short sleeves picked up a phone.

'Mr Lennox? It's Sandy on reception.' Henry saw the man look out towards her. 'There's a policeman here would like a word with you.'

Henry gave Lennox a little wave. He saw the man's mouth move. 'No, I don't know what it's about.' Sandy pressed the silent button and asked Henry, 'Can I say what it's about?' by which time Henry had had enough.

'I'll tell him myself.'

He set off towards Mr Lennox in his glass-fronted office.

Lennox was a fat, sweaty man with pools of damp under his arms and another across his chest underneath his large man-boobs. He didn't smell, which was a bonus, and was quite helpful – two things which endeared him to Henry.

'Ahh,' Lennox said, after Henry had explained why he wanted to see Ken Connolly. 'One of many, I suspect – well, several.'

'Several what?'

'Shady deals done by Ken Connolly.'

'What sort of shady deals?'

'We suspect Ken of skimming from the trade-in values of bangers against new vehicles. Unfortunately it's not something we could prove, so the management had a word in his lughole, told him we were on to him, and he decided to quit whilst the going was good.'

'What was he up to?'

'Falsifying trade-ins, getting cash from customers for a better on-paper deal ... something I suspect he's been doing for years at various places. He's worked all over the place.'

'Were the police ever contacted to investigate him?'

Lennox shook his head. 'It was only a suspicion.'

'And he never got challenged, either?'

'Not as such, just got told he was being scrutinized.' Lennox picked up an envelope on his desk. 'His P45's in here. I was going to send it to him today, if he's still there. He's a bit of a nomad, old Ken.'

Henry took the envelope, saw the address was in Rawtenstall, which was back on his home turf of Lancashire. Henry commented on the address.

'A lot of people commute into Manchester from there.'

'What exactly was Ken doing?'

'Basically getting a backhander from likely customers in order to get a better trade-in deal on their vehicles. Or, for cash buyers, getting a wodge of cash – by asking people to go and come back with cash-in-hand – from which he'd take a percentage, falsify the paperwork and get a whole load of drinking and gambling money. Happens all the time in the car trade, especially for sort of mid-sized concerns like ours with a pretty big turnover. There's a million scams going on.'

'Bloody hell,' Henry said, 'if you can't trust a car salesman, who the hell can you trust these days?'

'Is that ironic or facetious?'

'Bit of both, I imagine.' Henry smiled. 'So could that have happened to the Mondeo I traded in?'

Lennox shrugged. 'It's possible – and you turning up and asking about it maybe spooked him, too, made him decide to pack his bags a bit sooner.'

'I was after the name and address of the guy who bought it, though Ken did say it went for auction. He looked at some paperwork ... could you recheck it for me?'

'I could ... like, when?'

'Round about now, would be good.'

'Why is it so urgent?'

'Because the guy who bought the Mondeo is wanted for attempted murder and arson.'

Lennox gave an appreciative whistle.

'Also, Ken did mention that you had good surveillance cameras. Digital recordings, he said.'

'Yeah.'

'I wondered if there was any chance of seeing if anyone, a customer, showed an interest in the Mondeo? Ken said he'd do that for me, but he seems to have welched on his word.'

Lennox looked extremely pained. 'There is a chance of looking at the tapes, but the part-exes are usually put right at the back of the lot and they're not covered by the cameras. We could see, I suppose.'

'If you show me how to do it, I'll do the legwork, if that's what's bothering you.'

Lennox raised himself *Titanic*ally from his seat, which seemed to breathe a sigh of relief. He led Henry into another office off the service area in which there was a bank of four, four-by-four TV monitors on a desk, each giving a different view of the forecourt. Also on the desk was a personal computer. Lennox sat at the desk and pulled the keyboard up to his large gut and adjusted the computer screen so he could see it better.

'They're all linked up to this computer,' he explained. 'Very state of the art, but worth it.' He tapped a few keys, logged in and asked Henry what dates Henry was interested in. He searched for the first date, and the screen split into four. 'This is oh-six-hundred on the day you brought the car in ... can you recall what time you came in?'

'Ten-ish.'

Lennox fast-forwarded the day in question and stopped at ten, then clicked from screen to screen. One of them showed the entrance/exit of the forecourt, two others the stock on display and one cutting back and forth to the showroom itself.

There was a lot of coming and going and then a Ford Mondeo drew on to the forecourt, driven by Henry.

'My poor car,' he said.

Lennox looked over his shoulder. 'Right, sometime between then and when the car was sold, the guy who bought it must have come into the garage, unless it went for auction, as Ken says. If I show you how to scan through the images, can I leave it with you?'

'That would be good.'

'And I'll have a look at the paperwork for you.'

Thus trained, Henry began his task, part of his mind wondering what Karl Donaldson was up to.

'Why did you want to meet me here?' Andrea Makin asked. She and Donaldson were standing in the car park at Preston Royal Infirmary. 'Sounded mysterious.'

'I want to do a favour for a friend. I might need some help.'

'Riiight,' she said, drawing out the syllable suspiciously.

'And maybe do one for you.'

Inappropriately, she thought there was only one favour Donaldson could do for her. It had nothing to do with crime, but there might be some punishment involved. She cleared her mind of such meanderings. 'Go ahead.'

Donaldson's face darkened. 'I want to do something that you, the cops, can't do at this moment in time.' Andrea waited. 'You don't have to know I'm doing it and you can deny all knowledge if the brown stuff gets flung everywhere. However, I do need assistance from you in facilitating this thing.'

'It's not like you to beat about the bush, but I take it it's about Ingram?'

The American nodded. 'I want an off-the-record discussion with him.'

'He's not fit to be interviewed just yet.'

'This won't be an interview.'

'What will it be?'

'An exploration of his inner knowledge and self,' he suggested.

'You mean a baring of the soul? An opportunity to get something off his chest? An un-burdening?'

'These are all nice, appropriate terms.'

'But highly unethical and illegal to boot.'

'There's always a downside,' he said, and pouted. He gave her a naughty smile which sent a shiver to a certain part of her body. 'But sometimes that's the way of the world and the way I see it is this – if he can unload something valuable to me, it may prevent something very nasty from happening to someone else. And if there's nothing to confess, then so be it.'

Andrea looked at the hospital. Ingram had initially been airlifted to Rochdale Infirmary, but with a bit of connivance between the police and the medical world, once the patient had been stabilized he had been transferred to Preston under guard. Here it was easier for Lancashire police to keep track of him and provide the man-power needed to watch him. He was presently under twenty-four-hour armed guard.

Her mouth moved thoughtfully.

'In case you hadn't worked it out, I need to get access to his room ... sneak in, actually.'

'I think I'd worked that out, all right. Does Henry know you're doing this?'

'Absolutely not.'

'Then neither do I, is that understood?'

'Absolutely.'

Henry knew how difficult it was to look through CCTV footage and stay awake at the same time, even though the digital set-up he was scanning through was as fast as skimming through a DVD – or in this case, four DVDs.

With it he tracked his arrival in the Mondeo,

some discussion with Ken at the car; Ken checking it over and then a handshake as the deal was done – Henry even now feeling he had been ripped off by the salesman. He found the footage of the car being driven away by someone else and then couldn't find any other images of the Mondeo, which had probably been tucked away amongst the bangers at the back of the lot.

The next day's footage was more interesting.

The Mondeo was driven back into shot and Ken got into it, together with a second man. Henry sat bolt upright: Ken taking a customer for a test drive. The man wasn't clearly seen, but could have been one and the same as the guy in the photos taken by old Mr Jackson, the nosy neighbour.

Twenty minutes later the car and its two occupants drove back on to the forecourt. They parked up, in shot, and there was a discussion as they sat in the car, money issues perhaps. After a couple of minutes both men got out, had further discussion and then went their separate ways ... but not before the customer glanced up towards the lens of the camera recording the interaction. He looked only quickly, fleetingly, then jerked his head away as though he knew he'd been caught. Henry jammed his finger on the stop button, rewound slightly and then clicked the image forwards one frame at a time.

'Got you, you bastard.'

'Shush ... no need to say anything just yet.'

Karl Donaldson sat quietly on the edge of

Ryan Ingram's hospital bed. Ingram's eyes were closed. His face was contorted with pain, pale and ill-looking. The mechanics of the bed and a couple of pillows propped him up at a slight angle under his neck. His chest was bare and heavy dressings covered the two bullet holes in his body, two drain tubes running out of the wounds into a receptacle on the floor, rather like a siphon.

Various other tubes ran into and out of his body. His heart rate and breathing were being monitored and a clear solution of some sort ran from a drip bag held on a crane-like contraption by his side, down the tube and into his arm via a needle.

He was very lucky to have survived. Donaldson smirked when he thought that this was only due to Henry's poor shooting. Had it been him holding the weapon, Donaldson knew that there would have been a funeral by now, or at least an inquest, or maybe a cover-up.

Even at Donaldson's soft words, Ingram did not stir.

He said them again. 'Shh, no need to speak...'

Ingram moved slightly, wincing in agony, despite the painkilling drugs that had been pumped into him.

His eyes opened and his lips popped drily.

Donaldson smiled at him.

Ingram looked at him through watery eyes, but did not react adversely to the man in his room. He may not have seen the stranger before, but because he was wearing a white coat with a stethoscope slung around his neck, to all intents and purposes he was just another doctor checking him up, even though he was as good-looking as George Clooney in *ER*.

'It's OK, no need to speak,' Donaldson said again. 'I hope you're feeling better?'

Ingram's eyes fluttered.

'I was shot myself once, you know?' Ingram's brow furrowed at this revelation. 'I nearly died, so I know what it can be like. Very nasty indeed.'

'Eh?' Clearly the patient did not understand anything.

'I need to ask you a few questions, if that's OK?'

'Yeah, whatever,' he croaked harshly.

'You feel up to it?'

He nodded weakly. 'Need some water, throat dry.'

Donaldson poured some from a jug on the bedside cabinet into a plastic glass, which he held to Ingram's lips, assisting him to drink.

'Thanks.'

'No problems ... I need to make something clear, though.'

Ingram eyed him tiredly, wanting to get back to sleep.

Out of his newly acquired white coat pocket, Donaldson extracted a small, plastic box that he opened. In it lay a hypodermic needle. He took it out between his finger and thumb and held it up, with his thumb on the plunger. Inside was a colourless liquid. He made a show of tapping the needle with the nail of his forefinger, as doctors do on TV, but he didn't push the plunger, just held it up so Ingram could see what he was doing. Still, the wounded man showed no conception of his predicament.

Donaldson then stood up and inserted the needle into the drip so that the tip of it was in the liquid in the bag. He left it hanging there and reseated himself on the edge of the bed, smiling at Ingram.

'What's that for?' Ingram managed to say.

'I'll come to that in a moment ... firstly, as I was saying, you need to know that I'm not a doctor, as such. I know I look like one, but I'm not. Nah.' He shook his head.

Ingram licked his lips.

'I'm just here doing some research, you might say.'

'You're an American.'

'Good observation skills. However ... my research ... you need to know that whatever happens in the next few minutes, you'll never, ever see me again, either because you've answered my research questions to my satisfaction – or you're dead.'

Now Ingram's eyes suddenly came alive. His whole body stiffened as he took in a breath.

'Please do not think of shouting out, because if you do, you will definitely be dead before the first syllable comes out of your mouth. Trust me, I can do that.' He smiled winningly. 'That syringe' – he pointed to it – 'contains a chemical which, if introduced into your system intravenously, will kill you very painfully – nay, horrendously painfully – within about a minute. Doesn't sound a long time, but a minute, sixty

281

seconds, is a very long time when your heart feels like it's being squeezed by a vice and your brain has been set on fire. And, a plus point, the chemical won't let you scream, either. You think you're screaming, but nothing's coming out. Real clever.'

'Who the hell are you?'

'Someone who wants some answers and promises, which if I get will mean you live to fight another day. If I don't, you'll be dead in, say, three minutes max.'

'There's cops outside guarding me.'

'Don't kid yourself.' Donaldson gave him a knowing look. 'Would I sit here, chatting, with armed police outside? There's no one outside, pal. They've gone for a coffee.'

Fear, and a dawning realization that there was a cool lunatic in his room, were evident on Ingram's face.

'Easy or dead?' Donaldson said.

'Who the hell are you?'

'The seeker of truth.' Donaldson reached out to the hypodermic needle and rubbed his thumb on the plunger. 'This stuff, incidentally, will not be traced in a subsequent autopsy. Once it's done its job, it disappears.' His eyes, hooded and dangerous, roved slowly to Ingram. 'Your death will be put down to natural causes, probably a heart attack as a result of your gunshot wounds, which, as we all know, were given lawfully to you.'

'What d'you want?'

'Who told you Frank Jagger was an under-cover cop?'

'Is that it?'

'Was it Troy Costain?'

'Go fuck yourself.'

'Did Troy Costain tell you before you killed him?'

'As I said, go—'

Before he could complete his sentence, Donaldson moved quickly. He clamped his big left hand over Ingram's mouth, holding, squeezing tightly, then punched him with the power of a steam hammer on the dressings over his wounds. Twice. He held on to Ingram's face, preventing him from screaming and easily fending off his weak attempts to wriggle free and fight back. The man had no strength in him whereas Donaldson had ninety-five per cent of his back – and that made him fearsome.

In fact, Donaldson felt a resurgence of power within him, almost as though he had never been wounded. His face set like granite and, eyes ablaze, he held on to Ingram whilst he squirmed in agony, then eventually gave up. He withered and started to whine.

'I forgot to mention,' Donaldson said, his face inches from Ingram's, 'I'll cause you a lot of pain even before I plunge the needle, if I have to.' He glanced at the dressings, now saturated with new blood. 'You answer my questions, Goddamnit. You killed Costain, didn't you?'

Slowly, he peeled his hand off Ingram's mouth.

'Yeah.'

'What did he tell you about Frank Jagger?'

'Nothing.'

'Why kill him then?'

Ingram was breathing with difficulty now, his teeth grating, fighting the agony from his wounds, which had reopened with a vengeance.

'Why kill him?'

'To kill the debt.'

'Meaning?'

'Fuck you, whoever you are,' Ingram blurted.

'Doctor Nightmare, that's me.' Sharp and hard, Donaldson smacked a fist into Ingram's upper chest again. He re-clamped his face and held him down until the pain started to ebb out of his body. 'Tell me, or I'll release this death into your veins.'

'You fuckin' wouldn't,' Ingram gasped, as Donaldson lifted the hand from his mouth.

The American laughed. 'Try me.'

Ingram's eyes roved over every detail of Donaldson's face, the eyes, the skin, and the expression which told him with certainty that he was telling the truth.

'I was double-checking.'

'Meaning?'

'I'd already been told Jagger was a cop. I went to see Costain to double-check. But things took a turn for the worse. He argued about the debt, insisting that Jagger was a criminal, so I lost it and I killed him. I knew he was lying to me, but he didn't say anything about Jagger being a cop.'

'Who did tell you, then?'

'Someone else.'

'Don't fuck with me. I want a name, now, or I'll murder you.' He reached across to the syringe, put his thumb on the plunger.

Twenty

Rossendale was cold and grey. *Back again*, Henry thought as he motored into the stone-built town of Rawtenstall, the capital of the valley. Having spent a lot of his early career in these wilds, he knew his way around the place well, even now, but could not necessarily remember specific streets. He had to pull in and consult his *Lancashire A–Z*. He'd once thought about getting a satnav, but they took the fun out of finding places. However, on that day, being in such a hurry, he would have welcomed hi-tech assistance.

Even so, he found the street on the map quickly. He geographically imprinted it into his mind instantly and was on the trail again within a minute, heading up Burnley Road out of town. It was a terraced side street on the right-hand side of this main road, more or less opposite a pub he used to frequent in the days, long ago, when he was working as a uniformed cop down the valley.

He pulled into the roadside and looked up the street. It was a short, dead-end terraced street with maybe enough room to manoeuvre a car across the top of it along a tight alley and drop down into the next street back down on to the main road.

It was a street he had visited a time or two when he was a PC. He tried to recall why, but they must have been nothing jobs; kids causing a nuisance, maybe, no great memories. And now Ken Connolly, bent car salesman, lived in one of the houses on the left, number nine, in the middle of the terrace.

Henry checked the address on the envelope containing Connolly's P45. Definitely nine.

He rubbed his eyes. He was tired, aching, sore, but feeling confident, having that infamous arse twitch of his like he always did when he was on the scent. He got a surge of energy as he checked his shoulder, jumped out of the car and strode across to the mouth of the street which was still, amazingly, cobbled. Nothing progresses very quickly in Rossendale, he thought.

He rapped his knuckles on the door, a poorly maintained wooden one which needed either replacing or refurbishing. It rattled loosely, hollowly. Stepping back a few feet, he checked for activity, then looked through the ground floor window into the lounge. It was empty and cheaply furnished.

His knuckles hit the door again, but his cop sense told him no one was at home. He cursed silently, thought about knocking on a few of the neighbours' houses, but as he looked back down the street, his eyes focused on the pub, the Red Lion. He recalled that Ken had smelled of booze when he'd last spoken to him and just maybe, being a man out of work, he might be drowning his sorrows in the local.

It was worth a try. If it was a dead-end he'd do a few neighbours anyway, and then sit and wait in the pub for Connolly to roll home.

He dashed across Burnley Road and entered the pub.

This was somewhere Henry had been many times in the early 1980s when he was not much more than a kid in a uniform. He had never been to the pub whilst on duty, always off-duty and chasing skirt. In those days it had been one of the pubs in the valleys where cops congregated. And cop groupies went, too.

Treasured memories flooded back, but the reality of the pub on that day, as he pushed his way into the main bar, was of a place in urgent need of attention. It was a dive.

It was hardly busy, late morning just before lunch, and as he sauntered in he immediately spotted Connolly at the bar. He had a fresh pint in his hand which had been presented to him by a barmaid who could well have been in situ since Henry had last sauntered in twenty-odd years earlier.

Henry stood behind Connolly, who had not seen him enter, and noticed a racing paper on the bar in front of him, with a notepad and pencil, names of horses and odds scribbled down. *Ken the gambler, boozer and skimmer*, Henry thought.

He stepped sideways and dropped Connolly's P45 on to the bar.

'Pressie for you. Your P45.'

Connolly turned his head and squinted at Henry for a moment, then recognized him.

'Shit,' he said vehemently.

His eyes did an escape check, but, with half an eye on Henry, he saw there was no way of getting out other than trying to bowl Henry over, which was a task too far for Connolly who was slimmer, smaller and shorter than the detective. Resigned to whatever fate awaited, he turned back to the bar and took a long drink of his bitter.

Henry waited for further reaction, but none came

Eventually he did break the silence. 'Whaddya want?' he asked miserably.

'A chat, nothing more.'

'Buy me another pint and you got it.' He downed what remained in his glass, some three-quarters of his drink which, Henry guessed, must have gone straight down to his legs.

Henry eyed the barmaid. 'A pint of what he's having and a J20 for me, please, luv.'

Connolly hung his head as Henry slid on to the stool next to him. He did not meet Henry's eyes, but sat there with the cloud of doom hanging over his head.

'Ken,' Henry said, 'you are a fuck-wit – and don't even try legging it.'

'I won't.'

'But luckily for you, at this moment in time, your ex-employers are not pressing charges for theft and deception.' Henry paused. 'We do know what we're talking about here, don't we? We don't have to do this the hard way, do we?'

'We do and we don't.'

'Good, because the point is, if prodded just a

teeny bit, they would make a complaint, yeah?'

Connolly nodded glumly.

'How many altogether?'

'Eh?'

'How many cars?'

'Thirty, forty.' He shrugged.

'Nice little earner.'

'More than my commission, tight fuckers.'

'But still criminal?'

Another shrug.

'So how does it work?'

'I get into conversation, get a feel for a punter, get a cash sale – I mean cash, cash – get all the forms signed with no figures on them, which is easy, then I fill 'em in after the punter's driven off in a banger and take a percentage. Bob's your uncle. It happens throughout the car trade. Salesmen skim.'

The drinks were placed on the bar. Henry thanked the lady and they made eye contact. She looked quizzically at him and Henry did recognize her. A cold chill turned his tum. She'd been ten years older than him in 1982, which would have put her in her early thirties then, which wasn't so bad. A one-night stand in the days of his singledom and the sexual excess of being a young, good-looking cop in Rossendale which, if you wanted it, was a hotbed of sex and booze.

'Do I know you?' she asked hesitantly.

'Er, don't think so, love,' he denied.

'For a moment, I thought I did.'

He shook his head, smiled tightly and she withdrew along the bar, giving him repeated sideways glances. He scratched his head to hide his face.

'Carry on,' he said to Connolly.

'I only did it with cash-sale bangers and I diddled the paperwork to cover my tracks. Never had any comeback. Chances of being caught were minimal. You turning up and the company getting sus freaked me out, so I did a runner before the shit hit. Are you gonna lock me up?'

'Ken, I couldn't be arsed ... just so long as you tell me everything about the car I part-exchanged for the Rover and the guy who bought it. The paperwork seems to have disappeared.'

'The Mondeo?'

'That's the one.'

Henry fished out a screen-grab from the CCTV images he'd reviewed earlier. He showed the photo to Connolly. 'Him?'

Connolly barely glanced at it. 'Yeah, he just wanted the car, wanted to pay cash and it was a deal done quick.'

'How much did he pay for it?'

'It was on the lot for twelve hundred...'

'Twelve hundred? You only gave me seven-fifty for it!'

'That's business. Anyway, he got it for nine hundred on paper, I skimmed fifty and everybody's happy.'

'Except the company pay you a commission on the eight-fifty remaining, so that makes you a thief, Ken. I expect it pays for your bad habits, doesn't it?'

Connolly tilted his head in acknowledgement. 'I know. You want his name, don't you?'

'If you want to remain a free man.'

'Did he use the car on a job?'

'He tried to kill a member of my family.'

'Oh.' Connolly swallowed.

'Name.'

'I don't know it.' Connolly rubbed his temples.

'You do want to remain a free man, don't you?'

'I don't have his name ... it would probably be a false one anyway, under the circumstances.'

On that, Henry lost it slightly. It had been going on too long for him anyway. He grabbed the front of Connolly's tweed jacket and shirt in his right hand and twisted him off his bar stool and jerked him towards him so their faces were only inches apart.

'You're fucking locked up, then.'

'Let me go.'

'No ... let me tell you something you might not have picked up on, Ken. I'm not a happy soul at this point in my life and I'd just like to beat the living crap out of you for resisting arrest, you lush.' Henry's voice quavered.

'Resisting arrest...? I haven't—'

'Oh yes you have.' Henry shook him and rattled his alcohol-mushed brain.

'OK, OK, let me be.'

Henry eased him back on to his stool. Ken's shaky hand went for his pint which he just managed to get to his mouth without spilling, though he did bang the rim of the glass on his teeth.

'I want a name,' Henry insisted.

He was feeling something very unpleasant building up inside him now which, like projectile vomit, was close to coming out in a spectacular, ugly way. Something he was going to take out on Ken Connolly, who regarded him and sensed a bubbling volcano. Ken extracted a small notebook from the inside of his jacket pocket and flicked it open. It contained all the details of his criminal transactions.

The speed camera flashed, but did not slow him down. Instead he rammed his foot harder on the accelerator, swerved through a dodgy overtake, slotted back in and gunned the heavy car through the traffic.

His face was grim and determined, his mind focused on driving. He wanted to reach his destination swiftly and in one piece. But he was also focused on the name he had been given, desperately trying to work out what all this was about. To even start to do that, his mind, his memory, had to dig all the way back to 1982.

Twenty-One

Henry Christie's thief-taking potential had been spotted early in his career as a uniformed PC. From the outset he had loved the feel of a villain's collar and from his first day on the beat as a rookie, pounding the pavements of Blackburn town centre (his first posting), he had dedicated himself to depriving lawbreakers of their liberty. The traffic side of coppering had never really interested him at all, but crime fascinated him.

He had started at the bottom end and Blackburn had been a superb training ground for someone like him. Drunks were available all the time, day or night; shoplifters seemed to queue up to be arrested; there were assaults every day, mass fights spilling out of the clubs. It was great. He aimed for an arrest a day and on one occasion, following a brawl in a town centre pub which went on and on, Henry arrested ten people.

It was like shelling peas.

For a young cop with lots of energy, they were wonderful days.

Gradually he moved on to the more complex stuff when he was given a mobile beat covering one of the town's largest council estates. Then he began targeting burglars and one arrest, with which he was justifiably chuffed, resulted in 235 offences being taken into consideration.

His goal was to become a detective and in those days, the late 1970s, early 80s, one of the best stepping stones on to CID was via the uniformed Task Force, a mobile crime patrol used to target crime across the county and to assist in major investigations.

Task Force was on its last legs, though, and was due to be disbanded because of force restructuring. That did not deter Henry from doing his best to get on, and although rumours of its demise stated it would not last until the end of 1982, Henry managed to get a transfer on to the department at the beginning of that year. He was determined to enjoy it as best he could, short-lived though his time on it might be.

He was one of the last officers to join and the first thing he did was to get a clothing requisition signed by his sergeant and then race to HQ clothing stores and claim his car coat – a short cut gaberdine issued only to TF members. It was like a badge of honour, issued only to the elite (as they saw themselves, smugly) and Henry wore it with pride. It was one of the few items of uniform he owned over twenty-five years later, stuffed away in the loft of his house.

His only problem was that a move on to TF also meant a move from Blackburn to be based in Rawtenstall, from where the crime car operated. He was living in digs in Blackburn, being cared for by a little old lady who loved young cops – in a motherly way, of course. Henry travelled daily across to the Rossendale Valley to start with, but to save time, he found a small, damp flat near Rawtenstall town centre, which he shared with another PC on TF, by the name of Terry Briggs.

Life as a cop continued to be fantastic.

Henry found himself working around the county regularly on several high-profile investigations, including the infamous Mr Asia murder case, as well as around Rossendale and Accrington on general crime patrol.

He spent a lot of time assisting detectives, although he did try to avoid the DI who was based in the valley, one Robert Fanshaw-Bayley, who was later to become the Chief Constable of Lancashire. At that time he was a rotund, sweaty individual, who barked orders, blew smoke into people's faces, belittled anyone who disagreed with him and rode roughshod over feelings, rules and regulations, as it suited him. In those days, that was how DIs could operate and get away with it.

Little did Henry know that their love–hate relationship would begin in the valley and continue throughout his career. At that time he did his best to steer clear of FB, as people called him, whilst doing as much for other detectives as possible.

It was the summer of 1982.

The summer when the little girl went missing.

The briefing was at 8 a.m.

Arriving early, Henry made his way up to the refreshment room on the first floor of Rawtenstall Police Station, now commandeered as the incident room in the hunt for the girl.

He was first to arrive and spent some time looking at the walls, which were covered in charts and photographs, detailing all the information known about the last movements of the girl, her family, possible suspects, everything the police knew. Except what had actually happened to her, and where she, or her body, was.

There was a school photograph of her on the wall.

Her name was Jenny Colville and she'd been missing a week by the time the inquiry really got under way and the police took her disappearance seriously. Par for the course in those days.

Henry looked at the list of possible suspects.

Today, it was rumoured, would be the day when they would be rounded up for questioning. He wondered which one he would be asked to pull.

An arm shot past his shoulder and two stubby fingers with a cigarette trapped between them tapped on one of the names.

'That one.'

Henry looked round. FB was standing behind him. He took his hand away from the list and took a deep drag of the cigarette, exhaling the smoke up towards the ceiling. Henry coughed slightly.

'Sorry, mate,' FB said, squinting through the smoke. 'Anyway, my money's on that toerag,' he said, nodding at the list on the wall.

'Why's that, boss?'

FB took another drag. 'Gut feeling.'

Henry blinked. 'Do we need a bit more than that?'

'OK, he's a perv. Been done for exposing himself to kids, indecent assault, and last year he tried grabbing a little girl off the street. Well,' he said dubiously, 'I know it was him, but I couldn't prove it ... but he's my favourite.' FB raised his eyebrows. 'You wanna bring him in for me?'

Henry did not want to seem to hesitate, not particularly liking FB, nor his total reliance on gut instinct. Something more concrete was reassuring.

'Arrest him, you mean?'

FB looked at the young PC as if he was an idiot. 'Coax him in ... for a cosy chat, eh?'

A telephone on a desk rang. FB waddled towards it, but his body was twisted in Henry's direction, his two cigarette-bearing fingers pointing at him. 'I hear you've got a bit of a nose.' He picked up the phone. 'DI here.'

As he listened to what was being said, his eyes rested on Henry.

'Where ... who by? Exact location? OK, I'm on my way.' He slammed the phone down. 'They've found a body ... you got a car?' Henry nodded. 'Let's go then. Briefing's cancelled.'

The A6177, Grane Road, threads across the high moors between Haslingden in Rossendale, to Blackburn. In winter it can be impassable, in summer glorious, but always bleak and beautiful.

Directed by FB, Henry drove on to Grane

297

Road and towards Blackburn, climbing steadily, passing the two large reservoirs on the left-hand side before the road twisted slightly and on the right was a car park and visitor centre for the more adventurous souls who liked to don walking boots and brave the elements.

As they drew into the car park, Henry saw the liveried section vehicle, a Ford Escort, still called a Panda Car for some reason, even though the stripes had long since gone. A uniformed PC was talking animatedly to a pretty young lady, dressed for the outdoors, accompanied by a shaggy Golden Retriever. Henry drove up to the pair, stopped and both he and FB climbed out of the maroon coloured Vauxhall Victor, which was the favoured car of Task Force.

Henry recognized the PC. He was a fairly grizzled old-timer, stationed at Haslingden. They nodded at each other, but Henry's eyes were drawn to the female dog-walker. She was seriously pretty on close inspection and Henry's usually wayward heart missed a couple of beats.

'OK, what've we got?' FB blustered.

The PC, whose name was Stanforth, said, 'This young lady's been walking her dog on the hillside, came back down through these trees' – he pointed to the pine trees surrounding the car park – 'and she spotted some clothing in the undergrowth by the path. Her dog was off the lead...'

FB cut the PC short with a chopping motion of the side of his hand. 'Let's let her tell, shall we?' He turned smarmily to the woman. 'Hello, I'm DI Bayley' – in those days he did not use the

298

Fanshaw in his double-barrelled name; it was only as he moved up the ranks and further up his own backside that he started using it again – 'I'm from Rawtenstall nick.' He smiled – leered – at her. 'Now, don't get all upset or anything, love, but what happened here? Y'can tell me, I'm head of CID round here.'

'Oh, that's nice,' she said, amused and unimpressed.

'What's your name, love, by the way?'

'Kate Marsden.' She smiled at Henry, who had to catch his breath.

'And what've you seen, Kate?'

'Well...' she began.

'I want you' – FB jabbed his cigarette-holding fingers at Henry – 'to take this young lady home and get a comprehensive statement from her. You got that? Everything ... and then I want her clothing parcelled for forensic, OK?'

For the first and last time in his life, Henry wanted to give FB a great big hug.

FB spun around and left them. The circus had arrived and there was now a great deal of police activity on the car park and the surrounding woods.

'I didn't really see much,' Kate, the witness, said.

'Your evidence is vital,' Henry insisted. 'Like the boss said, I'll need to get a detailed statement from you.' In one of the strangest sensations he had ever felt, Henry found himself gasping for breath, even though he hadn't been exerting himself.

She smiled at him. His knees, literally, turned to weak rubber. 'Your place or mine?' she said playfully.

Henry's mouth opened and closed like a dumb goldfish.

She smiled again. 'You follow me in my car.'

'Yeah, yeah, sure,' he gabbled.

Kate Marsden turned and walked away, her dog at one heel and Henry Christie at the other.

Henry's life in Rossendale since moving into the flat off the town centre had been all work and play, nothing in between. He worked, he played; he caught criminals, he got drunk, ate poorly, chased women and had sex coming out of his ears – then he chased more criminals. The social scene for young cops was amazing, but eventually, it started to wear him down a little because it was so relentless.

But in Kate Marsden, a girl who worked for an insurance brokerage, Henry found some stability, though the morning after the discovery of the girl's body, the only thing he had found with Kate Marsden was exhaustion. They had easily fallen into each other's mindset.

Henry had taken the witness statement as directed. Done it long and slow, drawn out every last detail, every last word, just because he didn't want to say goodbye.

It had been Kate who finally smiled at him and said, 'Honestly, I don't think I can say anything else. You've drained me dry.'

She was more and more stunning the more time he spent in her company. Her young beauty grew on him. Her slightly crooked smile, one slightly misaligned tooth, the slight kink at the end of her nose ... all those trifling off-centre things went to make her gorgeous in Henry's eyes and he knew he couldn't let go of her ... but how to keep her? He was immaturely clueless at that point.

'Right,' he said collecting the statement forms, 'thanks.' He stood up. They were in the kitchen of Kate's family home in Haslingden where she lived with her parents. It was a big, detached house with a huge garden. Her parents were out. 'You've been very helpful.'

She walked him to the front door, pausing in the hallway.

She was tiny in comparison to him, and, having removed her walking clothes, which Henry had bagged up as instructed, and changed into jeans and a tee-shirt, Henry saw everything was just about right, where it should be.

'Um, er...' he said, lost for words.

Her eyes caught his, held them.

'Are you going to ask me out?' she asked cheekily. 'I'm between boys.'

Stunned, Henry garbled, 'Will-you-go-out-with-me?'

'Only after I've tested the merchandise,' her voice said, husky all of a sudden. She tiptoed up, placed a hand at the back of his neck and pulled his face towards hers...

'PC Christie!'

Henry's head shot up as he was dragged remorselessly back into the real world of the morning briefing of the night before, possibly the most glorious night of sex he had ever had in his short, penis-driven life.

He had managed to drag himself out of bed to make it to the hastily rearranged briefing at 8 a.m. on the morning after the discovery of the girl's body.

Henry knew he had fallen in love.

He looked at the stern face of the DI.

'You're away with the fairies, laddie,' FB said to the amusement of the rest of the people in the smoke-filled room. 'Still on the job?' he asked bluntly.

'No, sorry,' Henry spluttered, his face red.

'Right,' FB said. He took the last, deep drag of his ciggy and mashed it into an ashtray. 'You lot queue up for your jobs. PC Christie, you and me have some unfinished business to attend to.'

'Right, boss.' Henry stifled a yawn and wondered if his new lady friend had managed to drag herself out of his bed.

Five minutes later they were in the Vauxhall heading towards Haslingden, the most westerly town in Rossendale. Henry was at the wheel, FB in the passenger seat, constantly readjusting himself in his underpants.

'Wife's got me these newfangled boxer shorts,' he moaned. 'Can't keep the bloody tackle in ... need my usual ones, my Y fronts ... so bloody uncomfortable, these fuckers.'

'So what's the cause of death? Any inkling yet?'

'The PM's at noon today, but early indications are strangulation and sexual assault.'

'Shouldn't we wait until that's done?' Henry suggested meekly. 'I take it the guy we're off to see is the one we were going for yesterday?'

'I wanna rattle this guy's cage, get into his rubs, get him sweating.'

Henry raised his eyebrows. It seemed half-cocked to him, bull in a china shop, but he shrugged mentally. FB was the boss and had a reputation for taking that bull by the horns and shaking the shit out of it. Unpleasant though the man was, he did get results.

'Now the body's been found, he'll be on pins, waiting for us to hit his drum.'

Henry drove on to a council estate called Longshoot.

'Everything's fallen into place with him,' FB went on, making further adjustments. 'Firstly, he has a van and he works in a mill over in Black-burn ... uses the Grane Road everyday, so he knows it well. He's got pre-cons, as I said. Fairly minor stuff, but it's starting to escalate ... and he's related to the dead girl's mother, a cousin or something.'

Henry nodded, pulled to a stop in front of the address FB had given him.

As he did twenty-seven years later, all these historical thoughts having tumbled through his mind since leaving Ken, the car salesman, in the pub. The memories were still sharp, even now. The dead girl ... meeting Kate for the first time ... FB and his horrendous macho ways – which had not changed much in the interven-ing years, just his ability to hide them – and the

way in which the police operated with ruthless-
ness.

Robert Fossard came to the door bleary-eyed,
dressed just in a pair of jeans. Behind him were
his wife and ten-year-old son, drawn to the door
by the presence of a uniformed cop and a detective.

'Robert Fossard?' FB had asked.

'Yeah, what?' Fossard scowled.

'You're under arrest on suspicion of murder –
how does that sound?'

'What the fuck you on about?'

'Jenny Colville – abducted and murdered –
and I'm locking you up for it. You're not obliged
to say anything unless you wish to do so, but
what you say may be taken down in writing and
given in evidence. Now get dressed and get your
coat on.'

'This is madness. I didn't do it ... Jenny's a
relative!'

'Yeah.' FB looked coldly at him. 'And we all
know relatives kill relatives, don't we?'

'What's going on, Bob?' Fossard's wife, a thin,
rat-haired girl with thick glasses, asked.

'They're tryin' to fit me up for Jenny's
murder.'

'What?' she asked incredulously.

'It's bollocks.'

'Get hold of him, Henry,' FB said.

Henry grabbed Fossard's arm. 'You either
come easy, or hard,' he growled, but he knew it
would be easy. Fossard was a slightly-built man,
no match for the rugby-fit Henry who was all

trim and muscle at that age.

Fossard glared at him. 'I'll get dressed.' He shook his arm out of Henry's grip and retreated into the house, Henry close at his heels, not allowing him the opportunity to do a runner or hide anything that might be vital evidence. He followed him upstairs and he noticed the son watching him coldly, but with an air of worry. 'It's all right, Bobby Junior,' Fossard reassured his offspring, 'they've got nowt on me.'

At the front door, Henry heard FB arguing with the wife.

'It's bollocks, this,' Fossard complained as he pulled on a shirt, socks and shoes.

Henry shrugged. 'We'll see, eh?'

'You look like a real bastard.'

'I am a real bastard, but I don't kill kids.'

Henry saw that the son had sneaked up the stairs behind them.

FB clouted Fossard hard across the face, open-handed. The smack landed like a crack of lightning and the force of the blow lifted him off the seat in the interview room and sent him sprawling across the tiled floor, upending his chair. FB stood over the prisoner's prostrate form, breathing heavily from the exertion.

'Now then.' He wiped his lips. 'Let's start again.'

He aimed a kick at Fossard's ribcage which landed hard, winded him and made him curl into a ball, clutching his guts.

FB turned to Henry, a feral look on his face. 'Make sure nobody comes through that door,' he instructed the young cop, then took off his jacket, rolled up his sleeves, bent down and heaved Fossard up holding him against the wall.

Henry gulped, but stood guard by the door.

FB punched the prisoner in his lower belly then let him go as he doubled over, but bent down with him. 'Now then, you fuckin' lyin' piece a shit, tell the truth. You abducted her and raped her and strangled her, didn't you?'

'No, you got it wrong.'

'Wrong answer, pal.'

FB punched him again. 'Tell me the fuckin' truth.'

Fossard sank to his knees, gasping for air, snot and spit coming out of his facial orifices. 'That is the truth, I didn't do it.'

They kept him for twenty-four hours, but he did not break. FB grew more and more frustrated that his usually excellent interrogation techniques were having no effect on the prisoner – the variation from 'I'm your biggest pal' to 'I'm your biggest nightmare' seeming to get absolutely nowhere.

In the end he had to be released without charge.

There was no evidence to tie him to the girl other than the family link, no witnesses, no incriminating evidence putting him at the scene of the crime and his van was the cleanest in the world.

'I actually don't think he did it,' FB said sagely as he and Henry walked down to the charge office to tell the station sergeant to release him.

'I'm a pretty good judge of character in that respect.' He rubbed his hands together like Pontius Pilate.

Henry kept his mouth shut. It was the first time he'd seen a prisoner get such a beating.

'Take him home, will you?'

Henry nodded. 'Sure.'

Fossard was released and Henry did as he was told, driving him home. They did not speak on the journey, but as the car drew in outside Fossard's council house, he turned to Henry with a smirk of triumph on his face.

'Better luck next time, eh?'

'What's that supposed to mean?'

Fossard chortled. 'You bastards couldn't catch a cold.'

Suddenly, Henry did feel very, very cold. 'You did it, didn't you?'

Fossard simply looked at Henry, a smile on his face, then raised and lowered his eyebrows.

Henry gripped the wheel tightly, wondering what he should do. Rearresting him would not serve any useful purpose.

Fossard opened the car door. 'She fucked like a rabbit, enjoyed every second,' he sneered, then was gone, striding towards the front door of his house, which opened. His son ran out and hugged him, and shot Henry a fearful glance. Fossard's wife kissed him and the man turned to look once more at Henry, gave him a nod and an exaggerated wink, then entered the house. A guilty man walking free – something that Henry Christie, even at that point in his service, could never tolerate.

The investigation continued, got nowhere. Henry worked on the periphery of it, conducting house-to-house enquiries, assisting in searches of land and premises; he even arrested a couple more suspects at the behest of FB, but he knew they would be a waste of time because the real offender was still walking the streets, flicking a V at the police.

It had been rolling about a month, when late one evening after an arduous day, Henry found himself wandering along the first floor corridor at Rawtenstall nick, on which was the DI's office. The door was open, lights on, and FB was sitting at his desk, head in hands, fag in mouth. The room was filled with acrid smoke.

Henry knocked gently.

FB raised his head, the cigarette dangling precariously from his lips. 'PC Christie.'

'Boss, you all right?'

FB dragged deep on the cigarette, stubbed it out in the desktop ashtray and exhaled a fog of smoke. 'Y'know, Henry,' he said, using his first name for the first time, 'I'm pissing in the wind here.' He looked drained, beaten.

'What d'you mean?'

'I know here' – he held his right hand on his chest over the spot where his heart should have been – 'that Fossard's our man, and I can't prove it. I couldn't even verbal the twat up.' He sighed. 'The more I think about it, it's him. He was just good at holding out.'

'Can I tell you something?' Henry's voice was hesitant.

FB squinted through one eye. 'What?' he said warily.

'He kind of admitted it to me when I dropped him off.'

'What?'

Henry told FB what Fossard had said when he was getting out of the car. FB listened, open-mouthed.

'And you didn't think to fuckin' tell me?'

'His word against mine. He'd just deny it.'

FB's glare, one Henry would never get accustomed to, bore into his soul. For a few rocky moments, Henry expected him to explode. 'That man is a cold, calculating killer,' FB said. 'He blandly denied murdering the girl and then had the balls to say that to you! Cheeky, evil bastard.'

'I should've told you. Sorry.'

'Yeah, you should have ... but I don't think anything's lost by it. It has done one thing, though...'

'What?'

FB picked up a photograph from the desktop, one of the murder scene. He waved it. 'Made my resolve to convict this bastard even greater.'

He and Henry stared into each other's eyes, then suddenly FB rose to his feet and reached for his jacket. 'I need to do something,' he said, then left the office.

Next morning Henry was told to revisit Fossard's address, search the house again and re-arrest him.

'Why?' he queried.

'Because I'm right. He did it.'

'Suppose you're wrong?'

'Henry – PC Christie,' FB said, almost fondly, like he was talking to a stupid pupil, 'let me tell you two things, the rules around here. The first one is, the DI is always right.'

'What's the second?'

'If the DI is wrong, rule one applies. Now go and do what I ask of you. I've organized a team to go along and do the search and don't forget to search Fossard's van – thoroughly this time. And take this, just in case he gets nowty.'

FB handed Henry a search warrant signed by a local JP. It was one of the collection of blank, pre-signed ones FB kept in his desk for such occasions, but Henry did not know that.

Henry and the searchers were greeted by verbal abuse from the Fossard family, but he waved the search warrant in front of the suspect's mush and half a dozen pairs of size elevens trooped in and started to tear the place apart. Henry stayed with Fossard, who became increasingly angry.

The wife and kid were still at home, glowering and growling at the police, who showed little respect for their property.

'We can go and have a look at your van,' Henry told Fossard.

'You've already searched that as well.'

'Gonna search it again. It's listed on the warrant.' He held up the (almost) legal document.

'Do what you want,' Fossard said resignedly.

'I will. You want to come and watch me?'

'Why should I?'

'Then you can't accuse me of planting anything.'

He followed Henry out of the rear of the house to where the van had been parked in the back garden. It was an old Escort van, battered and on its last legs, common at the time. Fossard's son, Robert Junior, followed them out.

Henry opened the driver's door on creaky hinges and began a search, closely observed by the male Fossards.

'You won't find owt.'

Ignoring him, Henry continued – under the seats, in the glove box, behind the seats, in the back of the van – not finding anything. He had reached and felt under the two front seats and found nothing, but he decided to get down and use his eyeballs. He got the side of his face right down in the footwell in front of the pedals and stuck his nose in the gap between the seat and the bottom of the van.

A sprung wire mesh, rather like a net, supported the seat, and squinting, Henry thought he saw a rag tucked into the mesh. He tried to focus on it, but it was dark and hard to see. He squirmed around and slid his hand under the seat. The tips of his fingers gripped the rag and pulled it slowly out, like a magician revealing a string of handkerchiefs from a sleeve.

Except it wasn't a rag or a handkerchief.

It was a pair of girl's knickers.

From the moment Henry arrested Fossard, his first ever arrest for murder, and presented him to the station sergeant at Rawtenstall nick, he was completely sidelined from the investigation.

FB took full control and never gave Henry a second glance or thought, very much setting the scene for the way in which their relationship would be for the next twenty-odd years. Henry wrote up his statement and that was the last bit of involvement he had as the Task Force was disbanded, as expected, to be replaced by a sub-divisionally based crime patrol and Henry, for a short time, found himself behind the public enquiry desk at Haslingden Police Station before a transfer to CID.

All he knew was that Robert Fossard was eventually convicted of murder and was sent to prison for life, the crucial piece of evidence being the panties Henry had found secreted in the van.

There was an appeal which was quashed and Henry heard nothing more of Fossard. Ever.

And now he was about to knock on that same door again. He got out of the car and looked at the council house which had been refurbished, probably several times, in the intervening years. His mind was still running over the past, but his anger was welling up because of the danger Kate had been put in.

His mobile phone rang.

He picked it out of his pocket and looked at the caller display. It was Karl Donaldson. He considered rejecting it, but gave in.

'Henry, where are you?'

'About to knock on the door of the bastard who nearly killed Kate.'

'Robert Fossard?' Donaldson said.

'How the hell...?'

'Ryan Ingram ... he knows him...'

'How the hell does he—?' Henry stopped in mid sentence and a memory of something shot into his brain. Suddenly he recalled why there was something familiar about Ryan Ingram.

He ended Donaldson's call without a further word and marched up to the front of the house. He rapped on the door, standing close in and also at an angle so anyone who might be in the front room could not peer out and see his face.

He knocked again.

'Who is it?' came a male voice.

Through the frosted glass in the door, Henry saw a movement, a shape approaching the door.

'Mr Fossard ... council benefits assessment,' Henry replied through the door. 'We sent a letter saying we'd be calling. It's in your interests.'

The door opened on a chain.

A man peered out through the gap. It could have been Robert Fossard himself.

'Robert Junior?' Henry said.

It took no more than an instant for him to recognize Henry.

'Shit!' he uttered, and tried to slam the door on the detective.

Unfortunately for Robert Fossard Junior, Henry Christie had had more people trying to slam doors in his face than he cared to shake a stick at.

Twenty-Two

Henry paced the interview room, fists clenching and unclenching, desperate to get his hands on Fossard and strangle him slowly, sweetly. He knew he shouldn't be here, that his presence could have an adverse effect on the investigation, but he wanted to be present, beat the living crap out of him, and listen to his confession.

'I'm not saying anything,' Fossard maintained, eyeing Henry with the cowering sneer of the hunted and guilty.

'Well, you'd better just start.' Henry covered the gap between them and wrapped his fingers into the material of Fossard's tee-shirt and heaved him to his feet. The small man had a thin build and simply went with it, not fighting, not squirming, but maintaining the defiant eye-contact of someone who knew his rights.

There was a beat, the two men nose-to-nose.

'Go on then, hammer me,' he dared Henry. 'See how long it is before I sue the shit out of you.'

Henry felt it all rising in him. He knew he was going to lose it all very shortly, the arrogant, taunting prick – then someone laid a steadying hand on his forearm and a soothing voice said, 'Henry,' softly.

Still holding the prisoner, Henry broke the savage eye contact and his head slowly swivelled around to the voice.

It was Rik Dean, the Blackpool DI, Henry's old friend. Because the offences allegedly committed by Fossard had taken place in Blackpool, that was where he had been immediately transferred following his arrest so he could be processed there.

The red mist lifted slowly like pixels breaking up in front of his eyes and Henry dropped Fossard back on to the chair.

'Corridor, Henry,' Dean said.

Out of the corner of his eye, he saw Fossard smirk, heard him snicker.

Seething, he followed Dean out of the interview room.

'You can't be here for this, Henry,' Dean said in a whisper. Henry's mouth pursed tightly. 'You've done your bit by locking him up, but you're too involved. It's too personal. It could get mucky and we could lose it, especially if you have another go at him.'

'It is personal,' Henry said.

'I know it is, but by the same token it's not 1982 now. It has to be straight down the line, otherwise we'll lose it and he'll walk. You don't want that.'

Reluctantly Henry nodded. He didn't want that. He knew he could not get away with slapping Fossard, no matter how good it made him feel. What was important was the end result – getting him convicted and sent down, neutralized and punished.

315

'There's enough to get him convicted, even if he doesn't cough a thing.'

Henry nodded, coming down from the ceiling. 'Don't let me down, Rik.'

'Trust me Henry, I'm a DI.'

For Henry, the wait was interminable. Part of the problem was that he was homeless in terms of office space and did not actually know where to kill time. When he was on FMIT, covering Blackpool division, he'd had a cubbyhole for an office where he could hole up when necessary. Now that office had a new incumbent and Henry didn't even want to know who it was, so he avoided it at all costs. He could have used Rik Dean's excuse for an office, but would have felt uncomfortable in it. All this, therefore, left him wandering around like a lost sheep. His hand hovered momentarily over every internal telephone he passed, and he continually checked his mobile phone for that elusive call or text from Dean saying there had been a result. Neither came.

Finally, he'd had enough. Clearly Rik was not making any progress in the interview and it had all gone wrong, or surely he would have made contact.

Shortly before 8 p.m. he decided to drive home via his old burned-out shell of a house, just to pay his respects.

The building looked a sad mess. Since last seeing it, the blackened furniture which had adorned the front garden having been thrown out by the fire service had now been removed and

316

disposed of. The boarded-up house now stood alone, its brickwork charred and black. If it was a car it would have been an insurance write-off. Surely, Henry thought, the insurance company would decide to raze it to the ground and completely rebuild it from the foundations up? There was no way, in Henry's mind, that it could just be repaired.

He sighed, but inwardly was surprised to discover he didn't feel too much, then drove around to old Mr Jackson's house. The old man came to the door with the dirty-arsed Westie at his heels. It barked ferociously at Henry for a few moments, before he stared it out and it retreated, cowed.

'I wanted to say thanks for those photos, Mr Jackson.'

'Were they of any assistance?'

'Oh, yes, very much so,' Henry exaggerated. 'Someone's been arrested.'

Mr Jackson's face brightened considerably and he puffed out his chest. 'That's great news. I'm glad I was able to help. Maybe being a nosy old bugger isn't such a bad thing.'

'It's a good thing. I wish there were more people like you. Our job'd be much easier if there were. Thing is, we'll need to come and take a statement from you.'

'Not a problem. I'd love a day in court.'

I'll bet you would, Henry thought. They shook hands and Henry made his way to his newly rented house in Kirkham. There he found Kate and Karl Donaldson sitting in the conservatory, drinking tea and coffee respectively.

Both looked at him with expectant faces.

'No news,' he said glumly, tossing his jacket over a chair arm. He slumped down next to Kate and looked at her. 'However, love, I know Rik'll sort it and I'm one hundred per certain that this guy Fossard is the one, although all he did was squeal like a stuck pig when I collared the little shit, then wouldn't say anything to me.'

Relief flooded her face.

'You did good, pal.'

'And so did you, you big, good-looking hunka meat.'

'I'd pay you the same compliment, but I'd be telling a lie,' Donaldson retorted.

Kate said, 'I know it's early, but should I get the Glenfiddich out?'

'You two eaten yet?' Henry asked.

'Just a sandwich.'

'In that case, let's put the good stuff on hold for later, then go into town to eat ... they do a two-for-one in the new local.'

The food was simple, good and plentiful for the price. Henry ate with relish, realizing he had eaten sparsely that day. The other two did likewise, then they moved out of the dining area into the bar, which was crowded, but friendly and feel-good. They found three seats around a small, brass-topped table where they sat with their drinks, Henry with a Stella, Kate with red wine and Donaldson mineral water. Their conversation lulled for a while as their meals digested. Henry broke the silence by asking Donaldson, 'How's it going with Karen?'

'Henry!' Kate admonished him.

'What?' he said innocently. 'Karl doesn't mind, do you?'

'No.' But the American's Adam's apple rose and fell in his throat. 'She's avoiding my calls.'

'Sorry, mate.'

Donaldson shrugged helplessly. 'It's not looking good,' he admitted. 'You can't make someone do something they don't want to do, unless you beat the hell out of them, then their hearts aren't in it.' His big hand was dithering as he put his glass to his mouth. Kate laid a reassuring hand on his arm. Henry got the impression she was about to say something to him, but couldn't find the correct words. He looked quizzically at her, but she gave Henry an almost imperceptible shake of the head.

'Well, I wonder how it's progressing.' Henry exhaled and changed the subject. It was nearly ten o'clock. Then, on cue, his mobile phone rang, but it wasn't such a coincidence as he had been saying that out loud all night and sooner or later the phone had to ring. In his hurry to answer it he almost dropped it in his beer. 'Rik, pal, how's it going? Yeah, we're in there ... ten minutes? I'll have a drink waiting.' Henry snapped his phone shut. 'Rik's on his way.' He looked at Donaldson. 'Your round, I think.'

The four of them moved out of the increasingly cramped bar into the dining room, now sparse with eaters.

Three pairs of eyes, six orbs, focused attentively on Rik Dean.

'I'll take you through it stage by stage,' Rik began, after quenching his thirst with a long swig of his beer. 'I decided the best way to do it would be to get the offences boxed off with Fossard before moving into the whys and wherefores. Thing is, the evidence against him is pretty damning, so he couldn't really wriggle out of it and I had a bit of fun pinning him down and watching him squirm, the lying little git. We found the photographs of you, Henry, in his house with gun sights pasted on them like something from *The Day of the Jackal*. We found a pair of trainers which exactly matched the trainer imprint left in your flowerbed by the prowler the other night. He had a pay-as-you-go mobile phone which still had a copy of the text he sent you. There was also a balaclava which was similar to the one the prowler was wearing.' Rik screwed up his face. 'All in all, not a master criminal, here, but a cunning one nonetheless. There was also some paperwork from the car dealer he bought your old Mondeo from, with his name and address on it. All these things made my life easier. He also had possession of a can of petrol, matches and a map of Blackpool with your avenue ringed in it. To put it bluntly, after a long session of denial, he admitted everything. His brief just sat there and said nothing, looked glum.

'He admitted the road-rage, the prowling, and the arson, attempted murder.' Rik looked squarely at Kate. 'He was trying to kill you – but, he's not going anywhere and he won't be bailed.'

'Thank God!' she breathed.

320

Rik looked at Henry. 'He's been following you for about two years, building up his rage and courage to have a go at you. He did assault you outside Blackpool nick that night, but denies the assault outside the Tram and Tower, when you were with Karl, that night.'

Henry pouted. He'd put both of them down to Fossard.

'The reason for the breaks in the way he did things was due to him having a few short spells in the clink, minor stuff mostly, drink related.'

'But what was his motivation?' Henry wanted to know. He had told Rik about the circumstances of arresting Fossard Senior in 1982.

'He blames you for what happened to his father.'

'Because he killed a girl and got life imprisonment?'

'Because his father claimed he was innocent and Robert Junior believed him. He still remembers you finding the dead girl's knickers in the van, which he says you planted, and they proved to be a vital piece of evidence in convicting him, even though the police had already searched the van and found nothing. Apparently that issue was fudged when it came to trial, one search negative, a second fruitful.'

Henry's face contorted uncomfortably. 'I didn't plant them,' he said. But he had a bloody good idea who might have done. 'But that aside, what I don't get is why he started following me two years ago.'

'Because Robert Fossard Senior died in prison. Whilst he was alive, there was always a chance, he said – though he didn't elaborate what "chance" he was talking about. He blames you for killing him.'

'I didn't know he'd died.'

'You wouldn't necessarily. He died of natural causes ... but there's something else.'

'What?' Henry asked guardedly.

'Ryan Ingram.'

'I remembered where I'd met him and why he was familiar to me and why he thought he knew me, because he did. In passing, that is,' Henry said. 'Just as I was walking up to Fossard's house, it all clicked into place. Ingram used to live on the same estate as Fossard years ago. I spoke to him when I did house-to-house enquiries. Now I remember it plain as day. If we get the file out on Jenny Colville's murder, his name will be on the house-to-house sheets.'

Rik Dean nodded. 'And although he was ten years younger than Fossard senior, round about twenty in 1982, they mated about together – a lot.'

Henry went chilled. 'They both killed Jenny Colville, didn't they?'

'Fossard Junior says he overheard them talking about it. His memory of the conversation is that his dad "shagged" her, but Ingram strangled her. It could well have been the other way around, or they both had sex with her,' Dean said, 'but he believed his father didn't kill her.'

'Why didn't he come forward?' Donaldson said. He had remained silent up to this point.

'He was ten, for a start. He also lived in fear of Ingram, who was always a violent bastard – and he didn't trust the system.'

'Shit,' Henry said. 'Connections. All connections.'

'Do you still have the forensic for the case?' Donaldson said.

Henry said, 'We should have.'

'Then it needs reopening and the DNA cross-checking with Ingram's to see if there's a match.'

'And if we use Fossard Junior's DNA, we can find out if his father's DNA is on file, too,' Dean said.

Henry chuckled sardonically.

'What's so funny?' Kate said, who had listened intently to the discussion.

'It'll get FB's arse twitching. Thing is, once I'd found the knickers, I didn't have anything else to do with the case, really, other than general enquiries – which is when I came across Ingram.'

'Anyway, anyway,' Rik Dean cut in, 'because you were so easy to follow, Henry' – he raised his eyebrows – 'this guy was on your tail for a long time because you were his hobby. He managed to follow you to Manchester and actually saw you meeting Ingram, who he hadn't seen for years, by the way. He's not a master criminal by any means, but he put two and two together and decided to tell Ingram you were a cop. Ingram said he'd take care of you and Fossard decided to concentrate on Kate – and he almost succeeded.'

'And Troy Costain didn't let on you were a cop even when he was being beaten to death,' Donaldson said.

The statement dropped a bleak shroud across the four of them.

They drank their drinks silently.

The ringtone of Karl Donaldson's mobile phone shattered the reverie. He fished it out of his pocket and the display showed it was Karen, his wife, calling.

'Hello,' he said nervously. 'Right ... you're where?' he asked. 'Outside? Here? In, er, Kirkham? I'll be out in a second.' He closed his phone, a shocked but delighted expression on his face. 'That was Karen,' he blurted. 'She's outside.' He started to rise. 'She wants to talk.' He paused part-way to his feet and then looked at Kate suspiciously. 'You knew, didn't you?'

She gave him a knowing smile. 'I was sworn to secrecy.'

Donaldson swooped across the table and planted a big kiss on her cheek. 'Thanks,' he said rising to his full height. 'Wish me luck.'

Henry turned to Kate. 'You little matchmaker,' he said.

Even though it was a damage-limitation meeting, Dave Anger couldn't resist putting in a little taunt at Henry.

'So, once again,' he said, with his dangerous smile backing up his words, 'you made a judgement call which was entirely suspect?'

'Actually, it wasn't a judgement call as such,' Henry responded formally. 'It was a risk-assessed decision, overseen by Superintendent Makin and, I believe, countersigned by you ... *sir*.'

Henry tried to hide his look of triumph

because although it was, and always would be, a pleasure to stuff one finger up Anger, he was feeling very guilty about the course of events. In hindsight, that very precise science, Troy Costain should not have been conscripted into the operation against Ryan Ingram. But, to cover his backside, Henry did have the necessary documentation signed and dated by Costain in front of him and a risk assessment bearing the signatures of Makin and, crucially, Dave Anger.

'It was a quickly made decision, admittedly,' Henry conceded, 'but Costain knew the risks. Yet, having said that, no one could have truly believed that Ingram would hunt him down and kill him. It was considered, but given a low-risk rating.'

Anger's mouth twisted. He shifted uncomfortably.

Another week had passed and the force was now considering how it should respond to Costain's murder and what responsibility the organization had in respect of it. The Costain family were baying for blood and money like a pack of hungry wolves, but their main emphasis was on the compensation side of it. How much money could they squeeze out of the cops was their only concern. It was obvious that the litigation would be long, tortuous and very expensive.

'If we just tell the truth...' Henry began, but the words faded weakly. He knew there was little or no chance of the truth coming out – which, he had to admit, suited him to some degree. He may well have got Troy's signature on a disclaimer form, but he knew he would have to fudge the way in which it was obtained. To say there was a bit of coercion was an understatement.

The three of them, Henry, Anger and Makin, were in a meeting room at police headquarters at Hutton, near Preston. The discussion had been going in a circular motion for over an hour, and all three were flagging.

'I need to take something concrete to the force solicitor,' Anger whined. 'Something that'll give us a good defensive position.'

Andrea Makin cut in. 'The best defensive position we have is the truth,' she said. 'Let's go with that.'

Later that same day Ryan Ingram was discharged from hospital accompanied by his solicitor, who had made the journey up from London. He went straight into the back of a waiting police van and, escorted by an armed response vehicle, he was conveyed to the cells at Lancaster. This was the divisional headquarters of the area which covered Poulton-le-Fylde, from where young Gina Weyers had been abducted and the area where Troy Costain had been murdered. These were the initial offences for which he had been arrested and everything else would be added bit by bit as the police literally built up a case against him. Eventually it would include the abduction and murder of a girl called Jenny Colville in 1982, when his DNA was matched up with the DNA found on, around and inside the dead girl.

The clerk of the court read out the final charge

against Ryan Ingram at Preston Crown Court nine months later.

Ingram's running mate, Mitch Percy, had already been dealt with in court, having pleaded guilty to a double murder and several drugs trafficking offences. He had been sent to prison for life.

It had been a long list of indictments against Ingram and for each one he pleaded not guilty, even though he had admitted everything that had been put to him whilst under arrest. He had obviously changed his mind in the intervening months.

There then followed a series of legal arguments and challenges which were scheduled to last three days. The trial itself was listed for six weeks and it had been a work of great dedication and persistence to pull all the threads of it together, which had been Andrea Makin's job. She had done this brilliantly, having had to coordinate multiple lines of enquiry from the Met, Lancashire, Greater Manchester and Avon-and-Somerset police.

Fortunately, her second-in-command of choice was Henry Christie. He excelled in preparing good quality court files.

Both these officers, Henry and Andrea, were at court to see the trial begin, but they had no desire to spend much time listening to the barristers arguing for their money. They had done their job and now it was up to the legal profession to sort it out in court.

They sneaked out and made their way to the front steps of the court. It was a good, clear day and they walked across the busy dual carriageway towards Preston city centre.

'Well, fancy that,' Henry said. He was feeling good, having spent the last months helping Andrea, whilst at the same time repairing his family and home, structurally and emotionally.

In terms of the former, the insurance company had stuck to their guns and decided to repair the house rather than knock it down and start from scratch – at a cost of £204,000. But the end result was exceptional and Kate had relaxed back into it, especially when Robert Fossard junior was jailed for ten years, despite his pleas of mitigation which fell on deaf ears at court.

'Let's have a look then,' Andrea said. She reached for Henry's left hand and twisted it up so she could clearly inspect the shiny band of gold on his wedding finger. He blushed as she examined it. 'You finally did it.'

He nodded disbelievingly at the thought of finally making Kate an honest woman. The time had seemed right. Once the house had been repaired and they had moved back in, it was like a new start. One evening, whilst they stood together in the back garden looking up at their home, the question just came out, unrehearsed. Kate answered as quickly as it had been asked.

The remarriage was hastily arranged, taking place in a local registry office with close family and a few friends attending, including the newly reunited Karl and Karen Donaldson and their tribe. It had been a great day all round, followed by a couple of days in Lisbon for the happy couple. The honeymoon proper would take place after Ingram's trial, because Henry wanted to be present for every day of that. He had secretly booked a trip to the British Virgin Islands, even though he couldn't really afford it.

'God, I would have fucked your brains out, you know?' Andrea admitted. She let Henry's hand go.

'And if I'd got a hard on, I would have let you,' he admitted.

'But you didn't, because Kate was on your mind, wasn't she?'

'She was. Did you know that thirty per cent of erectile dysfunction problems are psychological? Not plumbing issues?'

'I'll remember that when my next lover can't get a stiffy,' she laughed. 'Anyway, whatever.' She turned and hugged him tight and rubbed herself naughtily up against him. They had reached and were standing in the covered walkway running past the entrance to Preston fish market. A vagrant with a dog and a blanket watched them through bleary eyes. And despite the location and the moment, Henry could not help but respond to her, so he pushed her gently away.

'Jeez,' he said. 'Blood rush.'

'Just testing,' she said cheekily.

Then, one of those incidents happened which had no rhyme or reason. As they stood facing each other, the door of the fish market opened and a lager-carrying youth of about nineteen came out, swaggering toughly. Henry saw him out of the corner of his eye. The lad, drunk even at that time of day, spotted the vagrant up against the wall. He yelled something and ran towards the man and simply kicked him in the head, sending him sprawling.

For the briefest of seconds the two cops were immobile, then Henry yelled, 'Let's get him.'

And before he knew what had happened, the youth with the lager had been arrested.

It took a couple of hours to process the youth, and by the time they returned to the court, there had been a lunch break and the prosecution barrister hurried towards them in his wig and robes.

'Where the hell have you been?' he demanded.

'Why? You don't need us yet, do you?'

'Not as such ... but there has been a major development,' the man said excitedly. 'Ingram has changed his plea – he's now going guilty on everything.'

Andrea and Henry swapped amazed glances.

'Why?' she asked.

'No idea, changed his mind over lunch. Court resumes in twenty minutes.' He left them and hurried away.

Stunned, the two stood in the court foyer, speechless. Then Henry had a strange creeping sensation.

'I wonder...' he said. He reached for his mobile phone and tabbed through to Karl Donaldson's number, which he called. 'Karl, it's Henry ... hi, pal ... I know this might sound a strange question, but have you heard about Ryan Ingram?

Henry listened for a moment, smiled and ended the call.

Andrea said, 'And?'

'Hasn't heard a thing,' Henry said. He folded his phone and slid it back in his pocket, an enigmatic smile quivering on his lips.

217.

.